Merciless Games

An Asha Kade Private Detective Mystery Thriller

Tikiri Herath

Merciless Games

Asha Kade Private Detective Mystery Thriller Series

www.TikiriHerath.com

Copyright ©2021 Tikiri Herath

Edition: 2021

Library & Archives Canada Cataloging in Publication

E-book ISBN: 978-1-989232-94-1

Paperback ISBN: 978-1-990234-07-1

Hardback ISBN: 978-1-990234-08-8

Audiobook ISBN: 978-1-989232-97-2

Large Print book ISBN: 78-1-7751956-0-3

Author: Tikiri Herath

Publisher: Rebel Diva Academy Press

Copy Editor: Stephanie Parent

Back Cover Headshot: Aura McKay

Tikiri

A Gift For You

Thank you for picking up my latest novel. There's a gift for you for picking up this book!

HER DEADLY END is a 250-page twisty serial killer thriller about an unusual murder-suicide case that Tanya (Tetyana), Asha, and Katy accidentally stumble upon while vacationing in Paradise Cove.

It's a pulse-pounding, nerve-shredding mystery of a devious serial predator stalking a small seaside town in Washington State.

You'll learn about the characters in the Merciless murder mystery series which features private detectives, Asha Kade & Katy McCafferty, and those in the new Tanya Stone FBI K9 series which features Special Agent Tanya (Tetyana) & Max, her K9 German Shepherd.

Join the VIP Red Heeled Rebels Club and receive your exclusive gift. Click the link below to join.

HER DEADLY END: A gripping thriller with a twisty end
https://books.tikiriherath.com/ts-b0-mmm-herdeadlyend

There is no explicit sex, heavy cursing, or graphic violence in these books. There is, however, a closed circle of suspects, many twists and turns, fast-paced action, and nail-biting suspense.

NO DOG IS HARMED IN THESE BOOKS. EVER. But the villains always are.

The Red Heeled Rebels Universe

The Red Heeled Rebels universe of mystery thrillers, featuring your favorite kick-ass female characters:

Tanya Stone FBI K9 Mystery Thrillers
www.TikiriHerath.com/Thrillers
NEW FBI thriller series starring Tetyana from the Red Heeled Rebels as Special Agent Tanya Stone, and Max, as her loyal German Shepherd. These are serial killer thrillers set in Black Rock, a small upscale resort town on the coast of Washington state.
Her Deadly End
Her Cold Blood
Her Last Lie
Her Secret Crime
Her Dead Girl
Her Perfect Murder

Her Grisly Grave
Coming soon!

Asha Kade Private Detective Murder Mysteries
www.TikiriHerath.com/Mysteries
Each book is a standalone murder mystery thriller, featuring the Red Heeled Rebels, Asha Kade and Katy McCafferty. Asha and Katy receive one million dollars for their favorite children's charity from a secret benefactor's estate every time they solve a cold case.
Merciless Legacy
Merciless Games
Merciless Crimes
Merciless Lies
Merciless Past
Merciless Deaths
One more to come.

Red Heeled Rebels International Mystery & Crime - The Origin Story
www.TikiriHerath.com/RedHeeledRebels
The award-winning origin story of the Red Heeled Rebels characters. Learn how a rag-tag group of trafficked orphans from different places united to fight for their freedom and their lives, and became a found family.
The Girl Who Crossed the Line
The Girl Who Ran Away
The Girl Who Made Them Pay
The Girl Who Fought to Kill

The Girl Who Broke Free
The Girl Who Knew Their Names
The Girl Who Never Forgot
This series is now complete.

The Accidental Traveler

www.TikiriHerath.com

An anthology of personal short stories based on the author's sojourns around the world.

The Rebel Diva Nonfiction Series

www.TikiriHerath.com/Nonfiction

Your Rebel Dreams: 6 simple steps to take back control of your life in uncertain times.

Your Rebel Plans: 4 simple steps to getting unstuck and making progress today.

Your Rebel Life: Easy habit hacks to enhance happiness in the 10 key areas of your life.

Bust Your Fears: 3 simple tools to crush your anxieties and squash your stress.

Collaborations

The Boss Chick's Bodacious Destiny Nonfiction Bundle
Dark Shadows 2: Voodoo and Black Magic of New Orleans

Tikiri's novels are available around the world, on all Amazon stores everywhere. The nonfiction books are available on Apple, Kobo, Barnes & Noble, Indigo Chapters, and all good bookstores around the world.

All these books are also available in libraries everywhere. Just ask your friendly local librarian or your local bookstore to order a copy via Ingram Spark.

MERCILESS GAMES

A MERCILESS MURDER MYSTERY THRILLER

The Photo

It was an image of a bloated, dead body.

He lay naked, sprawled over a cluster of rocks on a deserted and remote beach. The gruesome blood splatters on his back said he'd been shot multiple times. Whoever killed him had been vicious. Boiling with the desire for revenge.

They'd made sure he was dead.

Day One

Chapter One

"I don't like this," said Katy. "It's spooky."

"It's just a short trip," I said.

"Famous last words," she replied, making a face.

Though I didn't let on, my gut was churning, too.

Go home, it warned me. *Turn around now.*

But I was ignoring all the red flags, doing my best to pretend everything was just fine.

It was early afternoon, but the sky was already a dull gray and stiflingly low, so low, I felt I could get on my tiptoes and touch it.

I was glad we'd ditched our city dresses and heels for layered hiking gear and sensible flat boots.

A storm was on its way.

The swells rushed in, crashing furiously on the rocky shore. The howling wind whipped everything into frozen icicles, and the seagulls screeched as they got whisked up by the strong currents.

I brushed the long hair strands off my face, wondering about my crazy decision to come here and invite my BFF to join me.

"Maybe they made a mistake, Asha," said Katy, as if reading my mind. She pulled out the crumpled photo from her pocket. "Maybe this wasn't meant for us."

"They paid up, and they were generous, weren't they?" I said, pushing my fears to the back of my mind. "It had to be for us."

But it hadn't been an ordinary order for an ordinary cake.

I knew it as soon as I saw the gruesome image.

The unsigned message that had popped into my bakery's inbox four days ago had come with something extra.

A photograph of a dead man.

A naked corpse on a desolate beach.

A shudder went through me as I stared at the picture in Katy's hand.

The sand dunes and cactus in the background reminded me of a remote area I'd been to before. One at the Mexican border, where only outlaws dared to go.

It was this photo that had brought Katy and me to the small town of Trembling Cypress Bay, off the Oregon coast.

It was a place so remote it felt like the end of the world.

We were waiting now for the ferry on the town's fishing jetty, trying not to get soaked by the ocean spray crashing around us.

Underneath the muddy water near the pier, long strands of dark green kelp waved madly, like those wacky inflatable air dancers you find at county fairs.

It was like even they were warning us to stay away.

I pulled the jacket zipper up to my neck and curled my toes in my boots. The humidity on the West Coast soaked right into your bones and, I swore, chilled your blood.

We were a long way from home and our upscale New York bakery.

"When someone promises a weekend at an exclusive resort, I expect Laguna Beach," grumbled Katy, "not a dinky little fishing village in the middle of nowhere."

She poked me with her elbow.

"If they lied about this, how do we know they're not lying about everything else?"

She was right.

I had no idea what to expect.

Minutes after we got the cake order, they, whoever they were, sent a ten-thousand-dollar retainer. An electronic transfer from an anonymous payee, explained our bank.

Who pays that much money for a Dulce de Leche cheesecake?

Then came the message.

We were to hand-deliver the cake to a luxury retreat on a private island off the Oregon coast. Another twenty thousand dollars would be ours if we served the cake for dinner the first night and stayed the complete weekend at the resort.

The signature line simply said, *The Host, a friend of Madame Bouchard.*

That, I knew, was a call for help.

I could use thirty thousand dollars to expand the Red Heeled Rebels bakery and buy my chef team a set of new industrial-strength mixers. All I had to do was serve my cheesecake and stay the weekend at a resort? That would be the fastest money I'd ever made.

Of course, I said yes.

The money was nice, but as I stood on this remote ocean front at the other end of the country, I felt a knot forming in my stomach like those kelp strands under the sea tangling into a gnarled mess.

My mind swirled with unanswered questions.

Who is the Host? Why did they invite us? What did this exclusive island retreat in Oregon have to do with the photo of a dead man?

I wondered if I was going to regret my decision to come.

Chapter Two

"Look!" said Katy, pulling on my arm.

I spun around.

"It's the island," she whispered.

The fog was lifting in the distance, and a small black speck appeared on the horizon.

We stood in awe, watching the ghostly landscape unfold in front of us.

"Coffin Island," I whispered to myself as the eerie isle shimmered in the distance.

"Creepy," whispered Katy.

There had been very little information about the island or the retreat online. From what we'd dug up, the only structure on that rocky islet was a hundred-year-old lighthouse that was no longer in operation.

My mind buzzed as I speculated on where we'd sleep that night. In a tent? On the ferry boat?

But I kept those thoughts to myself.

My best friend, Katy, was a big city girl who loved her heels, her designer bags, and her beautifully tailored plus-sized dresses. She had been expecting to stay at a five-star luxury resort with white-gloved service.

I had warned her.

Our destination was a remote part of untamed Oregon. Not the celebrity-studded, sunny southern beaches of California. While she was having second thoughts now, the lure of a mysterious luxury retreat had been too tempting for her to stay away.

But it was too late to turn back now.

Still, she was no stranger to adventure and had that photograph of the bloated dead man tucked in her jacket pocket. It was our only clue to whatever we were going to encounter on that island.

Katy and I had taken a nonstop red eye from JFK and landed in Portland the day before.

We'd driven over in a rental car to the lone village along the coast with the only working ferry to the island, our final destination.

Ferry was a big word for an unimpressive boat.

It was an antique fishing skiff that smelled of dead fish and looked like it would capsize any moment. It was docked at the end of the jetty now, lurching back and forth so alarmingly, I was surprised it hadn't hit the piles and shattered into pieces already.

Mike, the ferry operator, was the strong and silent type.

Within seconds, he made it clear he didn't like city folk. He didn't have to say anything. The ugly scowl he shot our way when we approached him told us everything.

Mike wore a frayed captain's hat, dirty brown dungarees, and black rubber boots that sloshed when he walked. He communicated through impatient hand gestures and intermittent grunts, which meant we had to do most of the talking while he nodded or shook his head.

All we knew was we were waiting for two more people before the ferry would take off.

I stood at the edge of the pier and stared at the Pacific Ocean frothing in front of me, wondering what Madame Bouchard had planned for us now.

Most people knew me as the celebrity New York baker. Very few knew I moonlighted as a private investigator.

Because my former client, the now deceased Madame Bouchard's reach had been far and wide, I never knew from where I'd receive these calls for help. Some days, I wondered if she was scheming from beyond the grave.

The information I got was always sparse. Part of my sleuthing included uncovering as much about the person who summoned me as the problem that needed tackling.

These calls usually came from one of her upper crust friends at the most unexpected of times. It was either a request to solve a cold case, an appeal to uncover a concealed truth, or a plea to find a missing family member.

Above all, they required discretion.

Madame Bouchard had been a shrewd woman.

She had known my bakery team was made of street-smart, skilled trafficked survivors who knew a lot more than how to bake an award-winning cake.

We'd banded together in our youths to battle the criminals who'd come to hunt us and enslave us. Together, we knew how to fight a good fight, pick the right weapon, fire a clean shot, blow up a building and hack into their accounts, and expose their dirty deeds to the world.

We'd been on the radar of Interpol and the CIA and had escaped across four continents.

Madame Bouchard had known our pasts. She'd used us and our skills when she was alive, just like she was using us after her death.

She'd sealed the deal by promising our anti-trafficking non-profit a sizable donation from her estate every time I took a call from one of her friends. It was an offer I couldn't refuse. Even when the risks were great.

What I didn't tell my fiancé, David, my best friend, Katy, or anyone else in my found family was that I looked forward to these cases. Eagerly.

The lure of solving an impossible problem, of unraveling a mystery no one else could, wasn't just intellectually stimulating. It was an irresistible challenge.

There was also only so much I could take, catering to demanding, self-entitled socialites at my upscale bakery.

If I had to be honest with myself, I missed the lure of adventure of my youth. Even the worries whirling in my head now paled in comparison to the anticipation of what we'd find on that island.

Tetyana and David had wanted to join us, but they were held by contract to offer kickboxing classes for a Manhattan corporation's wellness program till Saturday.

I had promised David a quiet camping trip next week. Just me and him for once. But he and I both knew these cases never ended when I thought they would.

"There goes my romantic getaway with David," I said with a resigned sigh. "He's not going to be a happy puppy."

"Didn't he want to shut classes down and come?" asked Katy.

"We need the money to pay rent. It's not like Harlem's cheap anymore. Besides, we can't keep closing business every time Madame Bouchard's friends call us like this."

"Don't you think it's a little freaky?" said Katy, pulling her woolen hat over her ears. "We keep talking like she's alive when she died three months ago."

"Whatever her game, we can't say no to a million-dollar donation for the orphanage. There's so much we can do. A new school, more nurses, and teachers for the kids in NOLA. None of that comes cheap."

"It feels like she's still around," said Katy with a shudder, "the way she pulls on our strings. She always liked to play games."

"It was her plan, but it's her lawyer who's pulling our strings now. She made it clear in her will." I thought of the generous retainer that had arrived in our bank account this week. "Besides, this time, the client's paying us a tidy sum, too."

"Do you think this has anything to do with that letter we got?"

I turned to Katy, my brow furrowed. She was trying to look casual, but I could see she was bothered, too.

The letter had come to my bakery a week ago. It was a poison pen note with crudely cut-out letters from a magazine glued on cheap paper. The message had been short but nasty.

You're all nothing but dirt. You think you're big shots, but I won't let you forget your past.

We had scrutinized the letter from all angles. Tetyana had checked it for fingerprints and Win, our resident computer wizard, had examined it for hidden watermarks, but none of us had found a clue that would trace it back.

Katy had suggested we share it with the police, but that idea got overruled quickly. If it was a prank, we'd be wasting their time and opening doors to our past—doors we'd rather remain closed.

"That was just a silly letter. Could have been sent to anyone, anywhere," I said, more to myself than to her.

I felt a slight tremor in my voice as I spoke those words and hoped Katy hadn't noticed. I didn't want to alarm her.

Our past hadn't been easy. We had committed crimes in our youth to save our lives, to survive unspeakable circumstances. Was someone trying to muckrake everything after all we'd been through?

I shook my head to clear it.

What had happened was years ago and continents away. It had been another lifetime. We were safe in America now.

Or were we?

"Hey!" shouted a panicked male voice from behind us.

I whirled around, wondering who it was.

Chapter Three

A pale, thin man in a brown beret was running up the pier, a rucksack on his shoulders.

"Ahoy!" he yelled at the ferry captain. "Wait for me!"

"How did he get here?" said Katy, squinting at the figure. "I didn't hear a car. Did you?"

"Probably ran down from the village."

"Looks a little too sickly for a ride on these waves."

"That's one down," I said, scanning the horizon. "One more and we should be on our way."

We stood at the end of the pier, ignoring the ocean spray splashing against our pants, watching the man stumble uncertainly onto the boat.

Mike didn't even bother to welcome the newcomer.

He was crouched in the far corner of his boat, puttering around the engine. We'd heard the engine start and sputter for some time now, solidifying Katy's fears of us drowning in the middle of the ferry ride.

The new passenger turned his back to the driver. Choosing the corner of the deck with the most cover, he threw his rucksack down and huddled on the bench. He wrapped his arms around him and shuddered. I was sure he felt as miserable as he looked.

"I expected Ian Fleming in a tuxedo," said Katy. "This guy looks like he crawled out of a bat cave. So disappointing."

"He could be one of those flip-flop-wearing millionaire artists."

"These writers are crazy," said Katy, shaking her head, as the man retreated even farther into his corner. "Why do they torture themselves like this?"

"Maybe it's what makes their muse come alive."

Not wanting to stare, we turned back toward the ocean to watch the waves roll in, getting bigger and bigger as the wind gust turned into a small gale.

A ping came from my pocket and I pulled my phone out. It was David. I texted him back saying we'd arrived fine and were just ready to get on the boat.

"Tetyana can run the dojo and I can join you after today's class ends," he replied.

I typed back.

"Sweetie, we're fine. Our phones will work on the island, so we can talk anytime. Stop worrying."

I paused and sent another note before he could object.

"It's great here. Lots of fresh air and the sea. Love you, babe. XXXX."

The sound of car tires crunching on the gravel made me turn around.

"The second guest," I whispered as a young man struggled out of the cab with an extra-large suitcase. He was wearing a pair of worn cargo pants and a camouflage jacket.

"Are all novelists this scrawny?" asked Katy. "They look like they haven't eaten for weeks or seen the sun in months."

I shrugged. I was a baker, not a writer, and had little insight into the minds of eccentric story spinners. Besides, it was Mike who was worrying me now.

We could hear the boat come to life and die repeatedly as he kept pulling levers and pushing buttons. The smell of diesel was overpowering and made me wonder if we'd get to the island today.

Suddenly, the engine roared to life. Mike wiped his hands and stood up, hands on his hips, a satisfied look on his face.

"Time to head back," I said, nudging Katy.

We ambled over to the boat, trying not to breathe in the diesel smoke.

The man who'd just arrived was huffing his way across the pier, dragging his oversized suitcase behind him. It was a good thing his luggage had wheels. I wondered why he'd packed so much for just a weekend retreat.

"He's a kid," I said in a low voice, as we got within thirty feet of him. "Just a teen."

"Don't think so," said Katy, "malnourished maybe, but not a kid."

As we got closer, I realized she was right. He was in his mid-twenties at the most. Just as I was about to walk up and offer to help with his suitcase, he wobbled.

He was teetering too close to the edge of the jetty.

"Watch out!" I called out.

But it was too late. He fell into the water with a splash.

"Oh no!" cried Katy, her hand flying to her mouth.

"Man overboard!" I yelled, racing toward him.

He was flailing, apparently unable to swim. I looked around desperately for a life vest or a ring buoy to throw at him, but there was nothing around us.

"Help!" I shouted. But Mike had his head down next to the roaring engine, absorbed in his task, not hearing a thing anymore.

The first writer in the boat simply stared, his face pale.

What is wrong with these people?

Katy and I dashed to the edge of the pier and leaned over the dock. We extended our arms to the drowning man.

"Here!" I yelled. "Grab us!"

"Come this way!" shouted Katy.

But he seemed disoriented. Then, suddenly, he dipped under the water and disappeared from sight.

"Hey!" hollered Katy, jumping up and waving her arms at the boat. "We need a life vest! Someone help!"

But there was no time.

My heart pounding, I pulled off my jacket and shook my boots off.

Taking a quick breath in, I dove off the pier into the frigid water.

Chapter Four

I whipped my arms, spinning in the swirling water, heavy with seaweed.

Where is he?

Kicking with all my force, I headed down, ignoring the searing cold water seeping through my clothes.

There.

He was suspended a few feet beneath the surface, holding his breath, his feet moving gently back and forth.

His movements were strangely deliberate. Almost serene. These weren't the actions of a drowning man who couldn't swim.

But I didn't have time to think.

I pushed myself to the surface and swallowed a big gulp of air. With another powerful kick, I dove toward him and grabbed his arm.

I tugged sharply.

He didn't turn.

I yanked again, using both my hands.

With my petite frame and being only five feet tall, I was smaller than him. Summoning all my strength and with a quick prayer to the ocean gods, I pulled him toward the wooden pilings.

All of a sudden, the man seemed to get a second wind. He kicked his feet, like he'd just realized I was trying to save him.

When we got to within a foot of the jetty, I reached out and clutched the closest beam. Up above, I could see Katy silhouetted next to a second figure who was peering down at us.

Mike?

I guided the man's hands onto the beam. He nodded. Using the pile to guide us, we worked our way to the top, inch by inch. My lungs were ready to burst, and I was trying my hardest to not to lose it. But the man was no longer panicking.

Strange.

As we got close to the surface, two pairs of hands shot into the water and hauled him out. I scrambled onto the jetty after him, gasping for air.

The drowning man rolled over to his stomach on the pier and spluttered like a fish, while Mike tried to hold him down. We couldn't have him fall into the water a second time.

I lay limp on the jetty, my heart pounding, and my lungs struggling to take in every breath of air I could. I was wet, cold, and frazzled.

Next to me, the man was having a panic attack. Katy kneeled by him, ready to give CPR if needed.

Strange, I thought. He'd been more sedate a moment ago under the water.

Refusing any more help, he sat up and shook his head, as if to clear it of the sea water. After a few loud gasps of air, he mumbled a weak "thank you" my way.

I stared at him.

There was something odd about the way he'd reacted underwater. It was like he'd waited for one of us to rescue him.

Did he jump in deliberately?

Why would a sane person leap into the cold,churning sea like that? If he'd jumped, it had been a foolhardy move that could have killed us both.

With a loud grunt, Mike stomped back to his boat.

"You're going to get sick," said Katy, turning to me and giving my wet clothes a once-over. "We need to get you dry fast."

I nodded, too tired to respond.

She turned to the young man, a stern look on her face.

"You too."

He gave an imperceptible nod and made a move to stand up. His wobbly legs gave way, and he fell back on the jetty with a thud.

Katy and I took him by his arms and helped him get up.

We half pulled and half dragged him into the boat, while Mike grabbed his luggage and threw it next to ours on the main deck.

I cringed to hear the thump of the suitcase hitting the deck floor. He'd missed my cake carrier by five inches.

"Be careful," I called out. "That cake is worth a lot."

Ten thousand dollars, to be honest.

With another dismissive grunt, Mike stomped back up the jetty to rescue my discarded jacket and boots and brought them into the boat.

Then, as an afterthought, he opened a bench drawer and pulled out a stack of blankets. He threw one my way, and another at the wet man shivering on the deck.

Maybe Mike wasn't such a bad soul after all.

Without acknowledging my stammering thanks, Mike tromped toward the wheelhouse.

I wiped myself using the blanket, trying to control my chattering teeth. I looked down at my soggy clothes. There was no place on this boat to change, and I wasn't about to strip in front of these strange men.

As if reading my mind, Katy grabbed my blanket and held it up.

"Get into dry clothes or I swear you're going to get sick."

I picked up my bag and scooted behind the blanket to change. Anyone walking along the shore would have easily spotted my naked bum, but I didn't care. Besides, this place was so isolated I doubted any peeping toms were out here, anyway.

The boat began to move.

Mike was nudging it away from the pier.

I was shaking so badly from the rush of adrenaline that had coursed through my veins, and the exhaustion that followed, I was sure I'd fall off the boat.

I changed hastily, trying to keep a solid footing. It was a relief to get into dry clothes and towel dry my hair. But now, I looked more like a local ragamuffin than a well put-together businesswoman from the Big Apple.

What a way to meet our anonymous host, I thought.

After making sure I wasn't about to die of hypothermia, Katy helped the young man change. She ushered him toward a sheltered part of the boat and held the blanket up for him as well.

I noticed the first writer hadn't budged from his corner throughout this entire ordeal. He watched us, an unhappy expression on his face.

I had hardly taken my seat when the engine revved loudly. Mike had steered the boat away from the jetty, and we were facing the open ocean now.

Katy rushed over and plopped down. I huddled next to her, my teeth chattering, trying to stay warm.

Within seconds, we were careening over the ocean swells, heading to Coffin Island.

Chapter Five

The old boat jumped the waves, lurching and roiling, making the two writers' faces as green as vomit.

Katy and I had more experience on the high seas, but even my friend clutched the railing so tightly her knuckles had turned white. I looked away and focused my attention on keeping the contents of my stomach down.

From the shore, I hadn't realized how high the waves were.

We gathered speed as we approached deeper waters, and got drenched with every wave that crashed against the boat. I might as well have stayed in my wet clothes.

My only consolation was Mike.

While the rest of us huddled behind the wheelhouse, trying to keep warm, he whistled an old sea shanty and kept his eyes straight ahead.

Though he wasn't the friendliest of people, he looked like he knew this area well. Seeing him expertly navigate the rough ocean, my worries of drowning slowly dissipated.

Above us, the dark sky hung claustrophobically low. But it lightened, and the sea grew calmer the closer we got to our destination.

The black dot in the distance grew bigger and bigger to the point we could finally make out the outline of the lighthouse.

The island looked like a lonely speck out here in the open ocean. There wasn't any other land nearby.

I wondered how anyone would have thought hosting a luxury writers' retreat here was a good idea.

As Mike drove on, we kept our heads down and cowered under the blankets to keep as much of the cold spray as possible at bay.

After what felt like an eternity, I heard a change in the engine's sound and felt the boat slow down.

I removed the blanket and glanced ahead. We still had some distance to cross, but I could see the red and white lighthouse looming up like a massive church spire—a church to the sea gods.

The ocean was calmer out here, especially since we were no longer speeding over the waves like mad.

I licked the salt water from my lips and stared at the land mass ahead. That was when I realized why the island was named as it was. It was shaped like a long wooden coffin, a triangular head with a narrow body.

When we got to about a hundred feet to the rocky shore, Mike slowed down even further and started circling the island at low speed.

"What's he doing?" whispered Katy. "Doesn't he know where to dock?"

"It's the rocks," I said. "He's trying not to scrape the bottom of the boat."

If I'd thought the beach behind us had been bleak and lonely, I hadn't realized how much worse it could get.

The entire island was a high cliff that rose over fifty feet above sea level. It was ten square kilometers wide at the most, but little on it except for the imposing lighthouse, a large modern white building and a clump of trees in the back.

"That's possibly the biggest lighthouse in the world," said Katy, staring at the structure at the edge of the bluff.

The granite tower was much bigger than I'd originally thought, standing almost two-hundred-feet tall. Next to it was a large, beautiful three-story hotel, built in the colonial manor style.

Is this where we'll sleep tonight?

I had expected a crumbling place, untouched for decades, but as we circled the island, I could see someone had spent an enormous amount of funds to renovate the buildings.

If it hadn't been for the gloomy weather and the stark surroundings, this lighthouse cum hotel would have been an incredible holiday location.

"Check that out," said Katy, nudging me.

I glanced in the direction my friend was pointing.

Behind the resort building was a cluster of tall spruce trees assembled in a circle. It was like they were hiding something in their midst. Just as the boat turned the corner, I glimpsed the white cross in the clearing.

"A cemetery," whispered Katy.

We were cruising right beneath the lighthouse now.

On the shore, underneath it, lay a sandy strip. It would have been a nice beach if not for the blackened, craggy formations that had sprouted everywhere.

"Those rocks look as sharp as knives," said Katy.

Dark thoughts swirled in my mind as I wondered if anyone had ever fallen off that cliff and on to those jagged rocks.

"This place gives me weird vibes," I replied, wondering what I'd got Katy and myself into.

The boat steered closer to the island. A few yards ahead of us was a small aluminum pier.

"Thank goodness we're almost there," said Katy.

Near the pier was a wooden walkway that crossed the shore and wound itself up the cliff to the top. The wood was grayed out, like it hadn't been restored, in contrast to everything else here.

A faded sign near a clump of rocks caught my eye. It stood at an angle, like the wind had battered it down over time.

I read the sign as Mike nudged the boat closer to the jetty.
Suicide Cliff.

Chapter Six

Mike docked the boat at the small jetty, right under the lighthouse.

It was a secluded corner of the island.

Mike was now tying the stern to a pillar on the pier. I threw my blanket off and got up on shaking knees, cringing as I felt my wet clothes cling to me.

"Let me take that from you, Ms. Kade."

I turned around, startled, to see a petite woman standing on the jetty.

She was about my height, but about twenty years older. Her graying hair was piled up on her head in a messy bun and she was wearing worker's pink overalls and pink canvas shoes. Her weathered face was kind, but she wasn't smiling.

How did she know my name?

"Hello," I said, offering my hand. "Nice to, er, meet you."

Ignoring me, the woman leaned in and reached for my cake carrier.

What's she doing?

Without introducing herself or even asking, she plucked the carrier and turned around. I gaped as she marched away with my precious cargo.

"Hey! Excuse me?" I called out. "That's my cake."

She turned around briefly. "It'll be in the kitchen when you come up. I made space for it." Then she kept walking, without another glance back.

I'd brought my cake thousands of miles across the country, worried every step of the way that something would happen to it. And this stranger just yanked it from my hands?

I turned to Katy.

"What the...?"

"Don't panic," whispered Katy. "She knew your name, and she knew what was in that carrier. She probably works here."

"But does she know how much that thing is worth?" I said, shaking my head.

"Lighthouse folk," said Katy. "They don't like people much, that's why they live out here."

I guessed it took a particular personality to stay alone in a remote region for long periods of time. There were days in my busy New York bakery when I'd yearned for such a job.

Maybe they were the smart ones, I thought as I glanced around.

With the waves crashing on the shore, the seagulls squawking around us, and the ocean breeze smelling of salt and seaweed, I felt I'd stepped into a strange new world.

The two writers, who'd sat huddled wretchedly in their corners, stirred.

The younger man had recovered remarkably well from his drowning ordeal. He looked cold like the rest of us, but showed no sign of anguish you'd expect from someone who'd been near death only an hour ago.

The image of him floating calmly underwater with all that kelp and mud swirling around him flashed into mind. Part of me still wondered if he'd tripped or if he'd jumped deliberately.

I'd whispered my speculations to Katy, but she'd dismissed it. How could anyone jump into that hellish water by choice, she'd said, shaking her head.

But I couldn't brush off that image so easily.

I knew people reacted to crisis differently. Some panicked and ran away, others fought back, while others simply went limp. Maybe he was the freezing or fainting type. I hardly knew the man, after all.

"What a ride, eh?" said Katy, getting up and flashing the men a friendly smile. "Our weekend adventure begins."

Neither smiled back. The older man shivered visibly.

Katy nudged me and pointed discreetly with her chin.

There was a stranger among us now.

How did I not hear him arrive? Do people float around like ghosts on this island?

It was a man in his fifties, wearing a thick winter jacket and boots, and with a weather-beaten face, just like the woman. He was tying one end of the boat to a post on the jetty, focused on his task.

I turned around to look at where the woman was going.

She was making her way up the walkway now, one hand gripping the handle of my cake carrier and the other clamped on to the rope railing that ran alongside the walkway.

As I watched, a seagull swooped over her, making her stumble. My heart lurched at the thought of the cake slipping from her hands and crashing on the rocks below. But she caught herself just in time and kept climbing up.

"I'm going to have a heart attack," I said to Katy.

"Let's go find our room and get you into dry clothes," she said in a firm voice. "That's our priority right now."

She turned to Mike. He'd taken all our luggage out of the boat and stacked them on the pier and was now in the wheelhouse, fiddling with something.

"Hey, Mike, do you mind if we take these blankets with us?"

He shrugged, which I took to mean, yes. It would have been murder to let us walk up that cliff in this windy weather, soaking wet as we were, anyway.

"Ms. Kade?"

I swiveled my head to see the man we hadn't yet met standing behind us on the jetty.

His eyes were a pale blue but fierce, like he wasn't someone who'd let anyone get the better of him.

Is this our host?

I gave a weak nod, feeling like this was a terrible way to meet him. He'd paid ten grand for a private investigator and I turn up wet, weary and crumpled, like I'd been sleeping on the streets during a thunderstorm.

I extended my hand.

"Hello, I'm Asha Kade, the baker from New York."

"Yes, I know. The host told us you were coming."

So, he's not the host?

"Oliver Hudson. I'm the butler here. Please call me Oliver. My wife, Mary, is the cook. You just met her. We'll be taking care of you this weekend."

"And the host?" I asked. "Where is he or she?"

"They are currently unavailable."

I frowned. *Why do I feel like I'm talking to a robot?*

The butler leaned in.

"Ms. Kade, I need to ask you to surrender your mobile."

"I beg your pardon?"

"May I have your phone, please?" he said.

"Excuse me?" I said.

Oliver turned to Katy and the other two passengers, eyes squinting, but his face still expressionless.

"Ladies and gentlemen, I will have to ask you all for your telephones, tablets, or any other device that you have been using to communicate with the mainland."

"*What?*" spluttered Katy.

"This is a retreat, Ms. McCafferty," he replied in a patient voice, the one you'd reserve for children who're not just getting it.

"You can't confiscate our stuff like that," I said.

"There will be no communication with the mainland when you're on the island," said the butler.

Chapter Seven

"**A**re you out of your mind?" said Katy.

"They'll be held in a safe. Locked up where no one can access them for the duration of your stay."

"You've got to be kidding," I said.

"This is an exclusive writers' retreat," explained the butler, like he had all the patience in the world. "Everyone was fully aware before they signed on that when they arrive on this island, they will have no communication with the outside world until the retreat is over."

"Oh, for heaven's sake," said the older writer in a frustrated voice. "You're holding us to it then, are you?"

"I thought it was a joke," said the young man. "You don't really mean it, do you?"

"You signed a contract," replied Oliver, his voice unwavering.

"But…" said the young writer, giving the butler a flustered look. "I…"

"You knew this before you even got on the plane, Mr. Quinteiro. You shouldn't have packed any devices. We have high-quality writing pads and paper and lots of good pens that I personally ordered from the Mont Blanc store in Paris. You will have everything you want and need here."

"Except the phones," hissed Katy next to me.

Ignoring her, Oliver turned to the men and put his hand out.

"I'm afraid you must honor your word, gentlemen."

With a curse, the older writer ripped the zipper of his bag open and pulled out a phone, a tablet, and a laptop. He plopped them on Oliver Hudson's open hands.

He shot the butler a livid look.

"If anything happens to them, I'll sue you to hell."

Oliver answered with a slight bow.

"You can rest assured they will be secured. Thank you, Mr. Ward."

Grumbling under his breath, Ward hauled his rucksack on a shoulder, stepped out of the boat and stomped up the pier toward the walkway.

I turned to Oliver.

"We never signed any contract," I said, pointing at Katy and me. "We didn't come here to write."

I thought I detected a fleeting look of disappointment cross his face, but he covered it up too quickly for me to be sure.

"As you can understand, we cannot have different rules for different people, Ms. Kade. Besides, that would make the whole point of a writers' retreat moot, wouldn't it now?"

"I don't see how," piped up Katy. "We came to deliver the cake. Our job is done." She turned to me. "Asha, let's go. We don't have to stay overnight here. We can go back to Portland."

She was right. We didn't sign any agreement to hand over our phones.

But we didn't come three thousand miles to just deliver a cake either.

We came because of that call for help. There was a mystery to be solved and a ten-thousand-dollar retainer already paid, with more money promised. I couldn't pack up and go now.

"It's up to you, of course," replied the butler, seeing me hesitate. "You should know we've arranged rooms for you as instructed by the host. I think you will enjoy some quiet time on the island with the fresh sea air."

He's speaking in riddles.

"Who is the host?" I asked, frowning. "I'd like to speak to him or her."

Before the butler could answer, the younger writer who'd been quietly listening to our exchange stepped up. With a resigned sigh, he handed his mobile phone to Oliver and stepped out of the boat.

"Is this all, Mr. Quinteiro?" asked Oliver.

The young man nodded. "That's all I have."

He turned to me.

"Thank you for saving me," he said in a reserved voice, before turning around and walking toward the pile of luggage at the end of the pier.

We watched him as he dragged his heavy suitcase along the sand toward the walkway, making a clatter that would have woken the devil himself.

From their reaction, it was clear this no-phone requirement hadn't been a surprise to the writers. That was what they were here for, after all—to work in peace.

But I needed my connection to the world.

My phone was my lifeline to David and Tetyana, the two people I could rely on when things got sticky. I still didn't know what was expected from me, and I wasn't sure if the butler knew why we were here.

"Look," I said to Oliver. "Could you ask this host of yours if we could keep our phones? It's just for the weekend. I think they will understand. They know Katy and I aren't here for the retreat."

The butler's face remained stoic.

"I'm afraid my instructions were clear. Everyone, including you, Ms. Kade, must respect our policy with no exceptions."

"You can't do this!" said Katy, stomping her foot. "How am I supposed to call my daughter and talk to my hubby?"

"You're welcome to call them now, Ms. McCafferty."

"This is nuts."

"I'm just doing my job. The host informed me that you'll remain here till Sunday, at which time I've been instructed to hand over your phones with the full check for your catering order."

I squinted at the man, wondering how much more he knew than what he was letting on.

Did he know we received a hefty retainer before coming here, plus a promise for ten thousand dollars for every night we stayed on the island? He couldn't possibly imagine a cheesecake would cost that much, could he?

I turned to Katy.

"Would you mind if I stay? You can take the boat back home with Mike tonight."

Katy's eyes bulged.

"Are you nuts? You think I'm going to leave you alone here in this crazy place?"

It took all my willpower to not look at the butler.

"Katy," I tried again. "You don't have to stay, if you don't want to. Maybe it's best if you go home and let me—"

"As if I'd let you. I'm staying!"

Katy blew a raspberry and stomped to the other end of the boat to call Peace and Chantelle.

Everyone in my friends and family circle had a stubborn streak. Katy was no exception. When she made up her mind, there was no cajoling, convincing, or even bribing to change it.

I stepped away from Oliver to call David.

He was still in class, teaching his last students of the day. I left a short message, hoping he wouldn't panic and send a rescue helicopter with Tetyana brandishing a semi-automatic rifle.

With a resigned sigh, I handed my phone to Oliver. Katy gave hers shortly after, but not without shooting him a dark look.

"I get first dibs to use your phone, when I need to," she growled.

"I'm afraid we have no telephone at the hotel, Ms. McCafferty. Only an emergency radio we use judiciously," he replied.

While Katy stared at him, mouth open, he stepped around her, and handed all our devices to Mike.

The boat captain took them with a crooked smile. He opened a small safe in the wheelhouse, stashed everything inside, turned the lock, pocketed the key, and turned to Katy and me.

He had a smug look on his face.

Chapter Eight

"This way, ladies."

Katy and I stepped up to the walkway, following Oliver. He rolled our suitcases behind him, refusing to let us take them ourselves.

"Sounds like you've got a nice hotel up there," I said, trying to think of how to coerce more information from this tight-lipped man.

"They did a flurry of renovations last summer," said Oliver. "A lot of money was spent on this place in a very short time frame."

"Why the rush?" I asked.

"New owner," he replied.

"The host?"

"Indeed."

"Can you tell us who they are?"

"I would, if I knew."

I exchanged a confused glance with Katy.

"Do we get a sea view room at least?" asked Katy, still upset for having lost her phone to a smelly fishing boat captain.

Oliver turned back to glance at us.

"Oh, you will, Ms. McCafferty. I was given strict instructions to assign you ladies the lighthouse."

I thought I caught a glint in his eye when he said that. Or maybe it was just a reflection of the meager sun.

"Lighthouse?" said Katy, giving him a dismayed look.

Was he pulling our leg? Was it even possible for anyone to stay inside a lighthouse, let alone sleep in one over a weekend?

"You'll see," said Oliver, not looking back. "I think you'll like the accommodations the host has made for you."

Katy cursed under her breath. She wasn't the swearing kind. She didn't want to be here. I felt bad for dragging my friend into this now.

For her sake, I hoped we'd get at least a comfy bed in a nonsmoking room with a clean bathroom nearby. If not, Katy would totally flip.

Shoving my worries to the back of my mind, I kept my eyes on the path.

This walkway needed work. Most of it was made of solid planks with metal rivets that had been pounded to the ground to keep everything in place.

But where the cliff jutted out here and there, someone had added steps tied with rope. While most of the walkway was solid, the stairs wobbled.

Oliver didn't seem to have any trouble carrying our weekend suitcases up. He'd done this many times before, I thought, watching him.

Though I'd only seen his wife briefly, they looked fit and healthy, despite the gray hair. I'd put them in their fifties.

You'd have to be in good shape and in good health to live and work in a place like this. The fresh air no doubt helped too.

"Oh!"

I lunged toward Katy and grabbed her by the arm. Her foot had slipped through two steps, but she was holding onto me.

"I almost got killed!" she cried out.

Oliver, who'd been ahead of us by several paces, turned around, but he'd missed Katy's near tumble to the rocky shores below.

Leaving our luggage behind, he clambered down toward us, genuine concern on his face.

"It's slippery," I said. "Someone could get hurt."

"The rope has come loose here," he muttered as he bent down and tightened a knot.

"There," he said, straightening up and turning to Katy. "You wouldn't have fallen through. The steps would have held. This rope was just a little loose, that's all. It gave the illusion you were falling."

"Well, it was a pretty scary illusion," snapped Katy. "Sounds like you need to get your reno crew to fix this or ask for your money back."

Oliver gave her a meek nod.

"Please accept my apologies, Ms. McCafferty—"

"I'm not taking another step," declared Katy. "Isn't there any other way to the top?"

"I'm afraid, no. This is our only route to the hotel. My sincere apologies."

I turned to him. "How did the construction crew get up the cliff with their equipment and gear?"

"By helicopter, of course."

"Helicopter?"

"The new owner allocated significant project funds, so the construction company had a lot of leeway. They even rented a trawler to bring all the building material over. It was quite a sight to see."

"Sounds like an expensive operation."

"Yes. They anchored near the cove down there and used a chopper to transport everyone and everything to the island. They even built a landing pad up on top. Never seen anything like it before in my life, to be honest."

"So, tell me, who is this new owner?" I asked.

Oliver bent down to examine another knot. "Let me tighten this," he said, as if he hadn't heard me.

This was the second time I'd asked him about the host.

This was also the second time he had evaded my question.

Chapter Nine

"That's a long way down," said Katy as we got close to the plateau.

I paused to look behind me.

Surrounding the island was the great Pacific Ocean. The water changed from bright cobalt to a deep marine blue as it got farther away from land.

Tempestuous waves with frothy white crowns rolled toward the shore below us. The sun had lost its battle against the clouds and had retreated behind them.

But even in this weather, the view was grand.

To the west, in the far distance, was a craggy blue line. The mountain range along the Oregon coast, I gathered.

"That's where we came from, right?" I asked.

"The mainland," replied Oliver.

"Hey, there's Mike," said Katy.

We watched as his boat sped across the vast ocean, looking like a tiny toy from afar.

I felt a knot in my stomach to see our main transportation leave us, carrying our only means to communicate with the rest of civilization.

"He's gone," said Katy in a small voice.

As if sensing our unease, Oliver pointed in the other direction.

"You're missing the best part, ladies," he said. "Just a few more steps and you'll never believe your eyes."

We followed him to the top of the walkway and stopped, gaping at the sight in front of us.

This was possibly how the explorers from the Lost World felt when they'd trekked through the jungles of South America to the plains on top.

The message that came with our cake order had said this was a luxury retreat. They hadn't lied.

Even with the winds picking up, I couldn't help but gawk.

The lighthouse and the building next to it were in immaculate condition. They looked like something you'd find in a lifestyle magazine that targeted affluent, first-class travelers.

The main resort was three stories high and looked like a sophisticated five-star boutique hotel. The rooms on the third floor looked out to the sea and had floor-to-ceiling patio windows and wrap-around glass balconies. Whoever stayed there would never miss the magnificent view.

On the flat piece of land next to the building was the helipad Oliver talked about. In front of the building was a sprawling swimming pool with crystal-clear blue water and an extra-large hot tub.

"Heated," said the butler when he saw me look, "as long as it's not raining, it's very nice in there."

"Wow," said Katy, twirling around in place. "This was worth the climb." She smiled. "Now you're talking."

I had to agree.

This wasn't a place for anyone scared of heights, but the vista was stunning.

The only barrier preventing anyone from falling to the shores below was a line of large white boulders that had been placed strategically around the island.

"How come we don't get to stay in one of those rooms?" asked Katy, pointing at the resort.

"According to my instructions, all the writers must stay at the hotel. They have a strict work schedule," he replied. "You wouldn't want to be with them. Trust me."

I turned toward the tower we'd be spending the night in. Even from down here, I could see the enormous glass-encased light on top of the structure—a light that probably saved many lives in the olden days.

"Does it still work?" I asked.

"Untouched for a decade now," replied Oliver. "With GPS and satellites, no one needs a lighthouse anymore. They were going to get rid of it."

His eyes wrinkled in the corners, and I detected a sadness in his voice.

"That's too bad," I said.

He nodded. Oliver was opening up.

"So, what happened?" I asked.

"The government was going to take it down a few years ago," he said, "but everyone in the village rallied around, wrote letters and in the end, we saved it. They sold it to the village for a dollar. Lighthouse, building and the island."

Katy let out a whistle.

"A dollar?" she said. "For the entire island?"

"The village had to sign an agreement they'd renovate this place to modern standards and maintain it as a heritage structure. The repair work alone would cost millions of dollars. So, it wasn't truly a one-dollar purchase."

"Who bought this place?" I asked, crossing my fingers behind my back.

Are we finally going to learn the identity of whoever invited us here?

"The city sat on this property for a long time. They were looking for someone with enough cash to honor the government agreement. In the meantime, they paid Mary and me a small salary to stay and make sure local teens wouldn't row up and have late-night bonfires or drunken parties. It was late last year when everything changed."

Katy and I gave him a questioning look.

"What happened last year?" I asked.

"An investor paid three quarters of a million dollars to the village and took ownership of the island. It was a hundred grand more than they were asking."

"Someone wanted this place badly," I said.

Oliver pointed with his chin toward the mainland.

"The village had a big deficit from a storm cleanup a few years back. They were happy to sell at any price, to tell the truth. This sale was pure luck. Mary and I got lucky too, as the new owner wanted us to stay. Then, within months of buying the property, we had an army of construction teams come over to fix the place."

Oliver was sharing details I hadn't expected him to, but he looked away occasionally like he was avoiding eye contact. In those moments, I couldn't help wondering if he was misleading us.

My gut was telling me to stay on guard.

"So, who is this new owner?" I asked.

Oliver shrugged and gave us a blank look.

"I wish I knew."

"You don't know your own boss?" asked Katy.

"We communicate via email and through a law firm in New York. They paid us well after taking over, so we have nothing to complain about."

"Don't you have any inkling of who they are?" I asked.

"The mayor's guess is he's a billionaire from Russia or China who wanted to get their money out of their countries."

"Money laundering?" I said, raising an eyebrow.

Oliver shook his head.

"To tell the truth, no one really knows if it's a foreigner, or even if it's a man or a woman or a company. Could be a Silicon Valley millionaire who doesn't know what to do with all their money. What we do know is they want to stay anonymous."

"Don't you find it strange?" I said.

Oliver shrugged.

"My job is to follow instructions and not ask too many questions."

"Aren't you even a tad curious?" asked Katy.

"I get paid not to be curious. Our salary tripled after they bought this place."

"Is that right?" asked Katy.

I shot a warning glance Katy's way. We couldn't push Oliver too far or he'd clam up altogether.

Oliver gestured toward the main building.

"We live in a palace now. All we have to do is take care of the buildings and set up an annual retreat for their special guests once a year. Not bad at all, if you ask me."

A heavy gust of wind made me almost lose my balance. I clutched at Katy's arm and stepped away from the ledge.

"I apologize," said Oliver, stirring. He shot us a wry smile. "We just opened and haven't got any visitors till this weekend. When two curious city ladies like you ask questions about my home, I can get carried away and forget my duties."

"We don't mind at all," I said, smiling back.

"Would you like to see your accommodations now?" he asked, turning and walking over to the lighthouse.

We followed him toward the tower. Oliver put his hand on the handle of the large red steel door and smiled.

"I think you'll be surprised at what the host has arranged for you."

Chapter Ten

It was nothing like what I'd expected.

We'd walked into a mini museum dedicated to the relics of the sea.

On the wall hung oil paintings of tall ships of long ago. Miniature sailboats sat on a table and a ship's massive iron anchor leaned against the wall near the entrance.

An antique whalebone knife hung on a shelf between two paintings. Carved on the ivory handle was the final scene from *Moby Dick* when the whalers confronted the great white whale.

Someone had spent weeks, maybe months, creating that intricate detail.

"This knife belongs in a museum," I said.

"Aye," nodded Oliver. "The owner spared no expense."

"Spectacular," said Katy, wandering around the circular entranceway at the base of the building.

I walked up to the front of the lighthouse that faced the open ocean. The facade on this end was made of well-insulated, industrial-strength glass panes.

I could hardly hear the howling wind now. This was what you got when you had millions to throw into a reno project.

In the center of the first floor was a wrought-iron stairway that spiraled up to the landing above us.

I peered up.

"Your rooms are just below the library," said Oliver, making his way to the stairway with our bags. "Three floors up."

"There's a library up there?" I asked, following him up the stairs, my boots clanging on the metal steps.

Oliver stopped and looked down at us, his eyes shining.

"It was like they sent me a gift. I love to read and voila, the new owner built a library fit for a king, right here."

"Lucky you," I said with a smile.

"The owner was very precise. They sent a list of which books to order and how they were to be arranged on the shelves."

"Sounds pedantic," I said, "your new boss, I mean."

Oliver didn't reply, reverting to his butler's poise.

"Did they renovate the top floor too?" I ventured to get him talking again.

"The crew installed the windows and replaced the railing and balcony outside. But the old light stands where it sat for almost a century. They upgraded the electrical wiring and there's a newfangled gear box now. I don't dare touch it. They covered it in a glass panel anyway and you need a special key to open it."

"Who has the key?" I asked, curious.

Oliver shrugged. "I presume the new owner does."

"Are we allowed near the light?"

"I'm the only person who goes up. Mary doesn't like to climb up here. I polish the light every week. It's quite the sight to behold."

"Do we have this all to ourselves?" asked Katy excitedly from behind me.

"All yours this weekend, ladies," Oliver replied as he stepped onto the second landing. "I was instructed to open this for you and only you for the duration of your stay here."

He gestured to the open room that held three antique wardrobes and one full bathroom.

"Your dressing room," he said.

Katy and I gawked.

An entire floor of the tower dedicated to us showering and changing? Now, I wished I'd brought more clothes.

"Ooh, a dress steamer," said Katy, pointing at the contraption at the corner of the room. "I'll need that tonight."

I peeked inside the oversized bathroom.

"The entire world can see you taking a shower here," I said, making a face. "Did they forget to put up curtains or shutters?"

"Rest assured no one can see inside the lighthouse," said Oliver, "other than the occasional seagull."

"What about boats going by?"

"We're too high up. Besides, not too many boats come this way these days. You have nothing to worry about."

We trooped after Oliver to the third floor, wondering what our bedrooms were going to look like.

He turned to us and smiled when we got to the next landing.

"You didn't believe me when I said you'd enjoy your accommodations, did you?"

I gazed at the room that opened in front of us. It was the size of a premier five-star hotel suite and took over the entire third floor of the lighthouse.

Katy skipped up the stairs from behind. Brushing past me and the butler, she ran in, squealing in delight.

Thick wooden beams crisscrossed the high ceiling. Three queen beds snuggled against the walls on either side with a glass-encased wood fireplace in the middle of the room. Someone had lit a fire here recently, but it had died down, leaving warm red embers behind the grate.

Oliver placed our luggage beside the beds and walked over to the fireplace. He bent down to check a small white device that had been installed next to it.

A carbon monoxide detector. And a fire alarm beside it.

Oliver had been telling the truth.

Whoever fixed this place had done an excellent job bringing a century-old structure to modern safety standards. We didn't have to sleep in a rustic drafty room after all, I thought in relief.

From up here, it seemed like the ocean stretched on forever. If the view was this impressive now, I wondered what it must be like on a sunny day.

"It's absolutely gorgeous," said Katy, beaming. "It's a cross between a cozy hobbit's den and a five-star hotel, with an ocean view to boot."

She stopped to give a stern glance at Oliver, who was poking the fire with a long metal stick.

"This is why I wanted my phone," she said. "How do I take pictures for my daughter now? She'd love to see this."

He gave her a sympathetic smile.

"I can understand, Ms. McCafferty. I'm still waiting for further instructions from the host, but I don't see why you can't take a few photos once the retreat is over on Sunday. Mike will be back with your phones by then."

"How many writers are you having over for the retreat?" I asked.

Oliver paused, as if he wasn't sure he should divulge that information.

"Seven in total."

He paused again.

"I was wondering if we have enough cake to go around," I said, hoping that would egg him on to talk more.

"I was requested to send ten invitations, but only seven responded," he said. "Still, it will be a full house."

"Are you expecting us to cater more desserts this weekend?" I asked. "Our instructions were a little, er, cryptic."

"Your Dulce de Leche cheesecake is all we need for tonight."

"Do you know why the host wanted us to stay over?"

Oliver gave a small shrug.

"I presumed it was to make up for you coming all the way to Oregon. I'm afraid I'm in the dark as much as you are."

"Can you tell us who the other guests are?" I asked.

"You'll meet them all at dinner tonight," he said.

"Can you give us a hint?" said Katy, shooting him an eager smile. She knew when and how to turn on her charm. "All these famous people," she gushed. "I'm so nervous and I can't wait to see them."

Oliver smiled a small smile.

"Well, there's a children's book author, a cartoonist, a well-known novelist, a publisher, and, er, a very prolific writer of erotica." He gave us a side glance. "You've already met the poet and the screenwriter."

"The two men who came with us?" I asked.

He nodded.

"I thought retreats were specialized," said Katy. "Not that I know much about them, but don't they usually have one for novel writers, another for screenwriters or poets and all that?"

"I just follow instructions."

I was dying to ask more, but Oliver had already shared more than a normal butler would, and I could see he was getting a bit edgy.

I scanned the vista outside, as if I'd find answers out on the open sea.

Think, girl, think.

What do a photograph of a bloated dead man, a writer's retreat on a remote island, and an invitation for us to bring a cheesecake have in common?

Chapter Eleven

"Who invited us, Oliver?" I asked. "Was it you?"

Oliver's eyes flickered, and he glanced out the window.

"This is our first event," he replied, hesitating. "The owner wanted to launch the resort in spring with ten writers. I received instructions on who to invite via email."

"And us?"

"The owner invited you. They sent me an email last week saying to treat you like a guest."

"So is everyone here, except for us, famous?" asked Katy.

Oliver nodded, picked up a piece of wood from the log grate and threw it into the fireplace.

"Those who keep up with the literary news will know who they are."

"I keep up with celebrity gossip," said Katy.

"Novelists and poets aren't like actors," said Oliver. "Very few become household names. They're a reclusive bunch. When they hit the big time, they usually go into hiding. Not like Hollywood stars who'd kill for publicity."

"What's the younger writer's name?" asked Katy. "I'm sure I've seen him before. Was he on TV?"

"Francesco Javier Quinteiro," said Oliver, trying to re-ignite the fire. "Poet laureate from Mexico. He made it big at a very young age and surprised many people."

Katy turned to me.

"I swear there's something familiar about his face."

"He wrote some political poems," said Oliver. "He shot to fame about seven years ago at only twenty-seven. The Mexican government denounced him, but the outcry from the people was so strong, they eventually made him their poet laureate. Anyway, that's what his bio says."

"Wow," said Katy. "What a career."

"I thought he was in his twenties," I said, half debating whether to tell Oliver about this famous poet's near-drowning incident. "What about the older one that was all bundled up?"

"Mr. Elliot Ward?" said Oliver. "He used to be a well-known Hollywood agent but went quiet almost ten years ago. He reappeared recently as a screenwriter. One of his scripts got made into a movie that won an Oscar nomination. I hear he wants to set his next story on the West Coast. I think that's why he's here."

"That's super exciting," said Katy, brightening up.

"They all came to work here?" I said. "No phones, no parties? Just write all day like at a true writers' retreat?"

"Funny thing is...."

"Yes?" I said, quietly.

"Funny thing is, I was told not to call it a retreat on half the invitations."

"Oh?" I raised an eyebrow. "What did you write on those invites?"

Katy opened her mouth to say something, but I put a hand on her forearm to shush her. The butler had taken us into his confidence. We couldn't jar him awake and have him shut up now.

"In the remaining invitations, I was told to say they were going to meet VIPs from Hollywood who can help make their stories into movies.

The thing is, no one from the movie industry is here, except for that screenwriter, of course, but he's just...."

"Small potatoes?" I said.

Oliver turned to me and gave a start, as if he had just realized we were there.

"Unless you two ladies are disguised television producers?" he said.

"Who, us?" said Katy. "Oh, I wish. We're just bakers."

With an embarrassed look, Oliver got up and brushed the ash off his trousers.

"I'm sure you want to get comfortable and change. I should let you go. Drinks will be served at four and dinner will be at six thirty. It's a black-tie affair. Enjoy your stay."

With a small bow, he spun around and marched toward the stairway. We heard his footsteps on the lighthouse staircase. We stood still in our spots until we heard the steel door on the bottom floor clang shut.

That was when a chilling thought crossed my mind.

Is Oliver the owner, pretending to be the butler?

If Oliver was the owner, it would explain him opening up to us like this, sharing tidbits, paving the way to explaining why he'd brought us here.

Why would he do that?

I didn't know why I felt nervous, but my palms had begun to sweat. I turned to Katy and lowered my voice.

"What are the odds *he's* our host?"

Chapter Twelve

"We only have his word that he and Mary work here," I said.

"What about Mike?" said Katy. "He would know."

"Question is how to make him talk. Did you see his cocky face when he locked up our phones? He looked like the cat that got its cheese."

"Cream," said Katy. "The cat that got the cream."

"Whatever," I said. "Thing is, a normal butler isn't this chatty. He'd have left the bags down, bid us a good day, and left. Oliver didn't tell us everything, but he shared a lot. It was all very staged. Didn't you find that strange?"

Katy sat down on the nearest bed and shot me a quizzical look.

"This place probably cost millions to upgrade and we haven't even seen the main resort yet," she said. "Oliver doesn't look like a billionaire or even a millionaire to me."

"Have you ever met a billionaire?" I asked.

"Of course, I have. Madame Bouchard," said Katy.

"She's old-school and from another era. Billionaires don't go around dressed up like King Louis XIV and Marie Antoinette these days. They wear flip-flops in their private jets."

Katy frowned.

"You think Oliver sent that dead man's picture to us?"

"That's what we're going to find out," I said, pulling up my suitcase onto the luggage rack.

I unzipped it and pushed aside my thick socks, waterproof pants, and fleece shirts. I pulled out my black velvet gown, shook it, and hung it on my bedpost.

I was glad we'd brought our long coats to wear over our party dresses. It was going to be a chilly walk to the main building.

I glanced over my shoulder at Katy, to see her still staring at me.

"You getting ready for drinks and dinner, hun?"

With a sigh, she leaned over to pick up her suitcase and plopped it on her bed.

"It's beautiful here and all," she said, as she unzipped her bag and pulled out her long red satin dress, "but something about this place is giving me the creeps."

"We're here only till Sunday. If anything happens, which I doubt it will, we can ask Mike to take us on the next boat back."

"Oh!"

I turned around to see Katy bent over her bedside table, peering at something.

"What is it?" I asked.

She picked up a square piece of paper and waved it at me.

"Check this out."

I walked over. It was a small card, like one of those RSVP cards you get for fancy parties.

"It's for you," she said, thrusting it in my hands.

I read it out aloud.

"Dear Ms. Kade, thank you for coming. I knew you would. Madame Bouchard told me you always keep your promises when someone calls for help."

I stopped and looked up at my friend.

"It's from the host."

She nodded.

I turned back to the card.

"I invite you and your companions to join the black-tie dinner in the main dining hall tonight. Please serve your Dulce de Leche cheesecake after dinner. There will be one particular person in the room who will enjoy it immensely. Enjoy your stay on my island and be assured you're here, not as caterers, but as my esteemed guests."

I paused, my eyes widening as I glanced at the next line.

"What is it?" asked Katy.

I continued reading aloud.

"P.S. Seven guests arrived today. Not all will leave the island on Sunday."

Katy and I stared at each other.

"What does that mean?" she said finally.

I shook my head. I had no idea what to think. Was this a threat? Was it a call for help?

"Did they sign it?" whispered Katy, leaning over my shoulder.

I peered at the card.

"Welcome to Coffin Island, The Host."

I turned to Katy.

"Let's see that photo again."

She pulled out the printout of the photograph and smoothed it out. We sat on the bed and stared at the picture in her hand and the note in mine.

"There's a reason they sent this picture to us," I said, scrunching my forehead. "Is it someone we know?"

"I'd remember seeing a dead body on the beach."

"We saw a lot of dead bodies ten years ago," I said, frowning. "This could be any one of them."

"That was so long ago," said Katy, with a grimace. She hated it when anyone raked our past. It was something to be left behind and forgotten.

"Whoever sent this to us knew Madame Bouchard," I said.

Katy sighed.

"Maybe we're reading too much into this. Maybe this is just a simple stock photo. An actor playing dead. Could be a picture from a movie, like the one I watched with Chantelle last week. What was—"

"Zimmerman," I said, sitting up.

"What?" asked Katy.

"You said movies," I said. "That reminded me. Remember, Zimmerman was at the Mexican border when we caught up to him?"

"But we didn't see him die."

"Yes, but Emma Foster shot at his boat with an assault rifle and it crashed on the shore. Do you really think he survived that?"

"I thought he sank to the bottom of the bay. It's a bit of a stretch to think he crawled out and fell dead on the beach after we left."

"His body could have got washed to the shore," I said, staring at the picture.

The body was so bloated and bleached, it would have been hard to identify, even if he had fallen face up.

"But what does Zimmerman have to do with this place?" asked Katy. "This is a writer's retreat. Not a Hollywood executive party."

"Maybe you're right," I said, "maybe I'm reading too much into this, and maybe this is just a stock photo."

"Wait," said Katy, clutching my arm, her green eyes widening. "I know why they sent this pic."

"Why?"

"Because someone is going to die exactly like this. That's what this photo is all about."

I picked up the host's note and read it out loud again.

"Seven guests arrived today. Not all will leave the island on Sunday."

I looked at my friend. Something told me she had a point.

"Someone's going to die this weekend, Asha," said Katy, her face turning slightly pale. "I'm sure of it."

My heart beat a tick faster.

Chapter Thirteen

The dining hall was buzzing when we arrived.

"Are you our resplendent host?" boomed a male voice from the far end of the hall.

A shrill woman's laugh echoed across the room, bouncing off the crystal chandelier over the dining table.

It was Oliver who had welcomed Katy and me at the main door and taken our coats. As soon as he'd shown us to the dining hall, he'd disappeared carrying our coats with him.

Katy and I stood near the open doorway and surveyed the crowd.

No one had noticed us arrive yet. It was a perfect opportunity to take stock of this place and these people.

Five guests had gathered near the bay windows that opened to the balcony outside.

It was too cold to be out without a jacket, but there was still afternoon light outside. The panoramic view from up here was as striking as that from our lighthouse bedroom window.

The three men were in shiny black tuxedos with bow ties, while the two women had on long dinner gowns and a copious amount of makeup. One of the women wore a shimmering emerald-green necklace, the other a beautiful four-strand pearl choker.

The room smelled of expensive perfume and decadent alcohol. The row of empty champagne glasses on the buffet table said they'd started drinking a while ago. Either that, or they were fast drinkers.

The shrill laughter had come from the woman in the pearl choker.

She looked to be in her sixties. Her white hair was tastefully done up, and she looked stately in her long blue gown with that pearl necklace. With her ample girth and an almost double D bust, she upended Katy's theory that all writers were unhealthily skinny.

Facing her was a bespectacled man with gray hair around his temples. He was the tallest man in the room and was the type of commanding figure you'd expect to see featured in a business magazine about CEOs.

It was his voice we'd heard booming when we came in. He was dominating the conversation and seemed to enjoy making his presence felt.

To his left was the second woman who looked to be in her fifties. She was rail thin and wearing a floor-length lime green dress that clashed wildly with her brilliantly red-dyed hair.

While we watched, she gulped down her champagne and turned to the buffet table with a cross look, as if upset the butler hadn't come with a refill right away.

But neither Oliver nor Mary was anywhere in sight.

With a frustrated hiss, the woman slammed down her champagne glass on a side table and turned back to the group.

Standing next to her, with an amused look on his face, was a thirty-something African American man in a sharp black tuxedo. The only one without a drink, he was standing, hands thrust into his pockets, casually listening in on the conversation. But something about that smirk made me wonder what was going through his mind.

Completing the circle was the screenwriter who had come with us in the boat. He still had his brown beret on his head, but he'd changed from his scruffy pants and shirt into a wrinkled suit, which he most probably brought in that rucksack of his.

Though he was dressed up, he looked as miserable as he had been in the cold, wet boat. He hunched his shoulders and turned his face down, eyes on his half-drunk champagne glass. I couldn't imagine a more fitting picture of the suffering artist.

"Over there," whispered Katy, elbowing me.

I turned to look.

Away from the crowd and leaning quietly against a window was the young man who'd almost drowned on our way here. He looked out of place in this opulent gathering. I couldn't imagine this was the poet laureate of Mexico.

I wondered if anyone had even noticed him.

While the others were dressed for a black-tie event, he was still in his camouflage jacket and cargo pants.

A rebel for sure. But did he have a cause, I wondered.

He had self-exiled himself from this social circle, and was staring morosely out the window, a faraway look on his face. He was from a different generation from the boomer crowd, and looked like he'd rather have been in his room, reading or writing.

He was the only one who spotted Katy and me near the doorway.

He stared at us gloomily for a second, then looked away. He gave no hello, no wave, just a simple nod of recognition at me—the person who'd jumped in that cold ocean to save his life.

The image of his suspended body in the water crossed my mind again, making me shiver. It had been so spooky, even I was wondering if I'd imagined it.

I scanned the room.

"Can you guess who is who here?" I whispered to Katy.

"Can't even begin to imagine," she whispered back. "I could have helped you if this was a Hollywood retreat."

Finding that note in our room had awakened Katy's sleuthing spirit. She no longer complained about missing her phone or being stuck on the island. It was good to have my partner back.

"What did that note from the host mean? It didn't say anyone will die or get killed. Just that not everyone will leave."

"The host is playing a big sick joke on us," said Katy. "Either that, or one of these people will die before the weekend is over."

I nudged my friend.

"Come on. Time to find out."

I stepped toward the group after fixing a bright smile on my face, the kind you put on when you're walking into a room full of strangers you're forced to mingle with.

"Ah, I see we have more company," boomed the CEO man, spotting us walking over.

Katy had turned her charming dial up. She was an excellent actor, when she decided to take part. I was glad she was playing along.

"Thomas Ratcliffe," said the big man, taking my hand in his paws and gripping mine so hard I almost yelped in pain.

"Asha Kade," I said, trying not to wince.

The way he was looking at us made me feel like we were supposed to know who he was. I turned to Katy to see if she did. She was the one who read the gossip columns.

But Katy shook his hand with a lot less enthusiasm than she normally did when greeting our celebrity clients at the bakery.

"Senior executive at Ratcliffe and Shuman," whispered an English-accented voice in my ear. The mix of high-street perfume and cigarettes wafted to my nose.

I turned to see the red-haired woman in the green dress standing next to me.

"A big dog in New York," she said with a conspiratorial wink. "You'd know if you hang out in our circles. Personally, I can't stand the man."

"Oh?" I said, kicking myself for forgetting to put on my poker face. Now she knew we weren't in the publishing business.

I offered my hand. "I'm Asha Kade."

"Camilla Carter."

"Are you a publisher too?"

"Good heavens, no. I'm just a writer. Hahaha."

I forced a smile.

"May I ask what you write?"

She leaned toward me and lowered her voice.

"I make a killing writing hot and steamy novellas. *A killing.*"

I raised an eyebrow.

She seemed to me the most unlikely writer, let alone one who wrote erotica. Camilla was someone I'd have expected to meet at a high-end casino. Then again, what did I know of writers.

"Congratulations," I said, "sounds like you've done very well for yourself."

Camilla flashed a proud smile.

"Have you been an author all your career?" I asked, trying to make small talk.

She opened her mouth, then stopped. Her eyes journeyed from the top of my head to my toes and back up again, as if she was appraising me.

Strange, I thought. It was just a simple question, but she was gauging if she should answer me or not.

What's she afraid of?

Camilla glanced at her glass and made a face.

"Gotta get my champagne refreshed. Don't want to die of thirst. Hahaha."

Brushing past me, she took off toward the buffet table, making me wonder what hot button I'd pressed.

One by one, I got to know the guests.

Ratcliffe was the wealthy publisher from New York, and Camilla Carter was the erotica writer who'd flown all the way from London.

The woman with the pearl necklace was Sophia Knight, the children's book author from San Diego. Jason Taylor, who'd been listening with his hands in his pockets, was a cartoonist and graphic novelist from San Francisco.

Elliot Ward was our miserable-looking screenwriter from LA. And Javier Quinteiro was the Mexican poet.

Except Javier never made a move to introduce himself. I only knew his name because Oliver had told us earlier.

I watched him closely for a while, trying to remain as discreet as possible. There was something odd about him, something more than him just being a quiet introvert who preferred his own company. I couldn't put a finger on it, but something about him troubled me.

While Katy chatted with the others, I did a head count, trying to recall what the butler told us about each of these people.

Ten guests had been invited, but only seven had RSVP'd. There were six gathered by the side of the dining table now.

That meant one person was missing from this crowd.

Was that the mysterious host?

Chapter Fourteen

Oliver and Mary walked in with two trays of champagne flutes.

"There you are," said Camilla, brightening. "I thought you'd never come."

Mary had changed from her pink overalls to a pair of plain black pants and a crisp white shirt. She looked as serious as an undertaker as she presented her drink tray to Camilla.

The guests milled around with their fresh drinks.

Next to me, Elliot was trying to convince Ratcliffe to read his latest screenplay, while Ratcliffe was saying he was too busy to read submissions. That's what agents are for, he scoffed.

Jason was talking animatedly to a bored-looking Camilla now. Snippets of their conversation wafted over to me. If I believed him, he was a darling of Silicon Valley, a master of the perfect confluence of art and technology. One of his masterpieces was about to launch with national fanfare in LA next month.

Camilla didn't look impressed.

Sophia was telling Katy how her previous career as an Oscar-nominated movie star made her the perfect person to write a children's book. She could write a best-seller in days, she was saying to my friend, who looked sufficiently fascinated.

Katy was a good actress.

It looked like any fancy gathering of the annoyingly snotty upper crust, the type of friends Madame Bouchard used to hang out with. I sized them up one by one, wondering what was so special about this crowd.

Why would anyone want to target them? Who was in danger here?

But one question bothered me above all else.

What exactly did the host want from me?

Whatever it was, it had to be worth at least thirty thousand dollars, depending on how long we were to stay on this island.

I knew that wasn't a lot of money to a billionaire or even a millionaire, but it was a hefty chunk of change for an entrepreneur like me with high rent to pay in New York.

I racked my brain trying to think of how that picture of the naked dead man fit in with all this.

On our way up the walkway, I'd surveyed the area to see if I recognized anything from the photo. But that picture had been taken on the dry southern coast. There were no cactus plants or sand dunes in the cooler climes of the Pacific Northwest.

"Will the host be joining us for dinner tonight?"

It was Sophia addressing Oliver, who was lighting the tall candles on the dining table.

"What a magical idea it was to convert a historic lighthouse into a fancy resort getaway," gushed Sophia, "I can't wait to meet the new owner."

"I'm afraid, Mrs. Knight," said Oliver, "our host has confirmed they will not be joining us this weekend."

A murmur of disappointment went around the room.

"Why not?" boomed Ratcliffe.

"They're unavailable, sir, but they send their deepest regrets."

"Everyone was buzzing about this exclusive writers' retreat. I was the only publisher from New York invited, I might add," said Ratcliffe, a proud smile on his face. "Only reason I came all the way here was to see him. It's fitting we meet."

"Me too," said Sophia. "I'd always wanted to buy an island and renovate it myself. I have so many questions."

"I was going to ask if we can shoot the film for my next screenplay in this location," said Elliot Ward, moodily.

Jason nodded. "Me too. Imagine the exposure from hosting a new tech launch here. I bet you it'll get more business for the resort."

"I don't see how we can have a party without a host," said Camilla, her voice high-pitched. "It's simply not done."

"This is a retreat, not a party," said Javier in a quiet voice, the only dissenter in this crowd. "Why would the owner want to join us while we work?"

Ignoring the younger man, the publisher stepped up to the butler, towering over him.

"Why don't you call him and tell him Ratcliffe is here. Tell him I'd like to see him. Would you do that, my good man?"

Oliver gave him a sad smile.

"I apologize, sir, but I have no authorization to contact them this weekend," he replied. "I don't even have a phone number to call."

The group stared at him in stony silence, confounded someone had denied their request for once. Oliver was keeping remarkable composure, given the circumstances.

There was something strange about this scenario.

I couldn't help but feel that Katy and I were at a show, a show we weren't part of, but one we'd been invited to observe.

That was what the host wanted from me. The keen detective eye.

But what am I looking for?

Oliver gave the crowd a gracious bow.

"If there is anything else you need, ladies and gentlemen, please do not hesitate to ask."

Ratcliffe glared at him.

"Can I get a proper drink at least?"

"Certainly," said Oliver, gesturing toward the liquor cabinet at the end of the room. "What would you prefer, Mr. Ratcliffe?"

We watched Ratcliffe stumble over to the cabinet, with Jason following close behind. Elliot hurried over, like he didn't want to be left out.

"Do you like a good scotch?" we heard him ask the publisher. "I know a store on Madison Avenue that sells only the highest grade."

"Suck up," said Camilla under her breath. She downed her champagne glass, picked up another, and turned to me with a glare. *"Men."*

I felt someone poke at my waist. It was Katy.

"It'll get more interesting if everyone gets pissed tonight," she whispered. "We can pump them for info then."

Maybe. But I wasn't so sure.

I always found the truth came out when people were sober and knew exactly what the stakes were. Drunk people were unreliable. Useless for information.

A bell chimed near the doorway.

We all turned to see Mary ring the dinner bell.

We stepped up to the dining table draped in a fancy blue tablecloth. With crystal wineglasses, gold-rimmed plates and lace napkins, it looked like Oliver and Mary had prepared for mini royalty.

As I looked for my seat, I realized no one had asked Katy and me who we were or what we did. Everyone had been so absorbed in showcasing their status, they hadn't once shown any interest in getting to know us.

That was just the way I wanted it.

"This is your seat, Jason," said Sophia, picking up a name tag on a plate and putting it down. "Where's mine?"

"Mrs. Knight," said Oliver, pulling a chair for her. "I believe you're here."

Katy and I walked around the table, checking the name tags. To my surprise, I realized we had been assigned seats at the ends of the table.

Ratcliffe's face turned sour as he saw Mary pull out a chair for Katy at the end. He turned and scowled my way as I took my seat at the head of the table.

For the hundredth time that day, I wondered about our mysterious host.

Whoever they were, they had created theater tonight.

We were unwitting actors playing a part in a play. A play with a secret plot, and none of us knew how it would unravel.

This meant things were going to get interesting.

I looked around the room, my heart beating a tick faster.

Let the games begin.

Chapter Fifteen

"**T**his isn't your seat, young man," said Camilla, jabbing a sharp red nail on Javier's shoulder.

The poet scrambled up and held the chair for her, mumbling an embarrassed apology.

Once Camilla had taken ownership of her seat, Javier stepped around the table like a frightened gazelle, looking for his spot.

"Right here, Javier," called out Katy, waving his name tag at him. "You're next to me."

With a look of relief, he walked over and plopped on the seat next to my friend. Katy turned to him and flashed her charming smile. He actually smiled back.

I felt sorry for him.

Poet laureate or not, he seemed to be an extreme introvert and wasn't cut out for social gatherings. He was the most awkward person I'd met, and that was probably what made him a great poet.

Once Javier sat down, everyone noticed the empty chair in the middle of the table.

"Who's this place for?" asked Camilla, pointing at the single seat between her and Elliot.

"For the host?" said Sophia, looking at it expectantly.

"Didn't the butler just say he wasn't coming?" said Ratcliffe, impatience in his voice.

"It's for Helen Jenkins."

Everyone turned to Oliver.

"Helen who?" said Ratcliffe.

"I know her," said Jason. "She's a famous novelist. Won the Bookman prize last year, didn't she?"

Camilla gave him a dark look.

"Not like they'd ever give me one of those awards. Even though I make more money than any of these nominated so-and-so's."

"Maybe she didn't get to the boat on time," said Elliot, picking up a bun from the breadbasket and reaching for the butter plate.

"Maybe she refused to hand over her phone, and that captain threw her overboard?" said Ratcliffe, with a smirk.

Elliot let out a guffaw.

"She must have changed her mind," said Jason.

"Probably saw the boat and ran the other way," said Sophia. "Should have done that myself."

"Me too," said Camilla, picking up her wineglass which was already almost empty.

"I need a top up," she said, looking around her, an irritated look on her face. "Where did he go off to now? The service here, honestly."

Mary and Oliver had returned to the kitchen to check on our dinner. Their movements told me they were under strain. I would be too, I thought, if I had to service this demanding crowd.

My stomach sank as I realized my Dulce de Leche cheesecake would be dessert tonight.

I could just imagine their frosty looks and withering words. Why did the host ask me to bring this simple cheesecake, when I could make magazine-cover-worthy, intricately decorated, five-tier fondant cakes? I crossed my fingers under the table, hoping the guests wouldn't massacre it.

"We have among us someone even bigger than a Bookman prize winner."

Sophia was smiling genially at Javier, who was sitting across from her, hunched in his seat like he didn't want anyone to notice him.

"A young protégé," she continued, "and I never even saw you come in."

"It's a pleasure to meet you, ma'am," said Javier politely.

Everyone turned their attention to the poet, perplexed expressions on their faces.

"Did you know he's the youngest poet laureate in the world?" said Sophia to the table. "All the way from Mexico too."

"I grew up in San Diego," mumbled Javier, shifting in his seat. He spoke like he'd lived in America all his life.

Sophia pointed a long, manicured finger at him. "Didn't you win the grand Yeats award last year?" She paused and smiled. "Not bad for someone from Mexico."

I cringed.

Javier slinked farther into his chair and stared at his empty plate, as if wishing he could sink into it and disappear.

Jason looked at the young man like he was seeing him for the first time.

"I've read about you. I thought the Mexican government took you somewhere and tortured you or something."

"Jason!" scolded Camilla. "Must you bring such things up? We're at dinner."

"If they ever come and serve us," grumbled Elliot.

"Poets," sniffed Ratcliffe, taking a swig of his drink. "I never sign any to my firm."

Sophia turned a haughty gaze at him.

"My son, who is a tenured senior professor of political science at Stanford, has read some of his work to his class. You know how diversity is all the rage now? But his class loved it. He'd go gaga if I told him this man is here with us."

"Go gaga all the way," retorted Camilla under her breath, but I heard her.

"What an interesting collection we are," said Ratcliffe, looking around the table with a smile, as if to make amends for his stinging comment. "Poet laureate, Bookman winner, Emmy-nominated screenwriter, a tech artist superstar, and..." He dried up as his gaze landed on Camilla.

She scowled back.

I sighed, feeling like I had dropped into the middle of a daytime soap opera. I'd expected more from a group of supposedly brilliant minds.

The note left in our room flashed to mind.

Was it a joke?

Or was all this a demented game set up by a megalomaniac who didn't know what to do with their money other than play with people?

I knew the right thing to do was to share that message with the other guests. But that could cause panic. Plus, if the host was here, mingling secretly with us, that would only alert them and make them change tactics.

Something told me that would be a dangerous thing to do.

I scrunched my forehead, wishing I knew what this macabre game was. If I knew what was behind all this, I'd have some inclination of the rules. Right now, I felt like I was groping my way through a maze. In the dark.

Katy, on the other hand, seemed to be reveling in the conversation, finally seeing some drama. It wasn't the stodgy writers' dinner party she'd expected.

Seeing me look her way, she flashed a grin. I smiled back, thinking she was enjoying this way too much. Something told me this was more serious than she thought.

"You!" boomed a man's slurred voice.

I looked up to see Ratcliffe pointing my way.

I sat up in alarm.

What does he want with me?

"I'm talking to *you*," he hollered.

Chapter Sixteen

"Who are you?" he growled.

"I'm a baker," I said, feeling my back and shoulders tense up as I spoke.

Ratcliffe's eyes bulged.

Silence fell in the room.

I readied for the arrows to sling my way.

"Did you say *baker?*" said Camilla. "Like a common caterer? Can you even make a minimum wage from that?"

"We do all right," I replied.

"Why are you at the retreat?" asked Ratcliffe.

"We were requested to bring a Dulce de Leche cheesecake for tonight's dinner."

"Is this some joke?" said Elliot.

"You mean to say you're just the *help?*" said Sophia, turning to give me, then Katy, a look of severe disapproval.

Katy glared back.

"We hand-delivered tonight's dessert all the way from New York," I said, surprised at myself for staying calm under such intense scrutiny. But underneath, I could feel my heart hammering.

"I need another drink," said Ratcliffe, pushing his chair back and getting up. He walked over to the cabinet, shaking his head as if this was all too much for him.

"I thought you two wrote gossip columns like that Sex and the City woman," said Jason, the condescending smirk coming to his face again.

"We make cakes for diplomatic and celebrity parties," snapped Katy, barely able to hold herself back anymore. "We've even catered for royalty in Europe."

So there, I almost heard her say.

"And sometimes we take orders for small out-of-town events like this one," I added with a smile.

Sophia opened her mouth, then closed it.

"Well," said Camilla, sitting back in her chair. "I'm glad you're here. Come to think of it, having dinner with the same old people can become such a bore."

"What the dickens is this?" came Ratcliffe's voice from the corner of the room.

We all turned to see him standing near the liquor cabinet. He picked something up from the whiskey tray, frowning.

"What did you find?" asked Elliott, squinting at him.

I craned my neck to see that he was holding up a beige card very much like what we'd found in our room.

Ratcliffe walked over to the table, his eyes on the card.

"What is it?" asked Sophia.

"A love letter?" asked Camilla with a snicker.

"A note from the owner," said Ratcliffe, still not looking up, the lines on his forehead deeper now.

"Read it," said Jason.

Ratcliffe stood behind his chair and held the card up to the light.

"Welcome to my island," he read, half slurring. "I'm honored you joined this special gathering of ingenious minds."

He paused.

"That's it?" said Elliot.

Ratcliffe read the rest of the note.

"You have all connected before. Now you connect again here tonight. Enjoy the retreat. My best regards. The Host."

There was a moment of silence as everyone took the message in.

"So, we're not strangers after all?" said Elliot finally, looking around the table.

"But I've never met any of you before," said Sophia.

"Me neither," said Jason, with a perplexed shrug.

Javier glanced around the table, looking disoriented.

"Must be a silly joke," said Camilla.

Sophia turned and exchanged a quick glance with Camilla. I may have imagined it, but it looked like a warning.

Elliot seemed to notice it as well. He turned from Sophia to Camilla, before looking away as if he caught himself.

Do these three know each other?

"Funny way to greet us," said Ratcliffe, passing the card to Jason, who scrutinized it closely.

Where are Oliver and Mary?

I imagined Oliver had placed that card on the whiskey tray. The question was, who wrote it, or who instructed him to write it.

I was about to get up and find him, when Oliver entered the room.

This time, he had a stranger with him.

Oliver cleared his throat and gave a small bow.

"Ladies and gentlemen, our last guest is here. Ms. Helen Jenkins."

Our newcomer was a slightly overweight woman in her forties, wearing tortoiseshell librarian glasses.

She had on a tan skirt suit with a long black woolen coat opened in front. She looked like any nondescript professional you'd bump into on the subway during an early morning commute.

There was nothing special about her, except for her face, which had turned a petrified white.

She gave the room one look and clutched at Oliver's arm. Oliver held her, a worried look coming onto his face, as if he was wondering what was going on.

She stood by the doorway, swaying on her feet, her eyes flickering from person to person, taking us in, one by one. She gave Katy and me brief confused looks, but she seemed to recognize the others.

"Welcome, Ms. Jenkins," said Jason, getting up from his chair. "I enjoyed all your books, particularly the one that won the award last year. It was sublime."

She stared at him like he was a phantom.

Jason moved forward to shake her hand. With a startled jerk, Helen Jenkins stepped back, dragging Oliver with her.

"Ms. Jenkins?" said Oliver. "Are you feeling all right?"

Helen put a hand over her mouth, terror overcoming her features.

I glanced around the room, taking in everyone's reaction to the new guest. If I had to guess, someone at the table had spooked her. But my dinner companions looked as perplexed as I felt.

"Come on in, then," said Sophia, waving at Helen. "Let's not keep dinner waiting, shall we?"

Elliot turned around.

"Looks like you had a bad boat ride."

"I didn't know the boat ran this late," said Jason, sitting down, surprisingly not offended that the author hadn't shaken his hand. "Must have been a heck of a ride at this time of day."

Helen didn't answer.

Then, as if she couldn't take it anymore, she let go of Oliver's arm and spun around. With a stifled cry, Helen Jenkins ran through the corridor and clambered down the stairs.

Oliver reeled in shock. He dashed after her, calling out, "Ms. Jenkins!"

"My goodness," said Sophia.

"Whatever happened to her?" said Camilla.

"Weak-kneed," said Ratcliffe, shaking his head disdainfully. "Not the seafaring type, I gather."

"I don't blame her," said Sophia, uncharacteristically gracious. "The sea was rough today."

Camilla nodded. "I threw up after coming here this morning."

"I would have too," said Jason. "If I hadn't stuffed myself with Dramamine."

"It was so rough, I fell in and almost drowned," said Javier, his voice unusually calm. "Good thing they pulled me out fast."

I looked at him in surprise. He hadn't fallen out of the boat at sea. He fell from a perfectly stable pier, near the town.

He didn't make eye contact with me or Katy when he spoke. Something about his demeanor made me wonder whether he was having us on.

That was when I realized what had bothered me about him earlier.

Javier had huffed and puffed as he had dragged his heavy suitcase from the cab to the pier. It had made sense he'd fallen off the pier, as he'd wrestled with his luggage. But he had brought that same suitcase up that walkway effortlessly.

What was he hiding?

Chapter Seventeen

"We're writers, not sailors," said Elliot.

"I'm not looking forward to the trip back," said Jason, shaking his head.

A murmur of acknowledgment went around the table. It seemed like Javier's drowning comment hadn't registered with anyone.

Or were they just too self-absorbed to notice someone else's problems?

"Hors d'oeuvres."

It was Oliver walking in with a large silver tray in his hands. His face was white and drawn, looking even more under strain than before.

"Apologies for the delay," he said, placing the tray on the side table and removing the lid. The smell of caramelized butter and freshly baked pastry came our way.

"We were planning to set a buffet for the hors d'oeuvres, but I thought you might prefer to sit down and get to know each other before the main meal."

I turned to him.

"The new guest," I said. "How is she doing?"

"Ms. Jenkins needed some time to prepare for dinner, so she went to her room."

"Is she sick?" asked Katy.

"It's rough out today," said Oliver, not answering her question.

"Maybe some tea might help?" said Sophia.

"Mary is checking up on her right now," said Oliver.

"She looked in a terrible state," said Camilla, shaking her head. "I think you should open up that helicopter pad so people can come here in something other than a smelly fishing boat."

"Of course, Ms. Carter," said Oliver, placing a shrimp puff on her plate. "I will make sure to share your suggestion with the owner."

I picked up the beige card from the table and held it out.

"Oliver, what do you know about this?"

"Ah," he replied. "The welcome note from our host. You found it."

"What the dickens does it mean, my man?" said Ratcliffe, grabbing the card from my hand.

"It says we all know each other," said Jason. "That's not true."

"It's a joke, isn't it?" asked Camilla.

"I believe the message speaks for itself," replied Oliver. He paused like he was choosing his words carefully. "I'm just the butler here."

Ratcliffe flipped the card across the table, almost hitting him.

"Not much of a butler if you can't translate your owner's words to us, are you?"

What a douche.

"Sorry, sir," said Oliver, with a small bow. Without another word, he picked up his empty tray and walked out of the room.

"That wasn't very nice," I said to Ratcliffe.

"Neither is an absentee host," growled Ratcliffe, taking another swig of his drink.

His eyes were getting red, and the liquid in his glass was leveling down at an alarming rate. He was as bad as Camilla who was on her third glass of wine not counting the champagne, if I'd counted right.

"I'm surprised you didn't recognize Helen Jenkins," said Jason to Ratcliffe. "Didn't she sign up with one of your imprints?"

"I don't deal with writers directly."

Camilla shot an angry look at Ratcliffe.

"Do you care for your authors at all?" she asked.

"Absolutely," said Ratcliffe, picking up his whiskey tumbler. "They make me money. Better than a stable of horses."

"Horses? That's what you think of writers?" said Camilla.

"I said better than horses. I'm doing very well with unauthorized biographies written by no-name, ghost writers at the moment."

"But you don't recognize one of your own award-winning writers?" said Javier.

Ratcliffe gave a nonchalant shrug.

"Look, my boy, hiring writers is like hiring monkeys. You offer them a measly pay and a publishing deal and they'll happily sign away their firstborn. I let the agents sort through all that."

Sophia glared at Ratcliffe.

"Let me remind you that you're among a group of writers," she said finally.

"I didn't mean any offense to anyone, but business is business. How am I going to afford the company HQ in Manhattan if I didn't make sure the money comes in? I work hard at this game."

The looks everyone gave him were nothing short of murderous.

I wondered if Ratcliffe's days were numbered.

Was this what this game was all about? Pitting everyone against each other to see who was the most rotten to the core?

Then what?

Would someone shoot him in the back and leave him to die on the beach down at the shore, like in that photo?

Before anyone could respond to Ratcliffe, Oliver and Mary walked into the room, carrying our dinner plates, two in each arm. After serving the women, they returned to the kitchen to bring the remaining plates for the men.

We ate in silence for the next few minutes. I was glad for the quiet time to think.

If someone was at the risk of being murdered, I had to get to the bottom of this fast. I put my knife and fork down, wiped my mouth with my napkin, and glanced around the room.

Oliver and Mary had disappeared. Everyone had their heads down, focused on their plates, as if they had run out of topics to talk about.

But I could feel a sense of resentment boiling underneath. Even in the timid Javier.

"I'm curious," I said, picking up my wineglass. "is there any truth to the welcome greeting from our host?"

Sophia shot me a puzzled glance.

"What do you mean?" she asked.

There was no way to ask this, but directly.

"How do you all know each other?" I asked.

The only sound in the room was the clink of silver cutlery against the china.

I tried again, putting on my friendliest smile. "I'm just a baker, but I'd imagine the elite publishing world is quite a small one. You must have all come across each other at some point."

Sophia exchanged a quick glance with Camilla, and Elliot turned his face down. He was bent so low, his chin almost touched his plate.

There was something about those three. Something odd about the way they looked at each other.

Ratcliffe scanned the room, taking everyone in.

"Can't say I do," he replied in a gruff voice. "Haven't met any damn person here before this."

"Me neither," said Javier, shaking his head.

"I've heard of everyone, of course," said Jason, giving me that condescending look again. "We're all well known, you know."

Something nagged at me from the back of my mind. All of a sudden, I realized I'd been focusing on the wrong industry.

"What about Hollywood?" I said, leaning forward. "It must be an even smaller world, no, Sophia?"

"Small enough," she replied, not looking up from her plate.

"Must be super exciting to meet all those stars," said Katy, twirling her glass. "The actors, actresses, Hollywood directors and all. How amazing is that? You're so lucky."

"Bunch of bottom-feeding sharks," said Ratcliffe, spitting out the words. "At least we have some class in the publishing world."

I raised an eyebrow. From across the table, Katy caught my eye.

Thank you, Ratcliffe, for opening the perfect segue.

"I follow all the entertainment channels," said Katy. "They never share gossip from the publishing world, but the movie industry is stir crazy. There's a scandal every week."

A slight blush had come over Sophia's face.

"Hollywood's not that bad," said Camilla with a dismissive wave. "The media exaggerate things."

"How do you know?" asked Katy, with innocent wide eyes.

"Oh, I know Hollywood very well," said Camilla, giving Katy a searing look. "Much better than you do."

She threw her head back and gulped down her wine.

"From what I saw, Hollywood practically devours actors for breakfast," I said. "I've catered some events in LA and saw it all. It was pretty horrific."

No one replied.

"The casting couch isn't a myth," said Katy, picking up from me. "Happens all the time. Even today, doesn't it?"

"What do you know?" said Sophia suddenly on the defensive. "You're just bakers."

Ignoring her, I turned to Elliot, who seemed to have his face practically on his plate now.

"Didn't they break up a cabal of directors and producers who were abusing young actresses a while back?"

He shrugged, not looking up.

Katy shot me a look.

I gave her a discreet nod.

"No one said anything because they were too scared to lose their jobs," said Katy, shaking her head. "They had a good thing going on for decades until they got sussed out."

Everyone in the room had gone unusually quiet and wasn't making eye contact anymore.

"Didn't the head honcho get away in the end?" I asked, breaking a piece of bread. "Somewhere down south, I think?"

"Mexico," said Javier, suddenly sitting up. "I remember reading about it. Happened near my hometown at the border."

I nodded. "Big news ten years ago."

"It all blew up the day that actress, that poor girl, Maria Pablo, shot a producer who'd been abusing her, right?" said Katy. "What a horrible affair. The television stations had a field day."

"What was his name?" I said, pretending to think. "That exec who disappeared near the Mexican border?"

"Zimmerman," said Javier, "that was his name."

Sophia choked on her food and reached for a glass of water.

Camilla's face was now a beetroot red.

And Elliot had stopped eating.

I smiled to myself.

Gotcha.

I had discovered one small thread to this messy mystery at last.

Chapter Eighteen

Zimmerman.

I knew that name. I knew it well.

Over ten years ago when we were setting up our bakery, trying to get a foothold in New York, Madame Bouchard had snagged us a fancy catering gig at a gala in Los Angeles.

The Hollywood executive, Randy Zimmerman, had been a principal guest at that function, and we saw firsthand how he preyed on vulnerable young actresses.

We'd also been there when Emma Foster, in a fit of revenge, took a gun and mowed Zimmerman's boat down. She did it for herself, for her best friend Maria Pablo, and for all the other young stars hurt by Zimmerman and his evil cabal.

It had happened at the border of Mexico. That's why the background in the picture had looked familiar. We had been there. But we never saw him die.

No one had.

"That just made everyone go underground," said Katy, with a loud sigh. "I'm sure there are still predators out there, but they're more careful now, so they don't get caught."

"A sick business," said Sophia, her eyes on her plate. Her words, though, sounded forced and hollow, like she had no choice but to say something.

"Business is business," muttered Ratcliffe, more to himself.

I gave him a hard look, but said nothing. He wasn't putting on a show like everyone else, at least.

I thought of all the young women and men that cabal of criminals had harmed over the years.

It was easy to lounge in a luxury dining hall, eating a five-star meal, and casually chat about their lives like it was just another news story. But they were human beings with stars in their eyes and dreams in their hearts.

The lives of Emma Foster, her best friend, Maria Pablo, and all those other unnamed women and men had been irrevocably damaged.

All they had asked for was that the industry recognize their talents and hard work. What they'd got was torture and manipulation, and for some, even death.

They'd been discarded while most of the culprits got away with slaps on their wrists. As a trafficked survivor myself, I knew why Emma and Maria did what they did.

I was sure who was in that picture now.

It had to be Zimmerman.

Zimmerman was now dead.

Thank goodness for that.

But he was haunting us, and my task was to find out why. What did he have to do with anyone here?

I needed to clear my head and think. I couldn't do that in this room with all the sniping and the gossiping and the lying.

I pushed my chair back and got up.

"Excuse me," I said, and walked toward the door, "just off to the restroom."

I walked out of the dining hall and was about to step inside the women's washroom, when I heard loud voices coming from downstairs.

Sharp, upset voices.

Closing the bathroom door, I treaded softly toward the landing and climbed down the steps.

The voices were getting louder, but I could only make out a few words here and there.

The smell of delicious cooking wafted to my nose as I got to the main landing.

The kitchen.

I tiptoed toward the open door, following my ears. The double door to the massive kitchen was at the end of the long corridor on the ground floor. I walked quietly with my ears alert, passing the row of glass-paneled windows that looked out to the swimming pool and lawn.

"Why didn't anyone tell me?"

It was a woman's voice, speaking angrily.

That was Helen Jenkins, the novelist.

"But Ms. Jenkins, I had strict instructions—"

Oliver got cut off.

"I don't care about your instructions," snapped the novelist, sounding as flustered as she was furious. "If you'd told me who was going to be here, I wouldn't have set foot on this godforsaken island, let alone this state."

"There, there, now," said Mary, as if undeterred by the other woman's anger. I heard the tinkling of a cup against the saucer. "I made a hot cup of chamomile for you. It will be good to calm your nerves down."

"I don't need tea," said Helen, her voice rising. "I just want to go back home."

"I'm very sorry to say it's impossible to leave the island tonight," said Oliver. "Mike has already left for the mainland."

"Call him and tell him to get back then."

"Mike can't take the boat out after dusk, I'm afraid. It's simply not safe."

"There's still light outside."

"It will take him almost an hour to get here. Then you have another hour's ride back to the mainland and it will get dark—"

"Are you telling me I'm stuck here for the night?"

"You should have no worry about your safety here, Ms. Jenkins," said Oliver, his voice soothing. "Nothing bad will happen."

"You've got no idea what you're talking about!" snapped Helen. "You don't even know who you've invited here."

I leaned in closer toward the door, wondering which of the guests she was talking about.

Was it all of them? Or was she referring to a few particular individuals? Or one specific person?

"You make it sound like we have a murderer on the island, Ms. Jenkins," I heard Mary say, a tinge of frustration in her voice.

"You do!" yelled Helen. "I keep telling you!"

I drew back in shock.

Who is she talking about?

If I had to vote for one man out of the group who'd lost his morals or perhaps never even had any, it would have to be Ratcliffe.

But he was too open. It was the others I needed to consider. If I knew anything from my past, it was that the most insidious people hid their deepest and darkest secrets the best.

"I'm not spending one night on this island with those people!"

Those people.

That meant there had to be more than one.

"Look, my dear," said Mary. I heard the tinkling of the teacup again. "If it makes you more comfortable, we can change your room."

"What do you mean?"

"Instead of a guest room upstairs with the others, we can open up one of the smaller staff bedrooms next to ours. That way, you won't be too far from us."

"Do you seriously think that will make a difference? They'll find out who I am and then...then..." Helen sounded like she was choking, like she didn't know how to finish her sentence. "I spent my entire life working hard and doing the right thing. Now you've messed everything up by bringing me here with them."

"We'll figure something out for you—" tried Oliver.

"Nothing you can do will make any difference!" snapped Helen. "That boat man even took my phone. What an insane trip. I should never have said yes."

"Why don't you lie down for a few minutes, my dear," said Mary. "I know that boat ride wasn't that comfortable. Just a half hour nap will do you a world of good and I'll bring your supper up to you. You'll feel better soon, I promise."

"No! Leave me alone. For goodness sake... I need some fresh air."

Then, like she'd had enough, I heard heavy footsteps stomp toward the doorway.

I whirled around in panic and stepped away from the kitchen door.

But it was too late.

Chapter Nineteen

Helen barreled out of the kitchen, almost bowling me over.

Pushing me aside, she dashed through the corridor and out of the front door. Before I knew it, she had disappeared.

Oliver and Mary scurried through the kitchen door.

I spun around.

They gave me a startled look.

"Sorry, er..." I stammered, feeling my face go red. "I was looking for the bathroom."

"It's just outside the dining hall," said Mary, frowning.

"I heard a row and came to see what was going on," I squeaked, embarrassed for being caught eavesdropping, and realizing I couldn't pretend anymore. "Is everything okay?"

"She's not feeling well," said Mary. "She needs time to acclimatize to the island."

"Something is really bothering her," I said.

"If you ask me, she's overreacting," said Oliver. "Some folk can be a tad sensitive, you know."

"She sounded angry to me," I said.

Oliver let out a sigh.

"We did precisely what we were told. It's our job to follow the instructions sent by the owner. We can't help it if the guests can't get along with each other."

"Do you know what she was mad about?" I asked. "Who bothered her so much?"

"If I knew, I could do something about it," said Oliver, shaking his head unhappily. "I could talk to all the interested parties and find a solution. Make different room arrangements. Serve meals at staggered times. We're only two here, but we'll manage with the workload."

"I'd be willing to let her eat in the kitchen with us, if she doesn't want to join the others in the dining room," said Mary. "We want our guests to be happy, but she was so upset. I genuinely don't know what to do."

They looked earnest, like they were trying to accommodate everyone's needs, even Helen Jenkins who'd just stomped out on them. I wondered how much the owner was paying them to give personalized service to their guests like this.

Before I could ask any more questions, I spotted a shadow outside the building. I swiveled around, stepped up to the row of windows and peered out.

Helen Jenkins was the sole person out on the lawn.

"What's she doing now?" asked Oliver, coming over and standing next to me.

As the three of us watched, Helen paced the grounds, pulling at her hair, as if she was desperately trying to figure something out.

Behind her, the expansive ocean roiled and rumbled, as if agreeing with her dark mood.

I remembered that look of terror on her face when she spotted all of us around the dining table. I now knew it had nothing to do with seasickness.

"Good for her to let some of that steam out," said Oliver.

"City folks," replied his wife, shaking her head. "Always so wound up."

She stopped herself and gave me an embarrassed look.

"Sorry, I didn't mean…"

"That's all right," I said with a small smile, thinking Mary wasn't that unfriendly after all. "You're absolutely correct. Sometimes, we take things a little more seriously than we should."

"That's why I like to stay as far away from big cities as I can," said Oliver with a rueful smile.

Neither Mary nor Oliver seemed to understand the gravity of the situation. I wondered if I'd been wrong about Oliver pretending to be the butler when he was truly the owner.

They sounded sincere. Neither acted like anything tragic was about to happen soon. Their primary concern seemed to be keeping their guests happy.

I pondered whether I should tell them about the note we found in our room.

I looked back at Helen, stalking the lawn, muttering to herself. With the wind blowing her hair in all directions, she looked like a woman at the verge of losing her mind.

She saw someone she shouldn't have seen, someone she loathed or feared. Something told me she carried a key link to the mystery here.

I needed to have a talk with Helen.

"I can have a chat with her," I said. I turned to go when I felt Mary's hand on my arm.

"Leave her be. She needs to calm down."

I stared at her.

"It's time to serve your cheesecake, Ms. Kade," said Oliver. "The guests will be looking forward to it. Dinner will be over soon, and we'll be clearing up."

"I…"

"Would you help us?" asked Mary.

With a sigh, I nodded.

They already had their hands full with demanding guests and an eccentric boss. I didn't want to dump my duties on them too.

My Dulce de Leche cheesecake had been sitting in Mary's walk-in fridge all afternoon, and all I needed to do was slice it and plate it for Mary and Oliver to serve.

I walked back to the kitchen while they went upstairs to clear the table and prepare for the last serving. I was thankful they kept a spotless and neat kitchen. It made my job so much easier.

I badly wanted to talk to Helen, but Mary was right. If I was to extract the right information from her, I had to wait for the ideal time. I needed for her to calm down.

I focused on my task and helped Mary and Oliver carry the dessert plates to the dining hall.

When we walked in, the atmosphere appeared to have shifted. The conversation around the table seemed more amicable and everyone had settled down.

I placed a cake plate in front of Katy, and bent down.

"All good here?" I whispered.

"All good," she whispered back. "Don't worry. I've been taking notes."

"Good job," I said, and stepped around the table to place a second plate in front of Sophia.

I took my seat as everyone dug into the cake. No one was complaining. Yet.

An idea was forming in the back of my mind, one that began when I was cutting and plating the cake downstairs. It was a strange one, but I had nothing to lose by pursuing it.

I scanned the table and forced a smile.

"What an honor it is to be in the company of writers like yourselves," I said. "I wish I could write like you all do. I love reading twisty tales with surprising endings."

No one replied, their focus on their dessert.

I picked up my fork.

"So, tell me, how do you end your stories? How do you kill off the villains at the end?"

Ratcliffe looked up, a quizzical expression on his face.

"If I ever wrote a thriller," I said, smiling his way, "not that I'd have any talent, I know how I'd like to end it."

"How?" said Jason, looking up, a curious expression on his face. "How would you end a thriller?"

I glanced up thoughtfully, as if I was conjuring the scene right there and then.

"I'd set the last chapter somewhere in a tropical setting, maybe on a deserted beach in Southern California or Mexico. With cactus and sand dunes, you know?"

Ratcliffe squinted. Jason looked on. The others were too busy finishing their cake, so that I wondered if they were listening. I hoped they were.

"I'd make my heroine face the bad guy," I continued. "She has an assault rifle in her hand. Then, I'd make the bad guy run for his life. She shoots the blazes out of him. She watches him fall, facedown on the sand, convulsing with every bullet she rams through his body."

Silence.

The entire table was staring at me now, mouths open.

"My heavens," said Sophia, finally, "what an imagination you have."

I turned to my right.

"What about you, Camilla? How do you like to end your stories?"

It took a while for her to speak.

"I, er, I write erotica," she finally replied. "I'm, er, not ashamed to admit it. My genre is sexual asphyxiation, so when I want to spice things up at the end, that's how they die."

A murmur of surprise went around the table.

"Me," said Jason, seeming eager to share, "I kill aliens in my books using an old-fashioned knife. Mostly alien women because that's what my readers like to see."

"Misogynist," hissed Camilla.

"They're aliens," said Jason.

"Speak of your fetishes."

"You're no better," pointed out Ratcliffe to Camilla. "Cast no stones."

"I have equal opportunity asphyxiation in my books," sniffed Camilla. "I don't discriminate, gentlemen."

It sounded like another argument was about to brew.

"What about you, Sophia?" asked Katy.

"Oh, I write children's books," said Sophia, fanning herself with her hand, as if the room had got too warm. "No one dies in my stories."

"They do in mine," said Elliot, his mouth curving into a snarky sneer.

"In my last screenplay, the bad guy pushes the good guy off a high cliff. He falls screaming in terror, desperately clawing the air for something to hang on to. Then, he smashes his skull on the knife-edged rocks below."

Chapter Twenty

A chill went through the room.

Elliot grinned, seeing the reactions he'd elicited around the table.

"My readers love that scene," he said.

"Do not speak of such things in this place," said Camilla, giving a shudder and wrapping her arms around her shoulders.

"It's highly inappropriate," said Sophia, giving him a stern look.

"It's a quick way to die," replied Elliot with a shrug. "Compared to the slow agony of cancer, stroke, heart disease, and such we'll all die of."

"What about you?" I asked, turning to Javier, who'd finished his dessert and picked up a second serving plate I'd left on the buffet table in case they wanted more. He was eating the cake hungrily, like he was starved, though he'd just finished a full dinner.

Javier put his fork down and wiped his mouth with his napkin.

We waited.

He looked up at us.

"I don't write books where people kill other people," he said in a clear voice. "In my books, people kill themselves."

A shocked hush fell in the room.

"Suicide?" said Jason.

My mind wandered back to seeing Javier float underwater, serene and calm, as if ready for something. Ready for what? Definitely not for me to pull him out.

Javier nodded somberly.

"That's the best way to go, isn't it?"

The room fell quiet for a minute.

Ratcliffe cleared his throat, breaking the silence.

"You people are way too serious," he said.

"Oh, yeah?" said Camilla. "Do you even write any stories?"

"Of course, I do. I'm writing a new screenplay which is already being optioned for film. In my story, a nasty shark chows down on people. There'll be lots of teeth and big jaws. Tons of screaming and sexy girls in bikinis. And there's lots and lots of blood in the water."

"It's been done before," said Jason.

"That's what viewers want. They say they want original stuff, but no one buys that crap. You just pump out the same old crap and they lap it up. That's how franchises get made. That's how you make money, my boy. Listen and learn."

"You call that entertainment?" sniffed Camilla.

"Better than your cheap asphyxiation sex scenes, Ms. Carter," replied Ratcliffe with a sneer.

Camilla threw her napkin on the table, scraped her chair back, and stood up, wavering on her feet.

"I'm going out for a smoke," she declared before stumbling out of the dining room.

One by one, everyone got up.

Jason left, saying he needed a walk before bed. Javier excused himself to go to the restroom, and Elliot muttered something about hitting the sack. Ratcliffe and Sophia stepped out to the balcony with coffee cups in their hands.

I glanced out the window to see what state Helen was in now, but she was nowhere to be seen.

A wispy white fog was rolling across the green lawn. It must have got cold outside, and she probably went to her room. I made a mental note to knock on her door before we headed back to the lighthouse that evening.

I pulled Katy toward the liquor cabinet and pretended to pour us drinks.

In a low voice, I shared with her what I'd heard in the kitchen.

"What about you? Learn anything?" I asked.

"Only that they're all so entertaining, but I can't stand any of them," she replied.

"All of them?"

"Okay, that Javier guy seems polite. I feel sorry for him. Jason's not half bad too, plus he's hot."

"Katy, you can't let someone's looks affect your judgment."

"You asked me what I thought, didn't you?"

I let out a sigh. Despite her superficial tendencies, I valued my friend's point of view. There have been many times when she saw things I missed.

"Camilla's a snarky one," she continued. "I don't like her, but I respect her."

"Me too," I said with a nod.

"But that Sophia bitch—"

"Shh...," I said, turning around to make sure no one had come back into the room.

"Can't stand that snotty woman," whispered Katy. "That goes for that publisher too. Ratcliffe would eat his mother for lunch if he could make money out of it. He's the type of man I'd cross the road if I saw him coming."

"What about Elliot?"

"Can't make him out yet. He's always watching everyone with those beady little eyes. Creepy."

"What do you think of Oliver and Mar—"

A blood-curdling scream from the outside cut me off.

"Help!"

Katy and I rushed over to the window.

It was Camilla.

She was flailing her arms and rushing toward the house like she was running from a fire.

"Someone help!"

Her screams echoed across the lawn.

I banged open the balcony door and dashed outside, followed by Katy. From below us, we saw Oliver run out of the front door toward her.

"What in heaven's name is she shrieking about?" muttered Ratcliffe, leaning against the railing.

"Hey!" I hollered, waving my arms. "Camilla!"

Camilla stopped halfway across the lawn and looked up, her face pale with fright.

"What's going on?" I hollered.

"It's Helen!" she shouted. "She's dead."

"What in goodness...?" said Sophia.

"Where is she?" I yelled.

But Oliver had now reached Camilla. He placed his hands on her shoulders, as if trying to calm her down. Even from up here, I could see Camilla was shaking.

Tapping Katy's arm, I rushed out of the balcony and ran across the dining room toward the corridor. We scampered down the stairs and dashed out the front door.

When we reached her, Camilla was still shaking, hardly able to speak.

"What happened?" I asked.

"I don't know... She was lying there, dead..."

"Where is she?" I asked, trying not to hyperventilate myself.

"Down there," said Camilla, pointing a trembling finger at the walkway. "At the bottom of the cliff."

That was all I needed. I turned around and raced toward the walkway.

"Careful, it's slippery!" I heard Oliver yell from behind me.

Katy and I reached the cliff at the same time. I peered over the precipice, wondering why the construction crew hadn't put up a proper safety railing around the plateau. They'd had the funds. Instead, they'd placed a row of boulders next to the edge of the cliff.

Most were only thigh high, good enough to stop an inebriated guest from falling off the cliff at night. But if someone had deliberately scrambled on them, they could have easily slipped and fallen down.

Is that what happened?

My eyes swept the barren landscape.

The fog was thin and there was still late afternoon light, enough for us to see a body sprawled out below. All I spotted were sand dunes, craggy rocks, and waves crashing on the shore.

"Did she imagine it?" asked Katy next to me. "She was quite tipsy."

"This way," I said, walking along the ledge toward the lighthouse, peering over the boulders. "Maybe she saw her farther away."

Inch by inch, we scoured the area, but the beach below us was empty. There was no one, alive or dead, to be seen anywhere.

Chapter Twenty-one

"Ahoy there!"

I spun around.

It was Jason and Elliot, running toward us.

Closer to the building, Oliver was escorting Camilla back into the house. Ratcliffe and Sophia were still on the balcony on the second floor, drinking their coffees, watching the scene like this was theater for them.

"What's going on?" said Jason, breathless from running. "Heard someone scream."

"Camilla said she saw Helen down there," I replied. "But we can't see anyone."

"Is it true?" said Elliot, as he joined us, panting hard. "Is Helen dead?"

I turned to face him. Did I catch a hint of eagerness in his voice? Or was it frightened nervousness I was misreading as excitement?

"There's nothing there," said Katy, pointing at the shore below us. "We'd see her if she fell."

"Maybe the waves took her?" said Jason, bending over the rocks to get a better view of the shore below.

"Careful," said Katy.

"Impossible," said Elliot, peering over the stones. "The tide's not that high. See those lines on the rocks? You can see where the sea comes up to. If she fell, she'd still be down there."

"Maybe she's hidden behind some of those rocks," I said. "Perhaps we'll see her from another angle."

The four of us walked up and down the edge of the plateau, scanning the shore, shouting her name.

But we saw nothing.

I turned to the group.

"Guys, let's go down and check."

"The walkway is closed," said Jason with a shocked look. "They always shut it before dusk. It's dangerous to go down now."

"We can open it up," I said. "We'll find a few torches and wear good boots."

"Are you crazy? It's a long and slippery way down," said Elliot, giving a shiver. "It's tough enough coming up in daylight."

"But we can't leave her like that," cried Katy.

"There's no one down there," said Elliot.

"Do you want to sign your suicide card?" asked Jason. "I don't."

"What the dickens is going on?" said a gruff voice from behind us.

We whirled around.

It was Ratcliffe, walking over, a cigar in one hand and a coffee cup in the other.

"Haven't spotted Helen Jenkins anywhere," said Jason, shaking his head.

"She's a full-grown woman, for goodness' sake. If she'd truly fallen down, we'd have heard her scream like the devil all the way."

"Maybe she fell when we were having dessert," said Katy, "and that's why we didn't hear her?"

"She was pacing the lawn the last time I saw her," I said, "that was during dinner. She could have fallen anytime between then and when Camilla saw her."

"Bah! You believe that overimaginative, sloshed woman?" said Ratcliffe. He gestured grandly at the rocky shore below us. "Where's the body then? You people are wasting your time."

"Yeah, she's probably safe and sound in her bed," muttered Elliot, pulling his jacket close and his beret down. "Recovering from her boating ordeal."

"But Camilla looked terrified," I said. "She must have seen something."

"Her own shadow more like it," said Ratcliffe. "That woman was drunker than a skunk. She could hardly walk, let alone see straight."

Another possibility had crept into my mind, one I wasn't about to share with them. Maybe Helen was killed and pushed off to sea. Maybe we'd see her body floating in the waves tomorrow, I thought with a shiver.

"I was getting ready for a nice bath when I heard her yell," grumbled Elliot. "There should be a law against crying wolf like this."

"I was going for a walk around the block when she screamed," said Jason, straightening up and wiping the stone residue from his hands. "Well, it was presumably an innocent mistake. I'm going in for a cup of decaf."

Elliot and Jason turned their backs on us and ambled back to the main building, chatting amicably.

Ratcliffe pointed his cigar at us and narrowed his eyes.

"I'm watching you two," he said, in a dangerously low voice.

I raised an eyebrow.

"Oh, yeah?" I said.

"Something tells me you aren't just two catering chicks from the Big Apple. I've been in business for too long not to know horse manure when I see it."

Before I could offer a retort, he turned around and marched back to the resort.

We watched him walk away, Katy gritting her teeth and me suppressing an urge to run after him and give him a piece of my mind.

"Ass clown!" said Katy, shaking a fist at Ratcliffe.

"What a nasty fellow," I said, and turned back toward the ocean with a sigh. It seemed to be part of my job to meet people like him.

A chilly breeze came our way. Katy and I were in our evening dresses and heels, and it was getting cold out here. It was time to head back in.

"Ouch!"

I spun around to see Katy had tripped over something. I grabbed her arm and pulled her away from the rocks.

"Watch it, hun," I said.

She kicked something in the grass.

"My heel caught on this," she said, as she bent down to pick it up.

She held it up.

I gasped.

It was a pair of brown speckled librarian spectacles.

We looked at each other, horror coming over our faces.

"Helen Jenkins was here," I said. "Camilla wasn't lying."

"Maybe Camilla pushed her down," whispered Katy.

"But where is she then? It's not like there are any places to hide below."

"She could have dragged herself out of view after Camilla saw her," said Katy, and stopped as if she realized how absurd the idea sounded. "But why would she do that?"

I glanced up at the sky. It was going to get dark soon, and the fog was getting thicker. We had little time.

I turned to Katy.

"Time to check below."

"In these shoes?"

"Let's go change," I said, gesturing for my friend to follow me to the lighthouse.

"Ahoy!" called a voice.

We turned to see Oliver scampering toward us, waving his arms. His face had turned pink. That wasn't from the cold, I was sure. He was distraught.

"How is Camilla?" I asked when he got close.

"Shaken up," he said. "Mary's making her a tea. Ms. Carter is adamant she saw Ms. Jenkins below, but the others are all saying she imagined it." He paused. "To tell the truth, they all need sobering up, especially Ms. Carter."

"There's no one below," I said, and pointed at Katy's hand, "except we found this a foot from the ledge."

Katy held up the pair of glasses. "Something happened here."

Oliver sighed.

"Ms. McCafferty, there's a reason this place is named Suicide Cliff."

"Are you saying she jumped?" asked Katy in shock.

"Lighthouses do funny things to you. Make you see things."

"Come on, Oliver," I said. "I saw Camilla. She may have been a bit drunk, but she looked terrified."

He narrowed his eyes.

"The last lighthouse keeper went to investigate what he thought was a boat wrecked on the shore. He sent a distress signal before he did. It was a foggy night, much like this. When the Coast Guard came, they found him splattered on the rocks below. He could have been hallucinating, because no one found that boat wreck."

I gave him a shocked look.

We were hanging around here listening to fairy tales when we should be rescuing a possible suicide or murder victim.

Oliver turned to the building. "Please come inside, ladies."

"No, we're going down to the shore," I said. "As soon as we get our boots and gear on."

"You can't do that," spluttered Oliver, his face turning red. "It's dark and slippery. The walkway is closed, and the shore is out of bounds after six p.m. The Coast Guard would make sure I lose my job if I let any guests go down now."

"Oliver, if Helen Jenkins is alive down there, she'll be needing help," I said, surprised he was objecting. "I'll rappel down if I have to. We've done this sort of thing before."

"She's probably in her room," he replied. "I'll check on her as soon as we return, but I'm not letting you scramble down at this time."

"What if she's not in her room?" asked Katy.

Oliver shook his head firmly. "We wait till dawn to rustle up a search party with the proper gear."

"We don't have time for a search party," I snapped.

He turned to me with an angry frown.

"I can't have you go down, Ms. Kade. It's dangerous. If you do, I'll have to make plans for two more rescues. Don't do this to me. I can't allow it."

"But—"

His face clouded.

"Would you listen to me? I've lived here almost my entire life. Unless you two are members of the US Marines or the Coast Guard, I forbid you to go down. It's foolhardy. If you do, you'll be risking *my* life!"

Chapter Twenty-two

"She's not here," said Mary, closing Helen Jenkins's bedroom door.

Oliver rubbed his tired eyes.

Angry words were bubbling inside of me, but I stopped them from coming out. They both seemed as distressed as we were, and so far, all they had shown was concern. Concern for the safety of the remaining guests, including Katy and me.

"Wait," I said, pushing in between them and opening the door.

"You can't go in there," protested Oliver.

But I was already inside.

I scanned the room, searching for any clues to Helen's disappearance. The room was spotless. Only her unopened suitcase by the door and an untidy stack of papers on the bedside table showed someone was staying here.

"You can't barge into a guest's room like that," I heard Mary say. "It's against our privacy policy. The owner said so."

"She's probably gone for a walk," said Oliver. "She was upset and she needed some space."

I turned to the couple standing at the doorway, appalled looks on their faces.

"Your owner is playing a dangerous game," I said.

They gaped at me, uncomprehending.

"Mary, Oliver, we might have a murder on our hands," I said, speaking more forcefully than I expected.

"Murder?" gasped Mary.

"You can't be serious," said Oliver.

I lowered my voice.

"There's something you need to know," I said. "It's about this owner of yours."

"What about them?" asked Oliver.

"We found a note in our bedroom. It was a welcome message from the host," I said. "The last line on that card said, *Seven guests arrived today. Not all will leave the island on Sunday.*"

Mary gasped, and Oliver's jaws dropped.

They looked so disturbed, I wondered if they were innocent bystanders to all this drama after all. Maybe I had been too quick to judge them.

At the same time, I wasn't ready to strike anyone off the list yet. Even Oliver and Mary.

"Why don't you come in and close the door," I said. "It will be quieter for us to talk."

They stepped inside, exchanging nervous glances with each other.

They huddled next to the ornamental wardrobe in Helen's room, while Katy closed the door behind her and leaned against it.

"Don't you find it strange that your new boss invited us to bring a cheesecake all the way from New York in return for a hefty daily stipend?"

Oliver scratched his head.

"This isn't the first time we received unusual instructions. Rich folk do strange things. I mean, they bought a crumbling lighthouse on a remote island and transformed it into a mini resort with the biggest swimming pool in the entire state. They even built a fancy library on top. For whom? As I told Mary, anything is possible with them."

Perhaps even murder.

"I run a side business," I said, and paused to prepare them for what was to come. "I offer my services as a private investigator to my wealthy clients who seek discretion in their affairs."

"What are you saying?" asked Oliver, narrowing his eyes. "I don't understand."

"The cheesecake order came via our bakery website," I replied. "We normally refuse orders from out of state or chalk it up to a kid playing with us. But that order came with something that made us change our mind."

"What was it?" asked Mary, a curious look coming over her face.

"A request for help," I said.

"Who sent it?" asked Oliver. "It wasn't me."

"They did a good job hiding their identity and location," I said. "My resident computer expert checked the email and couldn't nail it down."

Katy turned to them. "It has to be the owner. Who else could it be?"

"Please tell me the truth," I said, looking them squarely in the face to see if I could spot a telltale micro sign of a lie. A twitch of the face. A flinch of the mouth. Rapid blinking of the eyes.

"Can you tell us who the new owner is?" I asked.

"We only wish we knew," said Oliver, shaking his head.

I sighed. I felt like we were going in circles.

"There was something else that came attached to our cake order," I said.

I turned to Katy.

"Do you have it?"

She gave me a warning glance.

"It's time we shared it," I said to her.

I had no confirmation if Oliver and Mary were playing some role in this charade. They looked and acted like the real deal, but they could also be stringing us along.

I knew I had to give them enough information to get more information.

Katy dug into her pocket, pulled out the photograph, and held it up to the couple.

They peered at the picture, Mary making a face at the sight of the naked, bloated body.

"Do you recognize this man?" I asked.

Oliver shook his head, seemingly too shocked to answer.

"How did he end up like that?" whispered Mary.

"My guess is he was shot in the back," I said. I didn't tell them I also had a good idea who the victim could be and who shot him. "I have a feeling this dead man is connected to your guests in some way."

"Oh no," said Mary, bringing her hand to her heart. "What have we got ourselves into, Oliver?"

"Asha?"

I looked up to see Katy pointing at something on Helen's bedside table.

"What is it?" I asked.

She walked over, picked up the stack of papers and brought it over.

It was a manuscript titled *It's a Man's World*. The author was Helen Jenkins. Stamped on each page was a copyright symbol with the word "confidential" written across it in red ink.

While it looked impressive, it didn't tell me anything. All I knew was Helen had most likely planned to work on it during the retreat.

"*This* was on top of it," said Katy, shoving a single piece of paper in front of me.

"Heavens," said Mary, her eyes bulging. "She got one too."

Katy put the photo she'd being carrying with her and placed it next to the new piece of paper. I gaped at the two identical images, feeling the knot in my stomach tighten.

Mary turned a panic-stricken face at me.

"What does all this mean?"

"Your guess is as good as mine," I replied, a grim look on my face. "What I don't get is how come we never saw Helen Jenkins below while Camilla did."

"She was quite drunk," said Mary.

"She could have been lying," said Katy.

"Someone was down there and pulled her under a crag of rocks or something," said Oliver, his face pale. "Though there are very few places you could hide an adult human without us seeing from up here."

"Remember how scared she looked when she came to the dining room?" I said. "Whoever she recognized around that table, recognized her too. They knew that she knew. And they tried to get rid of her."

Mary shook her head.

"Never heard anything like this in my life. Oh, my lord, what a horrible mess we've got into."

"Let's focus," I said. "I know this is not easy, but right now, we need to stay calm. We have no idea what else the owner is planning or even who they are."

"Are you saying they're here? On the island?" asked Mary, her eyes widening in horror.

"Have you met any of these guests before now?"

Oliver and Mary shook their heads.

"How do we know your owner isn't here in disguise?" I asked.

Silence.

Katy put a hand up, and counted with her fingers. "We were in the dining room with Sophia and Ratcliffe, so it couldn't have been them. But Jason, Elliot, and Javier left after dinner. Plus Camilla, of course. Any of them could have had something to do with this."

Mary crossed herself. "I'm not sure my heart can handle this."

I turned to her.

"When do you pick up laundry and do housekeeping?"

"After we serve breakfast in the morning."

"I'm coming with you. We'll check everyone's rooms discreetly. We just might find a clue to who the owner is."

Mary shook her head.

"All except Javier and Elliot asked for breakfast in bed, and those two said they don't eat in the morning," she said.

Oliver turned to me.

"We'll have to think of another way to herd them out of their rooms."

Day Two

Chapter Twenty-three

Katy and I were up before dawn.

I was sore from my unexpected swimming, boating, and climbing adventures the day before, and I was worn out from trying to figure out what we had on our hands.

I'd tossed and turned all night, worried that until Mike came back, we were completely cut off from the rest of the world.

My eyes were still bleary. Katy's eyes were red too, not having had a wink of sleep.

After our chat with Oliver and Mary in Helen Jenkins's bedroom the night before, we'd realized there was nothing more we could do immediately.

The best solution had been to get a night's rest and start a search for Helen first thing in the morning.

Within minutes, we'd raced down the stairs to see if the weather had cleared enough for us to get to the shore.

Outside, the morning fog was thick, like a white blanket had settled over the ocean and the island. It was eerie to see the smog swirling around us, its wispy fingers reaching through our jackets and into our bones.

Our first stop was the ledge where we'd seen Camilla run from the day before.

Katy and I hunched over the rocks and scanned the ocean and shore below for several minutes, hoping against hope to see Helen alive and calling for help.

The shore seemed the same as the day before. The sea was calmer, but that could change any minute.

"Nothing," said Katy, finally, shaking her head. "Even with the fog, we'd see if anyone was down there."

"We need to get down ASAP," I said, realizing with a sinking feeling that if we did find Helen, she might very well be no longer alive.

We hurried to the main resort building. It was quiet when we stepped inside, like everyone was still sleeping.

Katy turned right at the entrance to walk toward the kitchen when I stopped her.

"Let's check her room first," I whispered.

We tiptoed up to the third floor and walked toward Helen's bedroom. There was no one in the corridor and there were no signs of anyone being up and about yet.

When we got to Helen's room, I rapped on the door lightly.

Nothing.

After waiting a few seconds, I knocked again.

Still nothing.

"It's not locked," whispered Katy, pushing down on the door handle.

Crossing our fingers, we peeked inside the novelist's room.

The room looked exactly how we left it the evening before, but something was off. My tired brain whirred trying to figure out what it was, but it was just waking up.

"She never came back," I whispered.

"This means she's still down at the shore," said Katy. "Do you think it's time to call the police?"

I was about to reply when I realized what was bothering me.

"Where's the manuscript?" I said, pushing the door open and walking in. "Where's that photo you found?"

"Oh, my gosh," said Katy, closing the door behind her and joining me by the bedside table. "Someone took it."

"I thought Mary locked the door," I said.

We searched the room.

We checked inside the wardrobe, under the bed, and we even lifted the mattress to see if someone had stuck it underneath there.

We opened Helen's suitcase, feeling slightly guilty about going through her things. But, other than her clothes, a pair of black high heels, a makeup kit from an expensive brand, a curling iron, a velvet pouch containing a stunning red-stoned necklace with matching earrings, and a few multivitamin bottles, there was nothing out of the ordinary in her luggage.

Next to her suitcase was Helen's brown leather purse, with her wallet still inside. Her identification and five hundred dollars of cash were tucked within.

"A woman who packs her fancy jewelry, heels, and makeup didn't come here to jump off a cliff," said Katy, slamming the suitcase shut. "I swear someone did something to her."

"I doubt she fell," I said, getting up. "Let's go find Oliver and Mary. They must be up by now."

It was time to call David and Tetyana. I had a feeling this missing person mystery was going to turn into something bigger soon.

We closed Helen's door and tiptoed along the corridor. The other rooms were still closed and there were no sounds of showers working or taps running.

I glanced at my wristwatch. It was fifty-seven minutes past five. They were all still sound asleep.

After a quick check inside the dining room, Katy and I went down to the first floor. The smell of coffee brewing and butter frying came our way as we reached the main foyer.

"Good, they're up," I said, as we hurried toward the kitchen.

Oliver and Mary looked up as we burst in.

Mary was standing by the stove, a spatula in her hand, frying an egg. Oliver was on a stool, pulling his boots on.

"Any sign of Helen?" I asked.

"I'm afraid not," said Oliver, slipping into a yellow rain jacket. "I'm heading down the walkway to check up on her."

"We're coming with you," I said.

Oliver nodded. I thought I saw a sense of relief pass across his face.

Mary shook her head at her frying pan.

"Never has anyone gone missing in my forty years of lighthouse keeping. I don't think the Coast Guard will even believe us when we tell them. What a pickle."

She picked up a second egg and cracked it over her pan. She turned to us with a rueful smile. "When I get nervous, I cook. That's what I do best. I know it sounds strange, but it's soothing."

It was a sentiment I knew well. Learning to bake kept me sane through my hellish childhood. I smiled at Mary. I liked her.

But can I trust her?

Oliver picked up a small backpack that had been lying at his feet and stuffed a first-aid kit and a neck brace into it.

"You stay right here, Mary," he said. "These ladies and I will figure this all out soon enough. Just make sure the guests are fed so they don't make a ruckus."

Mary turned back to her pan with a sigh. "Be careful out there. The steps will be slippery, especially with the dew."

I turned to Mary.

"Did you lock Helen's door last night?"

"I did," she replied, "but I went back to unlock it."

I narrowed my eyes.

"Why did you do that?"

"I couldn't sleep thinking she had probably wandered off. I didn't want to lock her out, just in case she came back. All her things were in that room. Poor girl. She was in such a state."

"Did you go into her room when you unlocked it?"

"I peeked in to see if she wasn't already inside by some miracle, but I didn't go in. Why do you ask?"

"The manuscript was missing this morning."

"The what?"

"Helen Jenkins's work. The book she was writing. Remember, it was sitting on her bedside table last night?"

"The stack of papers, you mean? Are you sure you didn't see it?"

"Someone took her unpublished book, but left behind her jewelry pouch and wallet with five hundred dollars. Strange, isn't it? I wish I took the manuscript to our room now."

Mary gave me a confused look. "Why would anyone take her book?"

"Beats me." I shrugged. "Neither of you took it, by any chance, did you?"

"Good heavens, no," said Mary, giving me a wide-eyed look. "We wouldn't even know what to do with it. You're welcome to check our room if you don't believe me."

I shook my head.

If Mary was the thief, which I doubted, she wouldn't leave the manuscript in her bedroom for anyone to find. The person who took it had wanted it for a very specific reason, and they were most probably hiding it somewhere safe.

I turned to Oliver, who was picking up a folded stretcher from the floor.

"It's time to call the authorities," I said.

He nodded.

"I just did. Sent a brief message to the Coast Guard station this morning. Said we're going on a search mission first thing. Ms. Jenkins could be anywhere. I didn't want to cry wolf and get on the Coast Guard's blacklist. They have a penalty for false alarms, and it isn't cheap."

"But you said you had no phone," said Katy.

"We don't."

"Internet?"

"I have an old modem in my office. Just good for email. That's how I get instructions from the owner."

"It's how we talk to our kids too," said Mary, who had turned back to her eggs. "As long as Mike comes in with our weekly rations, we don't need to be connected to all the hubbub out there. We came here to escape it all."

Katy and I exchanged a look.

"How did you contact the Coast Guard?" I asked, wondering why they just couldn't answer a simple question.

Chapter Twenty-four

"VHF radio," said Oliver, seeing our faces. "It's how I talk with the Coast Guard."

He thrust the stretcher out toward us.

"Can you ladies help me?"

Katy took the stretcher, and I hoisted the bag that carried the plastic water bottles and the blanket for Helen.

Oliver shouldered the first-aid kit.

With a wave to his wife, Oliver walked out of the kitchen with us.

The walkway was slippery from the morning dew, but that wasn't going to stop us. At least we had full daylight and a rope railing to hold on to now.

I took the lead, walking gingerly down the wet steps.

"Did you hear anything last night?" Katy asked Oliver when we were at the halfway point. "Anyone walking around, opening and closing doors?"

"I'm afraid not," replied Oliver. "Our room is downstairs, next to the kitchen. They renovated this building to high standards, so everything is soundproof now. If someone was prowling in the middle of the night, we'd never have heard them."

I stopped at a flat part of the walkway to catch my breath and turned to Oliver.

"Oliver, what do you know about the guests?"

"Not much. The owner sent me an email with a list of names, their phone numbers and their designated room numbers. That was about it."

"But you seem to know a bit about each of them," I said.

He paused for a moment, his face somber, and then as if deciding to talk, he nodded.

"To be honest, I found all this a little strange. I was getting instructions from a boss I'd never met. I was supposed to invite a bunch of writers I'd never heard of. Then, this request to confiscate everyone's phones made me a little uneasy. So, I, er, did some digging."

"Digging where?" asked Katy. "You don't have the Internet."

"Used Mike's phone when he came over one day. Mary insists on him having a meal with us once a week. I told him what was going on, and the two of us used his phone to do some research, while Mary made lunch."

"Good thinking," I said.

Oliver shook his head.

"I'm not proud of it. It wasn't very professional of me to snoop on the guests."

"Given the circumstances," I said, "that was a wise move."

"Find anything?" asked Katy.

Oliver went silent for a minute. He stood against the cliff face, staring at the ocean.

Why is he hesitating? Is he debating whether to tell us the truth?

"Quite a bit," he said, finally. "They're all well known in the book circles, so it was easy to find them."

He fell silent again.

We waited.

It was no use rushing him. He was opening up. I only hoped he was as sincere as he looked and sounded. I had started to put some faith in the cook and the butler.

On the distant horizon, the sun was peeking out, and the fog was lifting. It was a relief not to hear the incessant crashing of the high waves on the pier below us. I hoped the weather kept improving. I didn't cherish the thought of trying to find Helen or her body in the pouring rain next to an angry sea.

"It was just that," said Oliver, speaking again, "a few of the writers seem to have sprung up overnight."

"Sprung up?" asked Katy. "What do you mean?"

"Take that screenwriter, Elliot Ward, for instance. You'd think someone who wrote for a film would have a lot more information about him, going back years."

He paused as if to recall what he had read.

"Same goes for Ms. Carter and Mrs. Knight. Their websites were simple, bare, and I could only find background going back two to three years. It's like they all popped up and became famous out of nowhere."

"They're writers," said Katy, "do they even have websites?"

He nodded.

"Mike and I checked other writers, and they had more comprehensive sites with their books, pictures of their dogs, what wine they like, and all the usual stuff."

I remembered how Sophia, Elliot, and Camilla had evaded my questions at dinner the night before. They got cagey when I broached the topic of Hollywood.

"That sounds fishy," said Katy, frowning.

Oliver nodded.

"I don't know too much about famous people, but I read a lot of books. And I know it takes more than ten years to become an overnight success."

"Maybe they worked somewhere else before they started writing?" I said. "In another industry?"

"We'd still have found info on their earlier careers, wouldn't we?" said Oliver.

"What about Ratcliffe?" I asked.

"He had the longest bio of them all. He's been in business for ages and he loves to talk about himself. It wasn't hard to find info on him."

"Jason?" said Katy.

"Lots of stuff about him too. He grew up in the online gaming world. But I must admit, some of his videos were a little... Let's just say, if Mary knew he made them, she'd have walked off the island and told me to call her back when he left."

"Risqué videos?" said Katy.

"Horrible. Had nightmares for days after watching one. Lots of gore and bad things happening. Mostly to young women...." Oliver trailed off, making a face, like he was trying to get rid of a foul taste. "Things that didn't look legal, if you ask me."

I raised an eyebrow. Jason came across as an intelligent and successful artist, but even he had a dark past.

"And Javier, well, he's the most famous out of the lot. He's a reclusive fellow, but you can find articles about his work in almost every major literary site."

"Helen?" asked Katy.

Oliver nodded.

"Prolific, well-known novelist. She seemed legitimate. She'd won awards and such and all her books are talked about. Nothing struck me as off with her."

That was all the information Oliver seemed to have found on the guests.

We resumed our hike down.

When we reached the bottom of the esplanade, we walked abreast and scoured the beach, advancing the shoreline, foot by foot.

Elliot had been right about one thing.

The ocean was more than a hundred feet away. Muddy lines on the rock faces told us where the tide came up, but it was too far for the waves to have washed Helen away.

We walked around the island, but spotted no place where a human being could hide or stay covered near the shore. The rock formations were too small for even a child to stay hidden behind them.

After circling the island a second time, we stopped to take a break near the jetty, just under the lighthouse. I put down my bag and looked up at the tower looming above, wondering about the stories it could tell us.

Katy let out a sigh.

"I hate being cut off like this," she said, looking out to the ocean. "Right now, I'd do anything to call my hubby and talk to my daughter."

"Don't you worry, Ms. McCafferty," said Oliver, "Mike will be here in a few hours. It will be a relief to see the boat."

"Wait a minute," I said, remembering what Katy and I had spotted from the boat when we came in. "There was a white cross on the other end of the island. Next to the clump of trees behind the building. Is there anything else out there?"

"The last keeper's grave. He wanted his remains to stay on the island. We planted those trees almost thirty years ago. The wind's nasty on that end and the soil breaks off every time a storm comes. Plus, we thought they would give some shade to his grave."

"Can someone hide back there? Behind the trees or a mausoleum, maybe?" I asked.

Oliver shook his head.

"No mausoleum, just the trees. The north wind is rough out back. You can only stay behind those trees for so long before you get whipped raw. I'm sure she isn't there."

Oliver rubbed his exhaustion-lined forehead. I imagined he'd little sleep, just like us.

He turned a puzzled face my way.

"What if all this is a hoax?"

"How so?" I said.

"Maybe Ms. Carter thought she saw Ms. Jenkins, but it was a...."

"A what?" asked Katy. "A practical joke?"

Oliver shrugged. "An illusion?"

"With a dead body?" said Katy.

"A dead body we haven't found," replied Oliver grimly.

Chapter Twenty-five

"Are you saying Camilla didn't see a body?" I asked.

"She would have to be a pretty talented actor to pull that sort of drama off," said Katy.

"When you're up on the cliff, the shore is quite a way down," said Oliver. "Ms. Carter said she saw someone facedown on the beach with a black coat on. She assumed it was Ms. Jenkins, but it could have been anyone."

"So, someone could have been pretending to be Helen," I said, looking at Oliver with renewed respect. He was trying to sort this out, or he was misleading us.

I had to take the chance.

"Good point," I said to encourage him.

"It was that," he replied, "or Ms. Jenkins was alive and well, but laying down on the beach, face covered. Anyone who saw her from the top would automatically think she fell."

"Why would she do that?" asked Katy. "Why would *anyone* do that?"

"If that was the case, it was because she wanted someone to think she was dead," I said, playing along. "She saw someone who scared her at the dining hall. Someone she said was practically a murderer. This was her twisted way of not making herself a target."

"But why make yourself disappear?" asked Katy.

"To make everyone think her body got washed away overnight?" I ventured. "If she planned all that, it was a dangerous move that could have actually killed her if she slipped down last night."

Oliver gave a dismal shrug and sighed.

"This is wishful thinking on my part. I don't want to think that anyone died suspiciously on my island. This is such a peaceful place. It's too horrifying to even think about murder."

Katy turned to me.

"That means Helen could be alive and well, and is up there, somewhere," she said, pointing up to the plateau.

How scared do you have to be to play an elaborate game like this?

Oliver stared out at the open ocean, a resigned look on his face.

"I don't know what to believe anymore. Maybe she's in with our new owner. Maybe they're all in this together, playing a nasty game on us."

I stood up.

"Time to head back," I said. "Next step, check all the rooms."

"They'll have a fit," said Oliver gloomily.

"We'll figure something out," I said.

We hiked back up to the walkway. I felt exhaustion settling in my body, but my mind was racing a million miles a second.

When we got to the top, we found all the guests had congregated under the awning just outside the front door. I wondered what had got them out of their rooms.

Didn't Mary say almost everyone wanted breakfast in bed?

She had turned on the outdoor heater near the main doorway and they all had coffee cups in hand. Camilla was standing to the side smoking, flanked by Sophia and Elliot.

They watched us walk over, anticipation on their faces.

Ratcliffe was the first to shout out to us.

"Did you find her?" His voice boomed across the lawn.

Ah, so it was curiosity that had drawn everyone out of bed. They were itching to find out what had happened to Helen Jenkins.

We shook our heads.

"I'll officially notify the Coast Guard of a missing person," said Oliver, when we approached the group.

"The Coast Guard?" said Sophia, making a face. "Do you have to bring them in? They'll be asking us so many questions."

"This place will be crawling with strangers," said Elliot, a look of distaste on his face, "we'll never get any work done."

"We paid good money for peace and privacy," muttered Ratcliffe.

Didn't they care for the missing woman?

"Maybe she swam back to the mainland," said Sophia. "I have half a mind to do it myself. This place is becoming unbearable."

"Unless Ms. Jenkins is a cross-Atlantic marathon swimmer with superb night vision, that would have been a very foolhardy thing to do," said Oliver.

"My publishing company owns buildings in New York bigger than this island, my good man," said Ratcliffe, glowering at Oliver. "How can you lose anyone in this place?"

"Maybe she's in her room?" said Jason.

Mary shook her head. "We checked last night and this morning. She'd not slept in her bed at all."

"I tell you I saw her on the beach and she looked pretty much dead," said Camilla, her voice even higher pitched than normal. Her hand holding the cigarette was trembling. "I didn't make it up!"

I looked at the group.

We needed time to search their rooms, but their nerves were already fraying. The last thing we needed was for them to do anything rash, while we waited for the Coast Guard to arrive.

"We have a missing persons case in our hands," I said. "This could get serious if we don't act fast."

Everyone turned to me, quizzical expressions on their faces.

"This could get plastered all over the news if we're not careful," I said.

Sophia gave a shudder, and Ratcliffe's face turned a shade darker.

"Oh, please, not the media," said Elliot, making a motion to leave the group. "I'm not getting involved in this."

"Wait," I said. "Maybe Helen is somewhere on the island, drunk, asleep, lost."

"Agreed," said Ratcliffe, straightening up. He put a hand on Oliver's shoulder. "No need to call for help yet, my good man. We'll find her and solve this fast enough."

Everyone breathed a sigh of relief. For different reasons, I was sure.

"I'm glad you understand." I paused and scanned the group. "We haven't searched the grounds yet. If we all pitch in, we can split up and take different sections of the island. There aren't many places to hide up here, but if we scour the area, we might find a clue to where she's gone off to."

"Happy to check the back," said Jason.

"I'll join you," said Javier, who'd been listening in quietly by the door.

"I'll come with you boys," said Ratcliffe. "I was a Scout cubmaster at one point. I can lead the way."

"We'll need to check the south side too," I said, giving the remaining three an anticipatory look. "Would you do the honors?"

"But there's nothing there," said Sophia. "Just the helipad and flat open land. We'd see from here if anyone is out there, wouldn't we?"

"You never know what you'll find," I said. "It's just a precaution."

"I'll do it," said Camilla, throwing her cigarette butt on the ground and crushing it with her shoe. "I still don't believe a dead body climbed all the way back up, but I'd be damned if I was going to stay and do nothing while you all make fun of me."

"We're not making fun of you," said Elliot. "I'll come with you."

Sophia put a hand on her forehead. "It's a little chilly and I feel a headache coming on. I'll stay behind, if you don't mind."

Katy turned to her.

"Fresh air is good for a headache. Might make you feel a lot better to take a stroll."

Sophia shot her a nasty look.

"What about you? Making us do all the work."

"We'll be searching the lighthouse," I said. "Not that anyone could have got in without us knowing, but better to double-check."

"Come on, Sophia," said Camilla, unexpectedly, pulling on Sophia's arm. "I need all the moral support now."

We watched as everyone fanned out and ambled away in their groups, coffee cups still in hand.

Interesting, I thought.

Elliot, Camilla, and Sophia pretended not to know each other, but these three had an affinity. I remembered what Oliver had told us on our way down to the shore.

All three of them had little info online—as if they weren't real writers at all.

Chapter Twenty-six

We had bought ourselves thirty minutes, forty, if we were lucky.

Katy and I hurried into the building with Oliver and Mary.
After a short debate, we divided the house and began searching, Mary and Katy taking the guest rooms on the third floor while Oliver and I checked the rest of the building.

Thirty minutes later, we had found nothing, not even Helen Jenkins's missing manuscript.

From the back kitchen window, I could see Jason and Ratcliffe having a chat, with Ratcliffe casually leaning against a tree, taking sips from his now lukewarm coffee. Javier stood by himself, in between two trees, staring out at the ocean.

"They're not searching," said Katy, shaking her head. "How lazy can you get?"

"They got out of the house. That served our purpose," I said. "That's all I care about."

"I'll go check the back," said Oliver, "after I call the Coast Guard."

"What about breakfast?" said Mary to her husband. "We'd better get to it or those people will riot. It's not like we need more trouble on our hands."

Oliver turned to us.

"She's right. We have work to do here. There's one other place we need to check," he said.

"The back?" asked Katy.

"The lighthouse," said Oliver.

"We slept in there last night," I said. "We would have heard anyone coming in."

"There's another way up," said Oliver, his forehead creased. "There's a ladder on the side. No one's used it for a long while, but—"

"You think Helen climbed all the way to the top of the lighthouse in the dead of the night?" I asked.

"That would mean," said Katy, "she walked down to the shore, pretended to be dead, then walked back up the walkway in the dark and climbed up the tower. I can imagine Jason doing that. Maybe even Javier, but *Helen*?"

Oliver shrugged. "You're right. Maybe I'm over thinking all this. It's just that I remembered there's another way up that tower."

I stepped over to the kitchen door, annoyed at myself for not spotting this ladder.

What bothered me more was the main door to the tower didn't have a lock. I shuddered at the thought of anyone sneaking inside while Katy and I were sleeping.

Is Helen hiding in the lighthouse?

"Katy, let's go check," I said, and turned to Oliver and Mary. "Keep them occupied and make sure they're in your line of sight at all times."

"What if they want to go into their rooms?" asked Mary.

"Make a batch of pancakes or something they'd all like and keep them in the dining room, would you?"

Oliver nodded. "We'll do our best."

Katy and I turned around and ran out of the main building.

It took us half a minute to spot the thin steel stairway that wound itself up from the ground to the top floor of the lighthouse, a relic from decades, if not centuries ago.

"A stairway to heaven," said Katy.

"Doesn't look like anyone uses it anymore," I said. "It's on the seaward side. That's why we didn't spot it yesterday."

After finding no other secret doors or entrances, we stepped inside through the main door.

Katy and I worked fast.

We checked the first and second floors, even feeling behind the paintings on the walls to see if anything was hidden behind them.

Once we'd thoroughly checked our bedroom, I stepped up to the staircase that spiraled up to the floor above us.

We still didn't know what the fourth and fifth floors of the tower might hold.

"Ready?" I said to Katy.

Taking two steps at a time, I dashed up to the fourth floor, with Katy clambering behind me.

I stopped in my tracks when I got to the landing and stared at our discovery.

We had stumbled into a book nirvana.

"It's the library," whispered Katy, breathing down my back.

The library spread across the entire fourth floor of the lighthouse.

It was the most opulent reading room I'd ever seen, with plush Persian carpets and gold-trimmed armchairs with velvet coverings.

Bookshelves built to spec covered every inch of the curved tower walls. The dark wood gleamed with polish next to the hardbacks with eye-catching covers. A rolling wooden ladder sat on its tracks, leaning against a shelf.

It was a room that would have turned even Marie Antoinette green with envy. The new owner had been serious about this library.

"I didn't realize we slept under *this* place," I whispered in awe.

"Remember that awesome library in *Beauty and the Beast*?" said Katy in a hushed voice. "This was made for Beauty."

"The owner is loaded," I said. "Can you imagine how much it would have cost to put this place together and get these books all the way up here?"

Katy walked over to the open window.

"Oliver forgot to close this," she said. "So much moisture coming in. I'm sure the sea air isn't good for these books."

I frowned.

Or did someone else come in after Oliver had made our rooms and opened it?

"What a view," said Katy, leaning out, "even better than the one from our room."

I stepped up to her. A sea gull swooped by the window, startling us. The salty smell of the ocean wafted to us.

"I thought we were going to sleep in a dump, when he said the lighthouse," said Katy. "This is incredible."

I pulled away from the window and turned to examine the bookshelves.

The only light came from the lone window and a handful of antique table lamps that sat next to the armchairs.

"I want a room like this in my house," said Katy, twirling around.

"In your New York apartment?"

"If they can put this inside a lighthouse, I can get one made for my place. You don't need to live in the Palace of Versailles to have an amazing library."

"When was the last time you finished a book, Katy? You're a movie buff."

"It'll be for Chantelle," said Katy, picking up a children's hardback that stood upright on the large coffee table in between the armchairs. "Hey, lookee here. Sophia wrote this book."

I walked up to the coffee table.

There were five hardcover novels and two spiral-bound documents laid on it.

I bent over to examine the titles and picked the one with a stunning purple cover. It was the author's name that had caught my eye.

It was a poetry book by Francisco Javier Quinteiro, our poet laureate from Mexico.

"Interesting," I said, as I shifted through the titles. "All these books were written by each of the guests staying this weekend."

Katy picked up a thick stack of papers that had been printed and bound in a spiral coil.

"That's not Helen's manuscript, is it?" I asked.

"Hers was a bunch of loose papers. This one's a screenplay by Elliot and this other one's from Ratcliffe. Seems like the owner got a hold of their unfinished work too."

"Doesn't this strike you as odd?" I asked.

Katy looked at the scripts in her hand.

"Maybe the owner wanted to make their guests feel special?" she said.

"Maybe," I said more to myself than her, "or maybe this means something more."

Katy raised an eyebrow.

"It's like those cards the owner left in our room and in the dining hall," I said.

"You mean this is another message?"

I stared at the books and manuscripts, wishing they could talk.

I couldn't help but feel like they were trying to tell me something—a subliminal message I couldn't decipher just yet.

Chapter Twenty-seven

We spent the next half an hour checking for latches or levers to secret rooms or spaces inside the library.

Anywhere an adult could stay hidden.

I even climbed the rolling ladder to check all the shelves on the top.

"Nothing," said Katy in a deflated voice when we were done. "Helen Jenkins is not here."

"One more floor," I said.

The stairway to the top was steeper. I felt my pulse quicken. We climbed up quietly, a sense of foreboding coming over me with each step.

"Wow," whispered Katy as we got to the top floor.

The library had blown my mind, but this had to be the most awe-inspiring room in the lighthouse.

The granite walls had disappeared, and in their place was glass. Floor-to-ceiling glass windows wrapped around the entire floor. Marine paraphernalia hung from the ceiling here and there, the only decorations in the room.

In contrast to the cozy atmosphere of the library below, daylight streamed in from all sides, making this open space feel even more expansive.

We gawked at the breathtaking, three-hundred-and-sixty-degree vista of the Pacific Ocean surrounding the island.

It was hard to take my eyes off the view, but I turned to look at the pièce de résistance.

In the center of the room sat the antiquated beacon that had kept seafarers safe for over a century. It was housed in an immense glass enclosure. I couldn't imagine what it must be like when that light turned on.

The only other piece of equipment in the room was a telescope installed on a mount near the window.

I jumped on it, placed my eye on the eyepiece and adjusted the focus.

"See anything?" said Katy, breathing down my neck.

I swiveled the telescope around.

Will we finally find Helen?

After turning it around the island twice and only spotting the other guests in various stages of searching, I passed the telescope to Katy.

"Maybe you'll have better luck," I said.

She took over while I walked around the open room, looking for any clues. Two minutes later, Katy straightened up and pushed the telescope away with a loud sigh.

"Nothing?" I said.

She shook her head. "If Helen's on the island, she is in a really good hiding spot."

Katy frowned and pointed at something over my head. "Hey, what's that thing over your head?"

I looked up.

It was a five-foot-long fish that had been stuffed and hung from the ceiling.

"Impressive," I said, and got on my tiptoes to touch the edge of its elongated bill.

"Ouch," I said, drawing my hand back hurriedly. "A stuffed swordfish," I muttered, examining the cut on my finger. "Its beak is sharper than a carving knife."

"Deadly," said Katy, handing me a tissue to soak up the bleeding.

After wrapping the soft tissue around my finger, I looked up at my friend. "There's no Helen Jenkins here."

"But there is a fantastic view," said Katy, walking over to the balcony and opening the door to the outside.

She stepped back as a powerful gust of wind crashed through the open doorway, blowing her back. She slammed the door shut.

Two hundred and fifty feet below us, the ocean was roiling, gigantic waves with white crests rolling along the top and crashing against each other.

"Looks like the sea is acting up again," said Katy. "Gosh, I hope she didn't come here, fall and get swept out to the sea, somehow."

A part of me went numb at the thought of discovering her floating body on the water.

"We'd have definitely heard someone fall," I said. "But it's impossible she'd climbed up the tower last night. Imagine trying to get up that ladder in the dark with a gale blowing like this, and it was worse last night."

Katy walked up to the telescope and put her eye on the lens, adjusting the focus and swiveling it around.

"See anything?" I asked.

"I think I see Mike's boat," she said after a while. "It's headed our way."

A rush of relief went through me.

I took the scope from Katy to see the small black blob in the distance, halfway from the mainland. It was moving fast toward the open ocean.

"Thank goodness," I said. "We get our phones back, the second he docks."

"Darn right," replied Katy.

Handing the telescope back to her, I strolled around the room, taking it all in.

The massive lantern in the middle of the room had a hypnotic feel, even unlit.

The newly installed electrical panel was set against the wall next to the light. Oliver was right. It was enclosed and locked in its own glass case.

I examined the panel, trying to decipher what it was for. There were no markings or signs, just plain black switches.

Maybe the light works after all, I thought.

Something Oliver said to us earlier popped to mind.

Lighthouses do funny things to you.

I wondered what wild stories this light could tell.

"What I don't understand is why the owner spent all this money sprucing up this place," I said. "This reno job cost way more than what the government ordered just to bring it to standards."

"It was for the luxury retreat," answered Katy, her eyes still glued to the scope. "But if they had asked me, I'd have told them they'd make way more money with Hollywood celebrities than this lot of sad writers."

"We don't know how much they paid for the retreat," I said. "I asked Oliver and Mary, but they got all cagey about it."

"I like those two," said Katy, turning to me.

"As far as I'm concerned, everyone on the island is untrustworthy until they prove otherwise."

Katy put her eyes back on the scope while I watched the boat get closer through the window.

"Wait," she said. "That's not Mike's boat. It's a Sea-Doo."

I took over the scope and scanned the horizon.

She was right.

"Maybe it's the Coast Guard?" I said. "Maybe Oliver got through to them, but they didn't have any boats ready, so they sent a recon guy out in whatever they could rustle up?"

"Sounds more like it," said Katy next to me. "Besides, Mike's too flabby and too slow to ride one of those."

I pulled away to see if I could make out the vehicle with my naked eye.

Katy took over the scope again.

I leaned my face against the window as the small vehicle got closer to the island.

Its outline was clearer now. The driver, in a wet or dry suit, was jumping the waves at a dangerous speed, leaving a frothy white wake behind them.

My heart beat a tick faster, the closer the Sea-Doo got.

Katy let out a loud gasp.

"You're not going to believe this," she said, reaching out and shaking me by the arm.

"What?"

She pushed the scope toward me, an astonished expression on her face.

"Look. *Look*, Asha!"

I put my eye on the scope, wondering what had got her excited.

It took me a while to adjust the focus again.

The vehicle was closer to the island. I could make out the Sea-Doo and the driver now.

I froze in place.

"It's Tetyana."

Chapter Twenty-eight

W e sprinted toward the lighthouse steps.

"What's she doing here?" cried Katy as we clambered down at breakneck speed.

"Something has happened," I said, trying not to hyperventilate.

We dashed out the front door and ran toward the walkway that wound down the cliff.

I glanced up only briefly.

The lawn was empty.

I thought I glimpsed something yellow flutter near the front door of the resort building. A woman's silhouette vaguely registered in my mind, but I didn't hang around to check.

I raced to keep up with Katy's long legs.

"Be careful!" I cried out as she reached the walkway to the shore. "It's slippery."

But Katy was already scrambling down.

The wind had picked up speed, and the waves were higher. How fast the ocean changed.

A quick look out to the sea told me Tetyana was still speeding toward us.

As I watched, she jumped a wave and landed with a loud crash on the surface. The water sprays shot so high that I lost sight of her, and for a sickening moment, I was sure she capsized.

I stopped and watched with my heart in my mouth until she reappeared again, surfing effortlessly on the waves.

"Slow down!" I yelled, knowing full well she couldn't hear me. The wind blew my frenzied words away, anyway.

Clutching the rope, I ran along the walkway, trying not to miss my footing.

Like David, Tetyana was a trained paramilitary operative who'd learned the skills of the trade at a young age. I knew I could trust her judgment. Even so, it was difficult to watch her put her life in the hands of the ocean like that.

The roar of her Sea-Doo got closer. Tetyana was almost at the jetty now.

For goodness's sake, slow down, I warned her in my head. *Watch out for those darn rocks.*

As if hearing me, the Sea-Doo engine cut off.

Tetyana was riding the waves next to the island, waiting for a good time to get closer to the jetty without getting smashed against the piles.

"Hey! Tetyana!" I heard Katy shout. She was about fifty yards down the walkway, waving at our friend.

Tetyana waved back, then turned her attention back to her task.

She made a striking figure. She was tall for a woman, with a strong athletic build and enough training to make her a shoo-in to any special forces team in the world. I was glad she was here, given our strange circumstances.

But why is she here?

Does this mean bad news back at home?

All the worst-case scenarios swirled in my mind like frantic whirlpools trying to suck me under.

Is David okay? Did he have an accident? Did the bakery burn down? Did Luc get into hot water with a high-flying client? Are we going to get sued?

I picked up my pace, holding on to the rope rail, and thundered down, my heart pounding like mad.

As long as no one is hurt, it will be fine, I told myself.

From somewhere behind me came a strange rumbling sound. I didn't think much of it, my focus on trying not to slip.

Was it thunder? Is another storm on its way?

When I heard the sound a second time, I stopped.

Tetyana shouted, her arms gesturing madly.

Something was wrong. And it was above me.

I snapped my head up just in time to see a white boulder, one that lined the ledge up on the cliff, come crashing down.

I flattened myself against the cliff face, screaming at the top of my lungs.

"Katy! Look up! Get out of the way!"

I covered my face as the rock thundered by me, drowning my voice.

I turned my head down just as Katy slammed against the cliff wall and the rock crashed by her. I gripped the railing, feeling faint.

I watched in horror as the boulder smashed on the cluster of rocks just below us, spraying debris in all directions.

Katy stood rooted to her spot, like she couldn't believe what had just happened.

She's alive.

I let out my breath.

"Hey!" shouted Tetyana.

Abandoning her attempts to bring the Sea-Doo to the pier, she'd dove into the water. She swam ashore and ran up the beach, hollering at us.

"You guys okay?"

"Okay!" I shouted back.

Katy ran down the remaining steps and jumped into Tetyana's arms for a hug. A red- hot anger welled inside of me, as I watched them.

That falling rock wasn't an accident.

Who tried to kill us?

"Someone pushed that on us!" I shouted at my friends, pointing to the top of the cliff.

Without waiting to say hello to Tetyana, I whipped around and scrambled back up the walkway.

"Hey! Where are you going?" I heard my friends shout at me from the shore.

I didn't have time to answer.

All I could think of was the things I'd do to whoever pushed that rock on us.

Chapter Twenty-nine

My climb up was slower, but my anger propelled me forward.

My heart was slamming inside my ribs, and my legs shook. The only thing that stopped me from crashing was the growing fury that someone had tried to kill Katy and me.

"Is everyone okay?" shouted someone from above.

I crawled to the top to see who it was.

It was Oliver and Mary, running across the lawn.

I scanned the grounds. There was no one else in the vicinity.

Where are the others?

I spotted two figures walking toward the building from the far end of the island. From where I was, it was difficult to make them out.

Oliver ran up to me just as I got to the top, his eyes wide in fear.

"What happened?" he asked, panting.

"Someone tried to kill us," I said through gritted teeth. "Did you see who it was?"

They stared at me like I was mad.

"What?" said Oliver, finally.

"My goodness," said Mary.

"Didn't you see that rock go crashing down the cliff?"

They exchanged a horrified glance.

"We heard a boat in the distance," said Oliver, reaching to help me up the last step. "I went to the third floor to check and saw it was a Sea-Doo. When I came down, I heard someone screaming. Saw Mary run out and I knew something was wrong."

"Somebody pushed a rock on us," I said, pointing a finger at the front door. "Did you see anyone hanging out there five minutes ago?"

"No one," said Oliver, shaking his head as if in disbelief. "I saw no one when I went upstairs to get a better look."

"I was in the kitchen, making pancakes," said Mary. "I came running out because I heard your screams."

"Did the others get back yet?" I asked.

Oliver nodded. "Most are back."

"Who?" I asked, my eyes narrowing.

Mary and Oliver exchanged another glance.

"I think the ladies are back with Mr. Ward," replied Oliver, scrunching his forehead. "I thought I saw Mr. Ratcliffe a minute ago in the dining room, but—"

"Didn't I tell you to keep an eye on them?"

"I... er... I'm afraid, it's like herding cats..."

"Cats are easier," murmured Mary, looking away.

"Something strange is going on here," I said. "I swear if I find the person who pushed that rock, I'd throttle them myself."

But Oliver and Mary were no longer looking my way.

They were staring down the walkway, eyes wide in surprise.

I turned back to see Katy and Tetyana were climbing up.

Oliver and Mary gave Tetyana a confused look. In her hooded black dry suit, she could have been mistaken for anyone.

"Are you from the Coast Guard?" asked Mary, giving my friend a once-over, when she came up.

"I'm with them," answered Tetyana, pointing at Katy and me.

Oliver turned to me with a puzzled look.

"She's with you?"

"This is Tetyana, a friend and colleague," I said. "Part of my family."
I turned to Tetyana.

"Oliver and Mary manage this place. They heard us scream and came running."

"Is that right?" she said, placing her hands on her hips.

She scanned the plateau, resting her eyes on the two men who were strolling toward the building, unaware of what had just happened.

"Who else was out here?" she said.

"N... No one was out here," stammered Oliver, shaking his head. "This is madness. I mean, I can't imagine anyone—"

Katy pointed at the rock debris at the bottom of the cliff and glared at him. "What does that look like to you?"

I looked up at the row of rocks that lined the edge of the cliff.

"You can see a boulder missing from the top," I said, pointing at a spot with flattened brown grass.

"Oh, my lord," whispered Mary, "what is happening?"

"Someone here means serious business," I said, "I'm beginning to think Helen Jenkins had good reasons to get scared."

Mary clutched Oliver's arm.

"I told you," she said, "they're coming after us all."

"Relax, Mary," said Oliver, "stop overreacting, would you?"

It was my turn to snap.

"Overreacting? We nearly got killed."

"Who's *they*?" asked Tetyana.

Oliver shook his head.

"We don't know, but Mary now thinks the owner is out to get us. I just can't think why."

He wiped his brow.

"There has to be a perfectly good explanation. Maybe the rocks got loose from the storm—"

"That rock needed leverage, Oliver," I said, trying not to grit my teeth. "Human leverage."

"Oh, my goodness," said Oliver, rubbing his forehead. "I don't know what to think anymore...."

Now that I'd caught my breath, I could think a little more clearly.

I turned my attention back to Tetyana.

"Why did you come?" I asked. "Everything okay at home?"

She looked from Katy to me.

"David got your message saying you had to give up your phones to the ferry driver."

"Did he panic?" I asked.

"Not till last night," she said. "I took the last flight to Portland and drove up to town. Wrangled a Sea-Doo from one of the kids in the village this morning."

"What happened last night?" asked Katy.

"David saw the local news. He'd been following the channel online, and he alerted me."

"What news?" I said, realizing how cut off we were from everything.

"The Coast Guard found the ferry boat smashed up on some rocks near the mainland."

"*What?*" said Oliver, his eyes bulging.

Mary put her hand over her mouth. "Oh, my lord, Mike! Is he okay?"

Chapter Thirty

"There was a big police presence near the fishing jetty when I left," said Tetyana. "They have divers out too."

"What about Mike?" whispered Mary.

"They haven't found him yet," replied Tetyana, her face grim.

I turned to Mary, who was tearing up.

"They'll find him soon," I said, unsure how else to pacify her.

"How does this happen?" Oliver shook his head as if in disbelief. "Mike's the most experienced local mariner. He grew up on that boat. He knew this area well, better than anyone."

He looked at us, the hair on his head looking grayer than before.

"If you told me he had an accident out at sea on a stormy day, I can imagine, but to crash on the rocks near the jetty? How is that possible?"

We had no answers for him.

"Oh, Mike," said Mary, wiping her eyes. "What about little Tod? What about Jayne? How are they going to get through this?"

"There's a massive search party underway," said Tetyana, tempering her tone after seeing how distressed they were. "I spoke with some first responders. They're giving it their all, so let's not jump to conclusions yet."

I turned around and gazed out at Oregon's coast. The town was too far away to see. If not for the shadows of the blue mountains in the distance, I wouldn't even have known which direction the mainland was.

I didn't know Mike well, and what little I knew of him didn't endear me to him. But I sent a silent prayer they'd find him alive soon.

As my eyes swept the horizon, I noticed something was amiss.

Wait a minute.

"Hey!" I spun around to Tetyana. "Where's your Sea-Doo?"

Tetyana whipped around.

"It's drifted out to sea!" cried Katy, pointing at the small white machine in the distance.

Without a word, Tetyana raced down, while Katy and I shouted at her to watch her step.

I turned to Katy.

"Let's go," I said.

Far away, the Sea-Doo was bobbing up and down on the ocean swells, drifting farther and farther from the shore with every second.

I was halfway down when I saw Tetyana dive into the waves and swim out.

"She's going to drown!" screeched Katy.

I heard a commotion from behind me and turned around to see Oliver and Mary were scrambling down too.

I ran down the walkway and up the jetty to get a better view of Tetyana. Katy was already at the end of the pier, hollering at her.

We watched Tetyana get pulled under by an enormous wave. My heart jumped into my mouth. Then I saw her head bob up. And she kept swimming.

I knew Tetyana was a powerful swimmer, but the sea was getting rougher and she was fighting the waves.

It's not worth it, I wanted to shout. *Dammit, girl.*

My brain whirled.

How are we going to get to her?

Between Katy and me, we had the swim experience of a nonathletic high school student. I could jump into shallow water to save someone, but swimming miles out to the open sea seemed like a Herculean task.

And a deadly one.

Tetyana was so far away now, it was difficult to spot her in that swirling surf.

I wanted to shake her. *Get back, now!*

Why does she have to be such a daredevil?

I scanned the beach, wondering if I could rustle up enough wood to make a raft, then let out a frustrated sigh. By the time we got a raft together, if we could make one at all, we'd have lost her.

The Sea-Doo was now miles away, a strong current dragging it away from her faster than she could swim.

My legs had gone wobbly, and I was sure my knees would give way at any moment.

It was a full five minutes later we saw Tetyana give up and turn around to swim back.

"Thank heavens," said Mary, who'd been watching with her hand on her mouth.

"I almost had a heart attack," said Oliver, sighing in relief.

Me too.

Katy and I ran down the jetty, jumped off it and got to the shore to wait for her to come in.

We stood on the beach, impatiently hopping from one leg to the other, as the waves crashed against our legs.

Swimming against the current now, it took Tetyana twenty minutes to get back to the island. When she was ten yards to the shore, Katy and I waded in to meet her.

When we got close, we reached for her through the surf and pulled her to her feet, as she panted from exertion.

"Don't ever do that again," scolded Katy as she took Tetyana's arm and draped it over her shoulder. I took our friend's other arm, and together, we stumbled over to the jetty.

After fussing over Tetyana and making sure she didn't have any injuries, Mary and Oliver walked back to the esplanade promising to make her a hot drink and get her some blankets.

Katy and I sat with Tetyana until she caught her breath.

Tetyana shook the water from her hair and put her head in her hands.

"I'm losing my touch," she said with an angry curse. "Should have tied that damn thing down."

"If that stone hadn't fallen, you wouldn't have abandoned it like that," said Katy.

Tetyana groaned.

"If I'd known what the heck was going on here, I'd have alerted the cops."

I put an arm around her shoulder.

"You came, didn't you? You did the right thing."

"It's just a Sea-Doo," said Katy. "We'll get another one for the kid."

"We didn't lose just a Sea-Doo, Katy," said Tetyana, her mouth set in a thin grim line. "My Glock and my phone were on that machine."

Chapter Thirty-one

"Wait, what's that?" Katy asked, pointing at something on the sand.

"What the frigging hell?" said Tetyana, sitting up.

I got up and ran over to pick it up. It was a small black plastic bag, made with a tough Kevlar-like material.

Tetyana stared at it when I returned with it to the jetty.

"That's my waterproof gun pouch," she said.

I could count on one hand the times I saw Tetyana look surprised. She plucked the pouch from my hand and felt it.

"Empty," she said.

"Fell out when the Sea-Doo capsized," I said.

"Impossible," she said. "For this to fall out, someone had to open the seat, unlatch the waterproof compartment underneath, take my bag out and pull the gun out of this pouch."

She looked up at us.

"Someone stole my gun. My loaded gun."

"They knew you had your gun in there?" asked Katy in a shocked whisper.

Tetyana shook her head.

"If I had to gauge this right, they rifled in the compartment because they knew that's where they'd find anything valuable. They just got lucky with my gun. The bastards."

A dark look came over her eyes.

"Whoever it was pushed the See-Do to the right spot so it would get taken away by the current. They knew exactly what they were doing."

Katy and I stared at her.

This case had just leveled up several notches.

"If they took my gun, they took my phone too," said Tetyana. "It was inside the same pouch."

"That's crazy," said Katy. "How come we never saw or heard them?"

"The wind is strong," said Tetyana, "and the waves are loud, but if we were looking down, we'd have seen the bastard."

I glanced up at the walkway.

Oliver and Mary were climbing up slowly, holding hands, looking like a sweet couple helping each other up.

"Do you think they distracted us?" Katy voiced what I was asking myself too.

Tetyana stared at the couple, her eyes fiery.

"We were looking the wrong way," she said. "Should have paid more attention."

"You're right," said Katy. "We were facing the island, but they were looking down. They would have noticed if someone pushed the Sea-Doo out to sea below."

"But they didn't breathe a word," I said, a sinking feeling coming to my stomach as I wondered if I'd put too much faith in those two. I felt a migraine coming and rubbed the sides of my head.

"Standard-issue Glock and a burner phone," said Tetyana, frowning. "No one can trace it back to me, but my worry is now someone on this island is running around with my gun."

She reached into her right leg pocket and pulled out a sheathed knife. It was her Japanese Tanto knife she liked to carry with her everywhere.

"I have this, at least," she said, unsheathing it to check it and sheathing it again.

We sat in silence for a minute to collect our thoughts.

"And here I was feeling bad for them," said Katy with a sigh.

"Wait," I said, trying to think despite my oncoming headache. "There's a chance they were so absorbed in Mike's story, they didn't notice anything. In a way, *we* distracted *them*."

"That's true," said Katy. "They looked shaken up. Then again, we've met some good actors in our lives, haven't we?"

Tetyana looked at us and raised her eyebrows.

"What the hell did you two get yourselves into? I thought you were just going to deliver some fancy cheesecake to a snotty writers' party."

"So did we," said Katy. "This is no normal party, I can tell you. One writer's gone missing already, and no one knows where she is."

"Are you kidding me?" said Tetyana.

"One thing I'm sure is that wasn't an accident," I said, pointing at the debris of pebbles on the beach. "Who pushed that down? Were they trying to kill us or distract us?"

"I was too far out to see, but I thought I spotted someone on the cliff just before the rock fell," said Tetyana. "I had my goggles on, and it had collected water, so it wasn't like I could see well."

"You came at the right time," I said. "We need all the help we can get now."

Between Katy and me, we explained everything we had discovered so far.

"David's instincts were right," said Tetyana once we were done. "He'd been losing sleep, antsy about you. But he didn't want to overreact. He knows how annoyed you get, Asha."

"He's a good man," I mumbled, feeling bad. David was a sweet, sweet man who cared. I needed to be more patient with him.

"There was nothing to pinpoint his worries until last night's news," continued Tetyana. "I came just to stop him from getting a stroke. Didn't realize it was this bad. I mean, how can things go wrong at a writers' retreat?"

"Things escalated quite fast," said Katy.

I turned to my friends.

"You know what this means, don't you? Someone doesn't want us to leave the island. Mike's boat was crashed, and he's missing. The See-Do is gone and the only phone in the island has disappeared too."

Tetyana got up and shook the sand off her dry suit.

"Let's see if we can track this idiot who took my stuff. They don't know what we're capable of."

For the next half an hour, the three of us scoured the beach, looking for tracks or telltale signs of the mysterious thief.

"These rocks," said Katy, after we circled the beach for a second time, trying not to erase any evidence on the ground. "That's what covered their tracks."

She was right. Whoever had taken Tetyana's stuff either walked on air, or stepped from the jetty onto the rocks on the beach, so they wouldn't leave any footprints on the sand.

"Hey!"

Katy and I spun around to see Tetyana waving us over. She was on the jetty. Taking care to stick to the rocks, we made our way toward the pier.

"Guess what I found," said Tetyana when we got to her.

She was standing next to the spot where Mike tied up his boat the last time we came. Two lifesavers were attached to the railing. In between them was a large wooden chest which I'd presumed contained boating equipment.

I thought I saw a padlock on it, but Tetyana had pried it open.

Katy and I peered into the box.

I was right. It was filled with boating and rescue paraphernalia, including a flare gun.

Tetyana pulled out a black bag that looked like it was made with the same material as the small pouch. "My bag," she said, unzipping it.

"Someone pulled this out of the Sea-Doo. They went through it and left my jeans and T-shirt."

"They took your gun and phone and dumped the bag here?" said Katy.

I rooted among the items in the box.

"Maybe your gun is in here too."

Tetyana shook her head.

"I already looked. They were smarter than that."

I pulled out a rope and the flare gun.

"I'm taking these. Might come to good use," I said, slamming down the lid.

I looked at my friends.

"I'm no longer playing the nice baker," I said. "It's time to confront everyone and see who's lying for once and for all."

Chapter Thirty-two

We stomped up the walkway and marched into the building.

My migraine was pounding the right side of my head. I grimaced in pain, but I wasn't about to let it stop me. Or let anyone get away with what they did to us.

Every step I took only incensed me further.

Katy and I turned right to walk into the kitchen when we heard loud voices from the second floor.

"Up here," I said, jumping up the stairs.

It was almost noon, and the scent of Mary's gourmet cooking wafted throughout the building. If everyone was gathered in the dining hall for lunch, we'd have a captive audience. A perfect time and place to ask a few questions and watch their reactions.

We got to the room just as Mary and Oliver were serving gourmet soup and sandwiches to the guests.

They all turned as we marched in.

They stared at Tetyana, who was still in her black Neoprene dry suit and diving boots. Even with her hood down and the goggles placed on her head, she looked like a strange deep-sea marine ninja.

She had her Tanto dagger unsheathed and in her hands. I hadn't realized she'd pulled her knife out as we'd walked up.

A quick glance around the room told me Camilla and Sophia were missing. I'll deal with them later, I thought, as I stepped up to my usual place at the head of the table.

"So, it was *you* who just came?" said Jason, pointing a curious finger at Tetyana. "I thought I heard a boat or Sea-Doo from my room."

"I heard it too," said Elliot. "Wondered what that thundering noise was. Who are you?"

Tetyana didn't reply.

"The question is, *what* are you?" sneered Ratcliffe. "A female wannabe *Die Hard*?"

She gave him a hard look, her eyes piercing. The knife in her hand glinted from the chandelier light.

That was all he needed.

Ratcliffe looked away, clearly out of his element. It was nice to see the man restrained for once.

With Tetyana and Katy flanking me, I leaned over my chair and placed my hands on the headrest. I felt my voice harden as I spoke.

"This is no longer a joke."

Everyone's attention turned to me.

"I want to know where all of you were an hour ago."

I turned around the table, making eye contact with each person, even Oliver and Mary standing near the buffet table at the end.

"What the heck?" spluttered Ratcliffe. He looked at the butler. "Serve my lunch, my good man. I don't have time for these stupid girls."

Oliver didn't reply, his eyes on mine.

"Which one of you pushed that boulder down the cliff?" I asked. "Did you realize you almost killed us?"

Everyone stared back, speechless.

"Someone tried to kill you guys?" said Jason, his eyes wide in shock. "Are you kidding?"

"We don't kid," I said. "Someone pushed our Sea-Doo out to sea and stole a mobile and a gun. This just got serious."

"Bah," said Ratcliffe, his confidence returned. "That would never happen to Bruce Willis."

I tried again. "Did any of you see anyone on the lawn an hour ago?"

Silence.

"Maybe it was that novelist who did it."

It was a quiet voice that came from the back of the room.

We all turned to Javier.

"Helen Jenkins," he said.

"Helen Jenkins?" said Elliot.

Javier gave a muted shrug as if to say *it's an idea*.

It was. A creepy one at that.

"Right," said Elliot, rolling his eyes. "She's dead and now her ghost is trying to kill us? Tell me another one."

"But are we sure she's dead?" asked Jason. "No one's seen her, right?"

"Utter nonsense!" roared Ratcliffe. "That's because she's been washed out to sea. I keep telling you people."

I turned to Mary and Oliver who were standing wordlessly, a teapot in her hand and a plate of sandwiches in his.

"You were there when Tetyana came in right now," I said. "Didn't you see anyone on the cliff?"

They stared back in response, their faces confused. Either they were excellent actors, or they were genuinely too terrified to speak.

I can deal with them later, I thought, and turned back to the table.

"If any of you had anything to do with any of this, I suggest you fess up now."

"Guns. Sea-Doos. Missing novelists. And now rocks falling down cliffs?" said Ratcliffe, thumping a fist on the table. "For goodness' sake, I just want to have my lunch in peace."

"It'll make a heck of a blockbuster movie, though," said Elliot with a smirk.

Jason gave Elliot a half smile.

"You write the screenplay and I'll create an anime version."

"Deal."

I wanted to stuff a few choice words down their throats, but I stopped myself in time. Yelling wasn't going to help.

I was the diplomat in our team, the one who talked to people and got the right information. But after what happened that afternoon, my blood was boiling, and I was having a hard time not letting my anger or my imagination get away from me.

If either of my friends had got hurt today, I'd have come here to see heads roll.

Before I could say anything else, a screech came from just outside the room.

We all turned toward the doorway.

"Who stole my scarf?"

Sophia tromped into the dining hall, her face in a scowl and her normally neat bun askew, like the wind had blown through her hair.

"Where's my mulberry silk scarf?" she demanded, glaring at the room. "The yellow polka-dotted one. It was in my bedroom this morning. Who took it?"

"Take a seat, Sophia," I said, giving her an icy glare. "We have bigger problems than lost scarves right now."

Sophia was about to retort when she spotted Tetyana.

She stared at our friend, her mouth open.

"Who the hell are you?" she said, pointing at her.

"Take a seat, please," I said, my voice hardening.

Elliot pulled her by the arm toward an empty chair next to him. Still gawking at Tetyana, Sophia plopped on her seat.

"Someone threw a rock at them and now they're a little sensitive," he said, his voice dripping in scorn but loud enough for everyone to hear.

Ignoring him, I turned back to the table.

"Who among you have been to this resort before?"

Shrugs around the table.

"Never been here before in my life," muttered Elliot, "and now I wish I never came."

"Me neither," said Sophia, "and I can't wait to leave."

"I'm a busy man," said Ratcliffe. "I don't have time for frivolous trips. Or for frivolous questions, for that matter."

"Whoever pushed the Sea-Doo out to sea knew where the currents were," I said. "That means it was someone familiar with this island."

All heads turned to Oliver and Mary.

Oliver's face went white.

"I'm a butler, not a boater," he stammered. "I can't even swim well. I had nothing to do with this. I'm as much in the dark as anyone else."

"If it wasn't you, who was it?" asked Katy.

"I wanna go home," said Sophia, pushing her chair back and getting up. "I don't know what the heck is going on, but I'm not staying here one more minute."

Elliot pulled her down again.

"Good luck with that," I said to her. "Whoever pushed our Sea-Doo out to sea, made us lose our one and only transportation to the mainland."

"What about that ratty boat we came in?" said Jason. "Wasn't that Mike guy supposed to come today?"

Mary let out a sob. Oliver put an arm around her shoulder and pulled her in.

I gestured at Tetyana.

"The reason my friend came was to let us know the ferry was destroyed last night. Crashed against rocks near the jetty on the mainland. Mike is missing and the police are searching for him as we speak."

A startled gasp cut across the table.

"Someone here is playing a dirty game," I said. "I'd bet anything Mike's boat crash and everything that has happened on this island are linked. Helen Jenkins is still missing. We don't know if she's alive or dead. Someone pushed a boulder down just when Katy and I were climbing down to the shore. Something strange is going on here. "

I glared at the guests.

To my surprise, no one wavered, averted their eyes, or showed any signs of guilt.

"I want to know what it is and who is behind this."

I turned to Sophia, the professional actor among this group.

"You seem in a hurry to leave," I said. "Where were you an hour ago?"

"How dare you!"

"Answer the question."

"I've no desire to answer any of your dumb questions."

"By any chance, you didn't take our gun and phone, did you?" I asked.

"Are you out of your mind?" screeched Sophia.

"Best to tell the truth because we'll be checking your rooms soon."

Sophia rose halfway. "Don't you dare! You come into my room and I'll... I'll... sue you to kingdom come!"

I turned to Tetyana.

"Search her."

Chapter Thirty-three

Tetyana stepped toward Sophia.

Sophia let out an ear-shattering shriek.

"Don't you touch me!" she screamed, flapping her arms.

"Who the hell do you think you are?" roared Ratcliffe, rising from his chair.

I spun around.

"I'm a private investigator," I said, glaring at him, making him sit back down. "You were right. We're not just bakers."

I scanned the room.

Jason opened his mouth to speak but then seemed to decide against it.

"The owner invited me to this island," I continued. "It was a call for help. They gave us a ten-thousand-dollar retainer to solve a problem for them and said to stay this weekend with all of you."

Elliot took a sharp breath in. Sophia gaped.

"I didn't know what problem they were talking about until Helen Jenkins disappeared." I paused. "I didn't realize the seriousness of this issue until someone here tried to squash Katy and me with a rolling boulder."

I gestured to Tetyana with my chin.

"Tetyana works for me. She's our security officer, and that's the reason she brought her gun. She came when she heard Mike's boat had crashed, leaving us isolated. That's what we're here for. To solve whatever this problem is and get us all back safely to the mainland."

I glowered at everyone.

"So, if any of you have our weapon, you'd better give it back now, or we're searching all of you."

Silence.

I turned to Tetyana.

"Continue, please."

Tetyana advanced on Sophia, who was now standing frozen in place. She patted her down while the others stared in numbed silence.

Once done, Tetyana turned to Elliot.

"You're next," she commanded.

I don't know if it was her demeanor or her knife, or maybe both, but Elliot got up immediately. He stood stock still, arms straight, while Tetyana patted him down.

"This is crazy. This is super crazy," grumbled Jason as he reluctantly got up next.

"If you have it, we'll find it," I said. "As soon as we get our phone back, you can be assured we'll be calling the authorities."

One by one, Tetyana went around the table.

Javier was easy, but I was surprised Ratcliffe had agreed without complaining. The knife seemed to have a powerful effect on him. Or maybe it was that he now knew who we were and why we were here.

Ratcliffe was a typical bully. He'd push his weight around and attack anyone weaker than him. That is, until he met his match. Or better than his match, in Tetyana's case.

I turned to Oliver in the back.

"Did you call the Coast Guard yet?"

He gave me a dazed look and fumbled to put the sandwich tray on the buffet table.

"I... I've been so... distracted by everything..." he stammered. "I'll do it right now." He stepped out of the dining hall, a worried expression on his face.

Why didn't he call already? I wondered, frowning. I'd taken it for granted that he already had contacted the authorities. Lunch could have waited. Didn't he realize how serious this was?

"Katy and I will check your rooms next," I said to everyone. "Tetyana will stay here with you until we're done."

"I did nothing wrong," said Jason in an angry voice. "You won't find anything in my room."

"I didn't take anything from anyone," said Elliot. "Let alone a gun."

"We'll see about that," I said, gesturing to Mary to join us.

"If you touch my manuscript," growled Ratcliffe, "I'll make you lot pay, you hear me?"

"We have no interest in your book," I said. "Just our weapon."

I turned one last time to the table before we left.

"My good friend here has fought the Russian militia with her bare hands. She's skilled in mixed martial arts and can move at lightning speed. If I were you, I wouldn't try anything stupid."

Sophia and Elliot gawked. Ratcliffe glared.

Leaving the door open in case we needed to come back in a hurry, Mary, Katy, and I walked up to the third floor.

With shaking hands, Mary opened each of the guest bedrooms for us.

Katy and I scoured each room, knowing the gun and the phone could be hidden anywhere on this island. It was a process of elimination. We would start here and then move outside.

We'd just finished Ratcliffe's room when we heard footsteps thumping up the staircase.

I whipped around.

"Mary!" came a shout.

It was Oliver.

He was running toward us, sweat dripping from his forehead. His face was flushed, and he was visibly shaking. His wife stumbled toward him, her face creased with worry.

"Are you okay, honey?"

Oliver leaned against Ratcliffe's door, trembling, as if trying to find the words.

"What's going on?" asked Katy.

"What in heaven's name has happened now?" asked Mary, shaking Oliver by the arm. "Tell me!"

He turned to his wife, then to us.

"It's our radio."

"What about it?" I said.

"Someone smashed it."

"You've got to be kidding," I said, feeling my stomach sink.

Oliver rubbed his face with both hands. He looked like he was barely holding himself together.

"The modem, too. Someone took a hammer to them both. I don't know how I never heard them. What do we do now?"

This was a strange place and getting stranger with every minute.

"When did that happen?" I asked.

"Was it when we were all down on the shore?" asked Katy.

"If it was, how come we didn't see them go up?" I asked. "They'd have had to take the gun and phone, push the Sea-Doo out and find a way up."

"Maybe there's another way to the top," said Katy, turning to the couple.

They shook their heads.

"Other than the helicopter pad, the walkway is it," said Oliver.

Katy turned to me.

"Maybe it's more than one person doing this," she said.

We stood in silence as we digested this thought.

Someone or some people were playing a nasty game and now had our loaded gun on them.

"They're trying to isolate us from the mainland," I said, trying to think. "But why?"

"If they wanted to get rid of us all, they would have used the gun already, wouldn't they?" said Katy. "Or are they waiting for the right time to pick us off, one by one."

"This has nothing to do with us," said Oliver in a whisper. "It's all those writer folk. Someone wants to get them, and Helen Jenkins was first."

"Oh, my lord, what in heaven's name is going on?" whispered Mary, her lips trembling.

I looked at the couple huddled next to Ratcliffe's doorway, arms around each other, looking beyond overwhelmed.

"Oliver, Mary, please tell us the truth. Are you involved in this in any way, shape or form?"

They shook their heads like they couldn't speak.

"Did the owner's emails give you any sign of this? Any hints about the guests? Or what would happen here?"

They shook their heads again.

"Do you know where or why Helen Jenkins disappeared? Or who pushed that boulder our way?"

After swallowing a few times, Oliver opened his mouth.

"Please believe me when I say we're as clueless as you," he said. "I just want this to stop. We never signed up for missing guests and attempted murder. This is too much."

I narrowed my eyes.

Do I believe them?

Did Oliver smash his own radio?

"This is a nightmare," said Mary, "a horrible nightmare." She turned to her husband, her face flushed pink.

"Why didn't you get one of those smartphones Leo's always bugging you about. Why do you have to be so stubborn?"

Oliver looked down at his feet.

"We might as well accept it," said Katy with a resigned sigh. "We're completely cut off from the world now."

Chapter Thirty-four

"Do we have enough provisions?" I asked.

This wasn't the time to give up. This was the time to formulate a plan.

Oliver nodded feebly.

"How much?" I asked.

"We stocked up for the retreat," he replied, still looking down. "We have enough food and water for a week for everyone. We have a saltwater purification system too, if it comes to that. Hopefully not."

"What about power?"

"There's an electricity generator in the shed out back, and I have enough diesel for a few days."

"A few days?"

Oliver looked at me, squinting, like he was trying to think. He'd regained some color and I could see he was trying.

Good.

"A week if we use it smartly. We also have two tanks of natural gas in the back. The kitchen stove and the fireplaces in all the rooms run on gas. The electricity is for lights and smaller appliances. We should be fine on that front for a week."

"Gosh, I hope we're not stuck here that long," said Katy, looking devastated at the thought.

"Oh, good lord," said Mary with a moan. "We're all going to die here."

"What about your family?" I asked Mary, trying not to get sucked into worst-case scenario ruminations. Prepare for the worst but expect the best, was my motto now.

"Where are they right now?" I asked.

"In Portland," replied Oliver. "We have two daughters and a son, and four grandkids."

"Do you call them often? Won't they worry when they don't hear from you?"

"We visit them for the weekend once a month and we spend a week over summer when we have some downtime. They have their hands full with their jobs and the kids. They hardly watch the news, so they probably won't hear about this for a while."

"When were you planning to visit them next?" I asked. "Not this weekend, I presume?"

"We were supposed to be working this weekend," said Mary. "They won't be expecting us till two weeks from now."

"So, no," added Oliver, realizing what I was getting at. "They won't know about our situation. Not for a while."

"What about the other guests?" asked Katy. "Won't their families try to contact them?"

Oliver looked down again and shook his head.

"The owner's instructions were explicit. No emails, no calls, no disturbances whatsoever till the retreat is over."

"So, nobody will call in till next week?"

"I'm afraid that's the case."

That left David and our families back in New York. I'd expect David to lower his guard now Tetyana had come. He wasn't going to start worrying for another couple of days. We had to find a way to survive until then.

I turned to Katy.

"Let's finish checking the rooms. Our priority is to find that gun before anyone else does."

Mary frowned.

"Why did she bring a gun?" she asked, narrowing her eyes. "What was your friend doing coming here with a loaded weapon?"

"Tetyana is my security adviser," I explained. "When I get hired for private investigations and I need extra help, she's the one I call."

"She's not some Mafia thug, is she?" asked Oliver, a troubled expression on his face.

"No. Her day job is as a martial arts teacher at my fiancée's dojo in New York," I said. "She's highly skilled and her goal during our missions is safety first for everyone."

I stopped, feeling bad for not being fully honest.

If I'd told them how we'd all met or divulged Tetyana's complete background, I'd frighten them. Right now, I had to figure out how to get everyone back to the mainland safe and alive.

The fewer distractions, the better.

"Think of her like a retired cop," I added. "If you're up to no good, she won't hesitate to hand you over to the authorities. If you're innocent, she's on your side. She's here to back us up."

Mary took a deep breath in.

"Thank you," she replied. "Makes me feel a bit better."

"Me too," said Oliver. "I'm glad she came when she did."

I nodded, but my mind was vacillating for the tenth time that day.

This means Mary and Oliver aren't playing games, right? Or are they that good at hiding their true motives?

"Camilla was missing from the dining hall," I said, returning to our task at hand. "Did either of you see her?"

"She came in after her search outside," said Mary. "She said she was tired from the walk and wanted to have a nap before lunch."

"Did she go straight to her room?"

"I thought so...I mean...why would she lie about that?"

"Do you have the key to her room?" I asked.

Mary pulled out her master key ring and picked one out.

"Can you show us to her room, please?" I asked.

Katy and I followed Mary as she shuffled to the end of the corridor on the third floor.

She turned to us when she got to Camilla's door.

"We really shouldn't be disturbing our guests," she said. "I'm not sure it's the proper thing to do."

"Don't you think these are exceptional circumstances?" I asked, surprised she'd even debate the issue.

Katy raised her eyebrows. "What if she's in trouble?"

With a sigh, Mary turned to the door and knocked.

"Ms. Carter?" she called out.

No answer.

"Ms. Carter?"

Nothing.

"Was she alone when she came in, or was she with Sophia and Elliot?" I asked.

"All three came back together. I served them orange juice in the garden behind the kitchen while you and the others were doing your checks."

"Maybe she went back to the grounds for some reason?" said Oliver, his brow knotted.

I stepped up to the door and put my ear against it. There was no sound coming from inside the room. I tried the knob. The door was locked.

I raised my voice.

"Camilla? Are you in there? Open the door. This is an emergency."

No answer.

I banged on the door.

Nothing.

I nodded at Mary. She gave me an uncomfortable look.

"We have a strict privacy policy at this resort," she said. "The owner made us sign it when they took over. I don't want to get in trouble with—"

"Let me then," said Katy, stepping up and plucking the key from Mary's hands.

"I didn't sign any policy," she said, as she nudged the woman aside and slipped the key into the keyhole. "If anyone complains, you can tell them I did it."

With a loud rap on the door, Katy turned the doorknob and pushed it open.

A rush of hot air came from the room.

I reeled back, stunned.

Camilla Carter lay sprawled out on the carpet next to her bed. Around her neck was a yellow polka-dotted scarf, tied so tightly, her face had turned purple.

Even from where we were, I could see Camilla was no longer breathing.

Chapter Thirty-five

Katy and I dashed inside.

Kneeling beside Camilla, I checked the pulse on her wrist. Katy stooped over her from the other side to examine the bruises on her neck.

Camilla's body still had a pinkish pallor. While her temperature was cooling, she was still warm.

A sliver of saliva dribbled from the side of her mouth, but it was her eyes that startled me the most.

They were wide open and staring out, dead to the world. But I could still see the terror in them.

She must have seen her assailant in her last moments. I wondered if those eyes reflected the horror at what was happening to her or the shock of seeing who was killing her.

Perhaps both, I thought grimly.

After probing for her pulse for a minute, I laid Camilla's stiffened arm back on the floor and looked up at Katy.

We paused for a moment, staring at her still body.

With her caustic attitude and the flaming dyed hair to go with it, she'd shown more personality than the rest of the group. It was shocking to see her lifeless.

Katy pulled at her shirt collar.

"It's boiling in here."

I looked at the gas fireplace. It had been turned on to the highest setting. I lifted my nose in the air and sniffed.

"Katy, is it just me, or do you smell that too?"

"You mean that stinky sm—"

"Ladies!"

We turned around to see Oliver at the threshold, gesturing to us urgently.

"Come out!" he shouted, waving his hands in a frenzy. "Get out of the room!"

Another glance at the fireplace and I saw what I should have spotted before I stepped into this room.

The smell of rotten eggs.

Someone had ripped both the small fire alarm and the carbon monoxide detector out of the wall. They lay discarded on the carpet, their battery compartments emptied, and the double AA batteries sitting next to them.

"Get out! Now!" yelled Oliver.

I jumped up, pulling Katy by the arm. I ran out of the room, dragging her behind me, and Oliver slammed the door shut.

"Downstairs!" he hollered, turning around and sprinting through the corridor.

Mary was scrambling down the steps, a hand covering her nose, with Oliver prodding her from the back now.

Katy and I bolted after them.

Tetyana was standing guard at the dining hall doorway on the second floor. She whipped around when she heard us rumble down.

"What the hell's going on?" she said.

"Get out!" screamed Oliver, as he streamed past her, pulling Mary along.

I came to a screeching halt near our friend.

"Gas!" I said. "We need to evacuate!"

Without a word, Tetyana spun around and headed into the dining room.

I didn't wait. I ran after Oliver, vaguely hearing Tetyana holler at the guests like a drill sergeant.

"Find the main valve!" I shouted to Oliver. "Turn it off!"

"This way!" he yelled as he dashed toward the end of the corridor.

It took a few minutes for Oliver to locate the central controls in the small electrical room next to the kitchen. I held my breath until he turned the valve off, and collapsed against the wall as soon as I heard the click.

Oliver leaned against the other wall, clutching his heart.

Katy came rushing in.

"What are you doing here?" she said, pulling on my arm. "We're supposed to get out of the house."

I pointed at the black lever that was now pointing down.

"Main gas valve to the house. Turned off just now."

We heard a noise and turned to see who it was. Mary stumbled into the room, her face white, her chest heaving.

"It's off, Mary," said Oliver, "we're okay now."

"Would that have blown up the house?" she asked in a shaky voice.

Oliver shook his head.

"Unlikely. But if we hadn't noticed the leak, we'd have all fallen like flies by dusk."

"The rotten egg smell," I said. "I smelled it but didn't make the connection." I turned to Oliver. "It came from the fireplace, right?"

"That's what it looked like," he replied in a quiet voice. "Someone tampered with it."

"What about that scarf?" said Katy. "I saw bruise marks on her neck. It was Sophia's scarf, wasn't it? But why would she turn on the gas to kill Camilla, then strangle her as well?"

"That had to be staged," I said, stopping to think for a minute. "Something tells me Camilla let someone into her room. Could have been Sophia. That person strangled her using the scarf, removed the detectors, and then turned the gas on before leaving."

"But the door was locked," said Katy.

"I saw the key," said Oliver. "It was on the floor on the *inside*."

"What?" I said, as my shoulders tensed at the thought. "That means someone has another key to these rooms."

"That's impossible," said Mary, showing her massive key ring. "This is the only master key set and I have it on me at all times."

Oliver nodded. "She sleeps with it on her bedside table. Whoever did this had to have gone in another way."

"What about the window? Her balcony?" I asked.

"Not unless they can leap twenty feet in the air from one balcony to the other," said Oliver, shaking his head. "They're all self-contained rooms and balconies. They'd have to use climbing rope, carabiners, a harness, or scaffolding at the worst. We would have noticed that."

"I can't imagine Sophia scaling the building," said Katy. "Plus, she's only a bit bigger than Camilla. She'd have fought back, wouldn't she?"

"I get this feeling someone's trying to frame Sophia," I said, frowning. "Those two looked like they knew each other. Remember how they were always hanging together with Elliot?"

"Sophia was upset about her missing scarf," said Katy. "Would she have used that if she killed Camilla?"

"Unless it was an act," I said.

"Of all the people to get killed," said Mary, shaking her head. "I can imagine someone going after that nasty Mr. Ratcliffe. He gets on everyone's nerves. But Ms. Carter? She was nice. She even gifted me one of her signed books when she came in."

Oliver shook himself, as if he was trying to wake himself from a trance.

"This is madness. I feel like I'm trapped in a never-ending nightmare."

"They're trying to confuse us," I said.

"Who?" asked Oliver.

"That's the thirty-thousand-dollar question," I said, feeling like we were grossly underpaid for the job at hand.

As if reading my mind, Mary clutched my arm.

"Didn't the owner hire you to find out?" she said, staring at me earnestly. "Find out who's doing this. Please. Spare us more heart attacks."

With a sigh, I stepped out of the small electrical room, followed by Katy. We walked over to the large window along the corridor that looked out to the front lawn.

It was a gloomy and subdued crowd standing outside. They had gathered behind Tetyana, like chicks huddling behind a mother hen.

Tetyana was holding them back and watching the house, hands on her hips, a stern look on her face.

"We'll have to tell them what we found upstairs," I said.

"It's one of them," whispered Mary, coming over and standing next to me. "They want to sabotage the resort. I just know it."

Oliver came over. "Precisely," he said. "Someone here was paid to do this by a business rival."

"A rival?" I asked, raising an eyebrow.

Oliver nodded, his lips set in an angry thin line.

"Mary and I've been doing some thinking. We think this has something to do with our new owner's business rival. They're trying to kill our business by creating chaos during our first ever retreat."

"But wouldn't your new owner tell us?" I asked. "They'd have given us the right information so we could tackle this problem. All we have is a cake order, a photo of a dead man, and strange notes left for us. They're playing cloak and dagger games with us."

"What if the new owner is a wealthy gangster?" said Mary in a hushed tone. "What if they're a Mafia family?"

"You're not serious?" asked Katy.

"Who else would have this much money to spend on crazy projects like this?" said Oliver. "Why didn't they tell you what their problem really was? Why don't they talk to us directly? They're being secretive because they're running an illegal business. I'm sure of it."

"Mafia gangs solve problems with bullets and concrete blocks," said Katy. "They don't pay for private investigators, or play elaborate games like kidnapping and killing writers."

"I can't think of any other explanation," said Oliver, his face weary. "I can't help but feel like we signed up to work for a Mafia boss."

I didn't reply, but something told me this was a more personal affair than anything to do with gangsters or business rivals.

Mary leaned over to me.

"I know who it is," she said. "I know who the rival is."

"Oh, yeah?" I said. "Who?"

"That Mr. Ratcliffe. He's the one."

I stayed silent for a while, contemplating their idea. From my experience, the most obvious suspect was the least likely to have committed the dirty deed.

Then again, Ratcliffe could be playing us, acting out the overbearing and rude personality to mask his calm and cool murdering interior.

But I was spinning myself into knots.

The note left in our room swirled through my mind.

"P.S. Seven guests arrived today. Not all will leave the island on Sunday."

"Have you thought of another, more likely, explanation?" I said, looking at the couple.

"Like what?" asked Oliver.

"Like it's your new owner who's orchestrating all this?"

Chapter Thirty-six

A stupefied silence fell on the lawn.

I could feel the chill going through the crowd as I told them of Camilla's sudden death.

Katy, Tetyana, and I observed them carefully, trying to see if we could catch a telltale micro expression that would give the murderer away, but we saw nothing.

It was a haggard, drained crowd that stood in front of us, eyes wide in shock, as if they had lost their ability to speak.

"We have more bad news," I said, feeling the next bit of information was going to jar them all awake.

I turned to Oliver.

His face flushed red as he cleared his throat and prepared to speak.

"I'm sorry to say, ladies and gentlemen, but, the, er, lighthouse radio is out of commission."

Ratcliffe jerked awake. "What do you mean, my good man?"

"Someone broke it," said Oliver. "Ripped out the wires and took a hammer to it."

"Are you saying we're stuck in this godforsaken place with no way to connect to the mainland?" hollered Ratcliffe.

"I'm afraid that's the case," replied Oliver in a quiet voice.

"Are you kidding me?" shouted Jason in shock.

"And the only transportation to this island has been sabotaged?" said Elliot, his eyes bulging.

"We don't know how it happened, sir, but the ferry is no longer working."

Chaos broke out after that.

Elliot cursed and Javier put his head into his hands and fell to the ground, as if he couldn't take it anymore. Then, Sophia fainted. Katy jumped to catch her just in time.

"You can't do this to us!" shouted Ratcliffe.

"It had nothing to do with me, sir," said Oliver, a weary look on his face, "I'm in this with you, ladies and gentlemen."

"How does a writers' retreat turn into a horror show?" asked Jason. "We paid good money for peace, not this hellhole!"

Ratcliffe glowered at Oliver.

"Who broke the radio? Tell me who it is, and I'll smash their face."

"Hey," said Elliot, shooting Oliver a suspicious look. "How do we know you didn't break it yourself? How do we know you didn't kill Camilla? You're the only one who knows how the gas fireplaces work."

"I can only give you my assurance," said Oliver, looking at least twenty years older than when we first met.

He looked helpless. I wanted to support him, stand up for him. If it hadn't been for him, Katy and I would have stayed in that gas-filled room longer. He had to be on the right side. But I also knew I couldn't make assumptions just because I took pity on him.

"My wife and I would never harm another person," Oliver was saying. "We've never had such a horrific experience in our lives." He paused unhappily. "Just like you, I can't wait to leave this place, this place that has been my cherished home for decades now."

Ratcliffe turned his snarl on me.

"What about you? You said you're a PI, didn't you? Ordering us around, searching us. Why didn't you stop this? You're useless!"

"We're doing our best to sort this out," I said. "Chaos and confusion aren't going to help right now. We need clarity."

I looked around the group.

"What we need right now is honesty," I added. "Frank answers from all of you."

A hush fell on the grounds.

Javier still had his head in his hands. Sophia had just come to and was leaning against a lawn chair. I wasn't sure if she had recovered enough to follow the conversation or if she was pretending not to. Either way, she remained silent.

"I think Javier's theory is right," said Jason.

"What theory?" asked Katy.

"This is all Helen Jenkins's doing. Everything went to hell in a hand basket, the minute she arrived on the island. We still haven't found her dead body—if she's truly dead, that is."

Elliot nodded.

"I've been thinking the same. She's the connection to all of this. I'd swear she's alive and kicking somewhere. She's Camilla's killer."

Wasn't it Elliot who objected to Javier's assumption earlier? That was a quick turnaround.

"If you ask me, Jenkins looked shifty," said Ratcliffe, giving me an accusatory look. "You need to stop interrogating us and go find that madwoman."

With decades of experience trying to suss people out and get out of dangerous situations, I knew there was one thing I could trust. That was my instincts.

And my instincts were telling me Helen Jenkins was in as much trouble as we were, or worse. I had no evidence. Just a gut feel.

"Sophia," I said. "We found your scarf around Camilla's neck. Can you tell us where you were an hour ago?"

Sophia's face turned white.

"How dare you!" she shrieked, pointing a finger at me. "Someone stole my scarf and you accuse me? How dare you, you little bitch?"

Everyone drew back as she jumped to her feet.

"I'm getting out of this mad place," she yelled. "I'm going home!"

Before anyone could do anything, she turned around and scrambled across the lawn toward the slippery walkway.

"Hey!" I hollered. "Stop!"

Tetyana caught up to her in seconds and grabbed her by the arm.

"Let me go!" wailed Sophia.

I ran up to them.

"Where do you think you're going?" I asked.

Sophia wiggled, trying to slip out of Tetyana's grip.

"I hate you!" shouted Sophia to me. "You nasty witch!"

A hand flailed near my face.

I ducked.

"Settle down!" said Tetyana, shaking her.

But Sophia pulled one hand out, reached over and slapped me across my cheek.

I stepped back, stunned.

Chapter Thirty-seven

Tetyana grabbed Sophia's arms and pinned them against her back, like she was arresting her.

"What the hell you tryna play at?" she barked.

Sophia let out a wail.

"Pull yourself together, for goodness sake," said Tetyana. "Do you realize, you're acting as guilty as heck?"

"It wasn't me!" cried Sophia. "I didn't kill her. I don't know how my scarf got on her...."

She started hyperventilating, her chest rising high and low, as if she was having a hard time breathing. As I looked on in alarm, her eyes rolled back into her sockets and she dropped her head, going limp.

Tetyana held her up. "Fainted," she said.

Mary walked over, concern on her face.

She patted Sophia's cheeks a few times until her eyes flittered back to life. Sophia looked around her, her movements still jerky and erratic.

"Where am I?" she croaked.

"Breathe. Breathe," said Mary, patting the woman's arm. "Slow down. Good. Keep breathing."

Sophia stared at Mary like she was seeing her for the first time.

"What happened?" she squeaked.

"Come, now," said Mary to Sophia, "we're going to sit down and breathe, okay?"

Mary linked her arm in Sophia's and escorted her back to the group. She shot me an angry look as she passed me.

"Why are you picking on her?" she hissed. "Why don't you ask that Mr. Ratcliffe questions?"

Tetyana and I followed them. I rubbed my burning cheek, wondering how much of a mess we had on our hands.

Ratcliffe glowered as we walked up.

"Why the heck didn't you let the banshee go?" he said, turning to me. "She could have got to the shore and called for help."

"Do you seriously think she can swim in this state?" I said.

"I want to go home too," cried Elliot, throwing his arms in the air. "I'm not hanging around here anymore. I want to go now!"

Jason turned to us.

"What are you going to do, huh?"

I glared at the crowd.

What a bunch of self-entitled, self-absorbed....

I had to take control of this group. I stood my ground, feet apart, shoulders squared.

"Whether we like it or not, we're stuck here together with a murderer on the island."

I paused to let that sink in.

"We believe Camilla died about an hour ago. Her body was still warm when we found her. If we're going to solve this, we all need to be honest about where we were in the past hour."

Silence.

"Okay," I said. "I'll go first. Tetyana, Katy, and I were down at the shore for almost an hour, searching for our gun and phone. Mary and Oliver can attest to that. We walked up about a half hour ago and came straight to the dining room."

"I saw you come up the walkway," said Javier who was now seated on a lawn chair, next to Sophia. "I saw you from the dining hall window."

I sent a silent thanks to the poet for sticking up for us.

"After that, we went straight to the third floor to check for our weapon in the rooms with Mary," I said. "We'd just finished Ratcliffe's room when Oliver came running up to tell us about the smashed radio. Then we all went to Camilla's room to see where she was. That was when we discovered her body. We have alibis for every minute of the past two hours."

I scanned the group.

"Who's next?"

Elliot stepped forward, surprising me.

"I came back from the search party with Camilla and Sophia two hours ago," he said. "We saw nothing, and I was bone tired. We came through the back door because it was the closest. Mary and Oliver were there, preparing lunch. I drank my glass of orange juice and went straight to my room to rest before lunch."

"Me, Javier, and Ratcliffe went to the back of the building," said Jason. "We split up and checked the woods but didn't see anything. We came in through the kitchen door where we saw Oliver and Mary. I went up to my room too, to change for lunch. Elliot saw me go in."

Elliot nodded.

"I saw him and he saw me."

But any one of them could have slipped into Camilla's room once the coast was clear.

Oliver turned to me.

"After we climbed back up from the shore, we came to the kitchen to make lunch. Everyone saw us there."

I nodded and turned to Javier.

"After drinking my juice in the kitchen," said Javier, "I went to my room to pick up my journal. I went to the dining room after that to write on the windowsill."

"Did anyone see you there?" I asked.

"Mr. Ratcliffe was in the dining room too."

I turned to Ratcliffe, who'd been unusually quiet.

"And you?"

"He's right. I was in the dining hall. Was there for the past few hours, reading my annual report." He glared like he wasn't happy to answer my questions. "I don't like being cooped up in my room and the hall has the best view."

"And me," said Sophia, suddenly speaking up. "I went to take a nap. I'll have you know, I had my scarf with me then. When I woke up, it was gone, and I came down to lunch soon after. Someone stole it and killed Camilla!"

She fell onto Mary's shoulders, sobbing.

I exchanged a glance with my friends.

They couldn't all be telling the truth.

Someone killed Camilla Carter.

One of them was lying.

Camilla didn't die by accident and it wasn't the act of a ghost, Helen's or otherwise.

We stood in a silent circle on the lawn, the wind blowing against our backs and the gloomy gray sky looking more ominous than ever.

"I'm ready for a swim," said Jason. "Better to die in the cold sea than hang around here for whatever crazy-assed drama is going to blow up next."

"Me too," said Elliot.

"I just want to get out of here," wailed Sophia.

"Look," said Tetyana, stepping to the front of the group.

"Things look bleak, but this isn't the time to rush into action without a proper plan."

"Oh, yeah?" said Ratcliffe with a sneer.

"I've been in worse situations than this, in places you people wouldn't dare to tread, and I've survived," she continued, ignoring the man.

"Here's my plan. I can build a raft that's stable enough to get a few of us back to the mainland and alert the authorities. I've been trained on rebuilding bridges and boats. If you can help me rustle up the right equipment and material, it should take me a day or two, tops."

"You gotta be kidding me," said Ratcliffe. "What are you now, Robinson Crusoe?"

Tetyana gave him a withering glance.

"If you have a better idea on how to contact the mainland, be my guest."

Ratcliffe fell silent.

"I wanna be the first on it, if you manage to build one," said Sophia, color back in her face again.

"The sooner we get over there the better," said Tetyana, ignoring her. "I'd say there's a strong link between the wrecked ferry and what's going on here on the island. I'm sure the cops will want to know what has happened here."

I sent a silent *thank you* to my friend for taking over the madhouse for the moment.

"I can help you build the raft," said Jason.

"Me too," piped up Javier. "I'll help."

Elliot gave a shrug. "If it works, it works. I'll give you a hand. Better than sitting around, going mad."

"But what do we do with, er, Camilla?" asked Katy. "We can't leave her like that. It's hot in her room."

"Take her outside," said Ratcliffe, "put her in the back or something."

"We can't leave her outside," said Mary, aghast.

Sophia shot Ratcliffe a nasty look. "That's like leaving her to the vultures."

I watched her. For someone who might have murdered her colleague, she was showing an unusual amount of compassion.

"I don't think there are vultures in this part of the world, Sophia," said Jason.

"Wolves then," said Sophia. "Anyway, that's just not right."

"There aren't any wolves on this island either," said Oliver, "but you're right. We can't leave her outside."

"We need a cool room that's secure, which we can lock until the authorities come," I said.

"We have a walk-in fridge," said Mary, "it's not perfect but—"

"You can't be serious," said Ratcliffe. "There's food in there. That's unhygienic."

"I don't know about you all, but I've lost my appetite," said Katy. "Someone just got killed here, people. I don't think I'm going to think of food for another week."

Oliver turned to me.

"Can you and your friend help me move the body?"

Katy and I followed Oliver toward the front door to get the stretcher and face masks from the first aid station, leaving Tetyana to manage the guests.

I was glad the three of us were sleeping at the lighthouse and not in the house with a dead body in the fridge.

But I had no idea what was to come next.

Chapter Thirty-eight

Elliot dropped a log on the pile and rubbed his hands.

"Think we have enough?" he called out.

"We need longer ones," said Tetyana, glancing at the latest addition. "Five footers or more. Try to find dry wood, people."

She turned to Oliver.

"I'll need a couple of axes or an electric saw."

"I have an axe in the work shed in the back. Do you need rope too?"

"Got some from the box in the jetty," said Tetyana, pointing at the rope and flare gun I'd brought up that were now lying on the lawn.

"I'll need floaters, one or two hammers, and some nails."

"We have tools and nails in the shed. There may be some empty diesel barrels there you can re-purpose," said Oliver.

"We'll need a lot more than a few barrels," said Tetyana.

"Come, I'll show you the shed."

Tetyana walked with Oliver toward the back of the building.

After Katy and I had moved Camilla to the fridge, we'd come out to the lawn to see Tetyana had put everyone to work.

Jason, Elliot, and Javier were collecting logs from around the island and had already stacked a pile of wood at the far end of the lawn.

Keeping them busy meant fewer panic attacks and less infighting, I thought in relief.

But two people were missing.

Ratcliffe and Sophia had separated themselves from the group. They were strolling along the far side of the lawn, near the edge of the cliff.

I watched as they moved their heads close together as if they were conferring about something important.

Strange, I thought, how rapidly Sophia had transformed from her suicidal panic attack to chatting calmly with a man whom I thought she disliked. A man who'd just mocked her and called her a banshee, no less.

Was that all an act?

Katy came running up to me.

"Tetyana needs more floaters," she said.

I frowned.

"Maybe there's something in the lighthouse we can use? Let's go check."

"You think this raft idea will work?" Katy asked in a low voice as we walked over to the tower.

"Better than nothing. Plus, it's keeping everyone busy and not descending into madness," I said.

"We just need something big enough for one person who can go to the mainland. I vote for Tetyana."

"We could have a riot in our hands."

"Oh gawd, you're right," said Katy, "Sophia and Ratcliffe will fight tooth and nail to be first on the raft. It won't be a fun sight."

"I don't think we have enough life vests for everyone. Even if we did, it'll be tough to build a barge large enough to carry ten adults all the way to the mainland without capsizing," I said. "Even for Tetyana."

"Better to try something than nothing at all, I guess," said Katy glumly.

I opened the lighthouse door, and we stepped inside. We scanned the ground floor ornaments.

"Stuffed fish, miniature sailboats, watercolor paintings, and a hundred-thousand-pound ship anchor," muttered Katy as we strolled across the floor. "Don't think any of these will float."

"Hey," I said, pointing at an empty spot on the wall between two paintings of tall ships. I was sure that white shelf had contained something, but it was now gone.

I gestured to Katy to come over and see.

"Do you remember what was here?"

She shrugged. "Nope. It was probably removed before we came here."

"I'd remember it, though," I said. "I was so impressed with what they'd done here. I'm sure I'd have spotted something glaringly missing."

Katy stepped toward the stairs.

"I need the washroom badly. Can we take a quick break please?"

I followed her upstairs, that feeling of unease growing in me again.

I tried to rack my brain and remember what I'd spotted on the wall before, but just when I needed it, my mind had slowed down.

It had been a long day.

My headache was still raging. My muscles were aching, and I was spent from all the running around.

Katy was right. I needed a break too.

With a tired sigh, Katy picked up a towel and stepped up to the stairway.

"Need a quick wash up and a trip to the washroom. Wait for me, okay," she said as she climbed back down to the bathroom.

A quick wash up might do me good too, I thought as I paced the floor. My brain buzzed with the events of the day, as I tried to make sense of everything.

Who killed Camilla?
And why?
Who tried to hurt us?
Again, why?

I could see why someone would steal Tetyana's gun and phone, but to push the Sea-Doo out into the ocean told me they were prepared to remain stuck on the island themselves.

How mad do you have to be to do that?

Who is this lunatic murderer among us?

Can I trust any of them?

"Asha!"

I jumped, startled. I scrambled toward the stairway.

"Katy? You okay?" I called out, clambering down the steps, my heart racing.

"Asha?"

"Katy! What happened?" I almost screamed. "Where are you?"

"In the bathroom. You've got to see this."

There was a tinge of fear in her voice.

I ran over and burst into the washroom to see Katy standing next to the vanity mirror, a dumbfounded look on her face.

She had a towel wrapped around herself which she was holding up in one hand, and in the other hand was her favorite pink lipstick, with the cover off.

She was staring at the window next to the sink.

"What are you doing?" I asked, walking over.

Katy pointed at the window, and that was when I saw it.

Words scribbled on the glass using pink lipstick.

"Why did you do this?" I asked, turning to my friend, wondering what on earth had come over her.

She shook her head.

"Wasn't me. I found my lipstick on the sink." She gave me a frightened look. "I was so sure I left it in my makeup bag in my suitcase upstairs when we left."

I leaned over to the window and squinted to read the message on the glass.

"Told you this trip would be fun. If you can figure out the motive, I might spare the remaining guests."

Chapter Thirty-nine

"What the frigging hell?"

Tetyana narrowed her eyes.

"No signature?" she asked. "No sign of who did it?"

We shook our heads.

"If they used pen and paper," I said, "we could have tried to find a match. Whoever left that message had been careful."

Katy nodded. "In all CAPS and written with lipstick to disguise their handwriting."

The three of us were standing abreast at the edge of the cliff, staring out at the open ocean.

The sea had become more turbulent over the course of the day. Enormous waves rumbled over and crashed on the shore, spraying everything in the vicinity. I wondered if the jetty piles would hold with all that thrashing.

The sea is incensed, I thought, unable to take my eyes away from the hypnotic scene. It was upset with what was happening on the island, came the absurd thought.

We were alone on the lawn.

An afternoon of scrounging, sorting, and hauling heavy logs up from the shore along a slippery and dangerous walkway had finally taken its toll.

By suppertime, everyone had disappeared inside the resort, pleading exhaustion and hunger. Even Ratcliffe and Sophia, who hadn't lifted a finger to help.

Katy and I had run back down after seeing that eerie message on the glass wall. But we'd had to wait until everyone had gone, before having a quiet chat with our friend.

After discovering her overnight bag dumped in the chest on the jetty, Tetyana had got out of her dry suit and changed into jeans and T-shirt. She was in good form for physical work, but I could see the lines under her eyes.

I was tired too. I was running on pure adrenaline, but we still had work to do.

Behind us was a crude pyramid made of logs. Next to it on the ground lay coils of shipping rope and a pitiful array of empty plastic barrels and buoys.

The only floating device Katy and I had discovered in the lighthouse was a fifty-year-old lifesaver, which was sure to crumble to bits as soon as it hit the water.

Tetyana wasn't too happy with what we'd found, but we'd have to make do.

"At least we know who's the murderer now," I said.

Katy swiveled around to me.

"Who?"

"The host," I said. "The mysterious, anonymous new owner of the island. Everything points to them. They invited us here asking for help. But they're here right now, goading us to solve this whatever this is."

"That's one sick dog," said Tetyana, shaking her head.

"So, who is it?" asked Katy, prodding my arm. "Ratcliffe?"

"Ratcliffe is too easy. Can't stand the man, but I don't think he's it."

"Sophia?"

"She's a self-entitled drama queen," I said. "I can see her throwing a kitchen knife at you if she didn't like you. But I can't picture her setting up an elaborate strangulation plot using her own scarf."

"I was seriously beginning to think it was the Mafia," said Katy. "Maybe Mary and Oliver have a point?"

Tetyana shook her head.

"I've dealt with gangsters before. Russian, Italian, Chinese, Somalian. It doesn't matter where they come from or what they call themselves, their strategy is like any big corporation."

"What do you mean?" asked Katy.

"Their methods are brutal, but organized crime has only one goal. To make money. Lots and lots of money as fast as they can. They wouldn't waste their time on schemes like this."

I nodded.

"This is someone with a personal vendetta," I said. "Someone bent on revenge for something someone did to them. I'm dying to figure out what everyone's connection is. There's a reason they're all so cagey about their pasts."

"Either that or someone royally flipped," said Katy, making a circling motion next to her head. "They invite a bunch of writers to a lonely island and scare the blazes out of everyone, including killing one. Then they tell us it's *fun*. You've got to be bonkers to do something like that."

"A demented dude who'd buy an island for their psychotic entertainment sounds more like a horror movie plot," said Tetyana, shaking her head. "I don't think this is some psycho. They planned this well and in advance."

"But what about us?" asked Katy. "Where do we fit in? Why did they ask us to come?"

A shudder went down my spine as I recalled the words on our glass wall.

If you can figure out the motive, I might spare the remaining guests.
I turned to Katy.

"That message was a challenge to us." I paused as another image came to mind. "Hey, Katy, do you remember those books in the lighthouse library?"

She nodded.

"I think that was a message from the owner too."

"But they're just books."

"A book by each of the guests."

Katy shrugged.

"If I had invited a bunch of writers for a retreat, I might have done the same. To show them I liked their work. Nothing out of place there."

"Except you're not a conniving killer playing a dangerous game."

"I don't know about these books, but this could mean more people are going to get in trouble soon," said Tetyana, her eyes on the darkening horizon. "When they're done with them, we'll be next."

Katy gave a gasp.

I nodded ruefully. "Camilla Carter's murder and Helen Jenkins's disappearance is just the beginning of this rampage."

Katy was about to say something when Tetyana made a discreet motion with her hand.

Quiet.

I turned around to see a lone figure was walking across the lawn toward us.

Chapter Forty

"Jason," I said.

"What does he want?" whispered Katy.

We watched him get closer. He ambled along like he wasn't in a hurry, but his face was a picture of anxiety.

"Hey," called out Katy.

Jason gave a gloomy wave back.

"Everything all right?" I asked when he got to within five feet from us.

He shook his head and with a loud sigh, turned to the ocean. He stood still, his forehead scrunched, as if he was trying to find the right words.

"Something you want to say?" asked Tetyana after a minute.

Jason turned to us, his eyes dull and his face ashen.

"What's going on here?" he asked, his eyes flittering between me, Katy, and Tetyana.

"We wish we knew," I replied. "We're as stumped as anyone else." I paused. "Do you have any ideas?"

He shook his head and kicked at a piece of wood on the ground.

"I'm scared," he said, not looking up. "I've never been this scared in my life and I don't know who to talk to. I feel like... this is going to sound weird... I feel like we were all brought here to be killed."

You got that right.

I bit my lips. I didn't need to add more fuel to this fire.

"You don't really believe that, do you?" asked Katy, putting a hand on his arm.

I watched him closely. Did he know about the message written in lipstick on our bathroom wall?

"It's a hunch I have," he said with a shrug. "I don't know what to do. And now we have no way to get home."

"Yet," said Tetyana.

He looked up, his forehead lined with worry. "I just can't trust anyone. You're the only ones…" He broke off and swallowed hard.

We waited, but he was staring out to the ocean again with that drained look on his face.

"Jason," I said, "is there someone here you recognize from your past?"

He shook his head.

"You write graphic novels, right?" I asked.

He nodded.

"Do you have a side hustle?"

"No, because I make good money with my anime books now."

"What did you do before that?"

"I used to edit videos and help studios with their technical productions. That's how I got to work with Silicon Valley."

"Studios?" I said, perking up. "Anything to do with Hollywood?"

He opened his mouth to speak and closed it.

"The more you tell us what you know, the faster we can all get out of here alive," I said.

"I worked for a movie producer," he said, looking down and shuffling his feet. "Nothing I'm proud of. Not something I can tell my mother."

He sighed.

"I've done some bad things in my life, just like anyone else."

"Jason, what kind of work did you do? It could be the key to all this."

He stared intently at his feet for a minute.

I turned to Katy.

"Hey, do you have that photo on you?"

She took out the dead man's photo from her pocket, unfolded the paper, and held it out.

"Do you know who this is?" I asked.

He gave a start.

"This is Zimmerman, isn't it?" I said. "That's who you worked for in Hollywood, right?"

He staggered back and gave me a glazed look.

Bingo.

"I... I have to get back," he stammered. "Mary's serving supper."

Before we could say anything more, he spun around and staggered across the lawn toward the building.

The three of us stared at his disappearing back.

"Zimmerman is at the center of this puzzle," I said.

"But he's dead," said Katy, looking at the crumpled photo in her hand.

"We can corner Jason tonight," said Tetyana, that steely look coming over her eyes. "I know how to make anyone talk."

"He's not the Russian militia, Tetyana," I said. "We have to use tact and diplomacy—"

Tetyana spun around to me, eyes flashing.

"With a mad killer running around? You do your diplomacy. I'll use my knife or my fist if I have to."

With a sigh, Katy wrapped her arms around herself.

"What a spooky place this is," she said, with a shiver. "All I wanted was a little vacation on the coast, and now we're stuck here on this kooky place."

"Not if I've got anything to do with it," said Tetyana. "Come hell or high water, I'm making that damned raft and going myself if I have to."

"I need to find out who the new owner is," I said, looking at the resort building behind us. "I bet you anything they're here, pretending to be a guest or a worker."

"Jason's right," said Katy. "We can't trust anyone."

"I don't think they trust us either," I said. "They're only tolerating us because we promised to build a raft."

Tetyana kicked glumly at a log on the ground. "We're in a rain forest at the tail end of the stormy season. Everything is dripping wet. Nothing's going to float."

The building material we'd all scrounged up for the raft had disappointed everyone.

Though no one had said anything, I felt the tension rise when Tetyana explained what little was possible with what we had.

Jason, Elliot, and Javier had helped, but their motivation was more out of desperation than anything else.

"Oliver said we're good for a week," said Katy, "at least we have food, water, electricity, and gas here. It's not like anyone's going to starve."

I looked at her.

"Except we might all get murdered by then."

Chapter Forty-one

"How are you going to make them talk?" asked Katy.

"The trick is to isolate them, one by one," I said. "They seem more open alone than when they are together."

"Let's go see what these clowns are up to," said Tetyana, stepping away from the log pyramid and turning toward the house.

We heard Ratcliffe the minute we stepped inside the building.

"More dry sandwiches?" his unpleasant voice boomed from the kitchen.

We walked down the corridor, listening to Sophia and Ratcliffe's angry voices among the more hushed tones of the others.

My mind whirred as we got closer.

One of these people was the owner of the island.

One of these people was playing a dangerous sport.

I stepped into the kitchen, feeling a bitter taste in my mouth.

"These aren't normal circumstances, Mr. Ratcliffe," Mary was saying. "We're all trying to cope. You have to understand."

"We paid a tidy sum for our stay here," he said. "You could at least serve a hot supper."

Did he already forget Camilla Carter? Strangled to death and now lying in the walk-in fridge, wrapped in plastic garbage bags?

Mary straightened up and squared her shoulders. She glared at Ratcliffe like she'd just been injected with a shot of confidence.

"Mr. Ratcliffe, if you don't like what I'm serving, you're welcome to return to your room without supper," she said in a firm voice.

Without waiting for an answer, she turned around and marched toward the stove.

It was nice to see Mary come to her own. I'd thought she was a reclusive woman who'd kept to herself, but there was strength in those eyes. She was no longer playing the accommodating service person.

At the other end of the kitchen, Oliver was pouring tea. He waved at us when he saw us.

"Take a seat, ladies," he said. "I'm making you all some hot drinks."

Please don't let them be the new owners disguised as the workers, I prayed. I just wished I knew their backgrounds and any connections to the others here.

Huddled around the modest kitchen table were the remaining guests. No one looked up, absorbed in their meals.

Elliot, Jason, and Javier slumped on one corner of the wooden bench, eating quietly, their eyes on their plates. They'd all put in a few good hours of manual labor that day and looked like this had been the most physically intensive work they'd done in their whole lives.

Javier had shrunk, Jason looked spent, and Elliot was scarcely holding his head up.

It was hard to believe any of them would be planning all this. I'd eat my hat if any of them turned out to be the new owner, I thought as I observed them.

The two people who seemed bent on making things difficult for everyone were sitting at the other end of the table.

As if on cue, Sophia turned to Oliver.

"When are you going to fix the heating? It's freezing in my room."

I could see Oliver struggle to rustle all the patience he had in him.

"Mrs. Knight, I closed the gas valve for your own safety."

"Do you seriously think someone murdered that woman?" said Ratcliffe. "She took out the detectors and turned up the gas herself, because she wanted her room piping hot. People make these stupid mistakes all the time."

"And she accidentally asphyxiated herself?" I asked, not able to stop myself. I turned to Sophia. "And choked herself on your scarf."

"She stole it!" said Sophia, her face flushing. "She's the one who took my scarf."

"I saw the bruises on her neck," said Katy. "That wasn't self-inflicted."

Sophia raised her voice. "I tell you—"

"Hey!" shouted Mary, looking up from the stove. "Could we have at least one meal in peace?"

That silenced the debate.

Oliver walked up to us with a small tray of sandwiches.

"How are you two holding up?" I asked him.

"It's not like we have a choice," he replied. "It's good to keep busy. Besides, we all have to eat, drink, and sleep."

Mary shot us a stern look. "And remain civilized."

She was right. This was not the time to lose our heads.

"I won't get much sleep tonight, that's for sure," said Oliver, rubbing his eyes.

"A good rest will do us all good," said Katy, taking a sandwich.

Tetyana turned to him.

"I should have the raft done by tomorrow. Then, we'll have to make some serious decisions."

Oliver nodded somberly.

"I tried to repair the radio, but whoever smashed it, did some pretty bad damage. I'll keep trying."

A stir at the table made us look up.

Elliot, Jason, and Javier were getting up. The three men took their empty plates and cups to the sink and then walked toward the door.

"You can have our seats," said Javier as he passed us. "See you tomorrow."

"Thank you," said Katy, walking over to the table with her teacup and sandwich, and taking the farthest spot from Ratcliffe and Sophia.

"Hey, those are my scissors!" cried Mary, staring at the door.

I spun around.

Elliot was at the doorway, and in his hands was a pair of scissors.

"Give that back," said Mary. "It's mine."

I recognized that brand.

It was the popular stainless-steel, serrated shears I had in my kitchen as well. They worked much more efficiently than a regular pair of scissors and were much sharper too.

One stab and you'd be done for.

Chapter Forty-two

"Put that down now," growled Tetyana.

She made a move to jump on Elliot, but Oliver stopped her. "Wait," he said. "He's just scared."

Elliot turned to us, a petrified look in his eyes.

"I'm going to my bedroom and I'm locking my door and I'll have this under my pillow." He paused and glowered at us. "If any of you weirdos are planning anything tonight, I suggest you count me out. You hear me?"

He turned around abruptly and stomped out of the kitchen.

No one spoke for a while, as we listened to his footsteps echo along the corridor.

"Jeez," said Jason, shaking his head, "I need some fresh air badly." He turned around and walked out.

Tetyana and I exchanged a glance.

Everyone was on edge.

Even us.

We walked over to the table to join Katy when Ratcliffe got up and turned our way.

"You girls better finish that raft by tomorrow," he snarled.

"Or what?" snapped Tetyana. "You gonna swim to the coast? Be my guest."

He turned away with an angry scowl.

Sophia got up and faced us.

"If anyone knocks on my door tonight, I swear I'll pluck your eyes out with my tweezers." She glared at us. "Don't think for a moment I can't do it."

With that, Ratcliffe stomped out of the kitchen, with Sophia on his arm.

"How did those two become friends so fast?" said Katy, moving to make space for us. "I thought they hated each other."

Shaking his head, Oliver stepped up to the kitchen door and locked it.

I raised an eyebrow. If Tetyana hadn't been with us, I'd have been worried.

As much as I was growing to like the Hudsons, I knew we had to be on guard.

"I don't trust anyone," said Oliver, turning to his wife. "I just can't. Not after all this."

They joined us at the table with resigned sighs. *What a madhouse,* they seemed to say.

We ate together for the next half an hour, while I gently probed them about their history, their family, their work and their new owner. But I learned nothing new.

They seemed to be a typical, quiet, middle-aged couple who loved the outdoors and the fresh sea air, and who'd watched over lighthouses all their lives.

"I get the feeling something will brew tonight," I said, when we had finished and were cleaning up.

"We need to keep vigil," said Tetyana, nodding.

"Count me in," I said.

"Me too," said Katy.

"Tell me which hours and I'll keep watch too," said Oliver.

"Good," said Tetyana with a nod. "I'll take the first hour. Katy, you're up for the next two hours, then you're on, Asha. I'll take over after that."

We nodded.

She turned to Oliver.

"Can you do four to six in the morning?"

"Yes, ma'am."

There was a glint in Tetyana's eyes that told me she wasn't planning to sleep when Oliver was up. This may be just the test to see where he stood.

"It's not going to be comfortable," Tetyana continued, "but we'll have to camp out in the dining hall."

"Why?" asked Mary.

"Because it's central and the windows open to a major part of the—"

That was when we heard the gunshot echo across the grounds.

Tetyana was the first to spring toward the entrance. She yanked the door open.

The smell of smoke and the crackle of fire came to us.

"The house is on fire!" screamed Mary, putting her hands to her head. "Noo!"

Tetyana darted out. I ran after her.

Outside, it looked like the sky was glowing red.

"Oh no," I heard Katy say from behind me.

"What in tarnation is going on?" cried Oliver.

We dashed through the corridor toward the main entrance. Tetyana slammed the front door open. We spilled out of the building to confront the biggest bonfire I'd seen in my life.

Someone had lit the pile of wet logs. The air was thick with smoke, and the potent smell of burning diesel stung my nose.

Three plastic jerry cans lay discarded on their sides, next to the fire.

"My diesel!" shouted Oliver. "Who did this?"

"Wait! Who's over there?" I shouted, seeing something big and lumpy near the edge of the cliff.

We ran around the fire, holding our shirts up to our noses so we could breathe.

"Oh no," said Katy, stopping in her tracks when she saw it.

Sprawled near the boulders was a body lying on their stomach.

"Jason!" shouted Katy.

She was right. Even with my eyes watering from the smoke, I knew it was him.

We sprinted toward him.

Tetyana stepped up and turned him over. Katy and I gasped out loud. A dagger stuck out of Jason's chest.

I recognized it.

It was the ivory-handled, *Moby Dick* whalebone knife that had been on the wall in the lighthouse.

"The missing knife," I whispered to myself.

Tetyana was checking Jason's pulse, but we were too late. He'd already lost an enormous amount of blood and his eyes were lifeless.

"Oh, my heaven's," cried Mary. "What in the good lord's name is going on?"

"What's happening?" screeched a female in the dark from near the front door. It sounded like Sophia, but I didn't look.

I cursed myself. I should have noticed that missing knife on the lighthouse wall. I shouldn't have let Oliver lock the kitchen door.

Did he lock it to keep us away?

Was it so we wouldn't suspect another murder was being committed?

I gave him a side glance. He looked appropriately horrified, but I was no longer sure of him now.

"What about the gunshots?" I said to Tetyana. "I was sure I heard shots."

She nodded, a dark frown on her face. Her eyes swept the lawn.

"Look!"

We spun around. It was Katy, holding something in her hand.

"A gun," she said to Tetyana. "Is it yours?"

We scrambled over.

"That's not my Glock," said Tetyana. "It's the flare gun from the jetty."

"I found it next to the diesel containers," said Katy.

"Jason could have fired it to get the attention of a boat going by," she said. "But then, maybe someone came behind him and stabbed him?"

"No, he was dead before that shot was fired," said Tetyana. "I doubt any boats were out at this time of the night."

I looked out at the inky black ocean. I couldn't see anything in the dark, but I could hear the crash of the waves down on the shore below.

This is lunacy, I thought. Complete and utter lunacy.

Mary and Oliver had retreated to the building and were trying to calm Sophia and stop her from scampering toward the walkway again.

Near the front door, Ratcliffe was demanding answers and Elliot was shouting something incomprehensible.

Javier was on the threshold, staring at the bonfire, frozen in place, the red flames creating strange flickering shadows on his bewildered face.

Did someone kill Jason after they saw him try to talk to us?

The message on our bathroom wall flashed to mind.

"It was the killer who fired the flare gun," I said, turning to my friends. "Whoever stabbed him wanted us to know another person is dead."

"Oh, my god, you're right," said Katy. "They lit the bonfire, but we didn't notice because the kitchen door was closed. So, they shot the flare gun."

I gave my friends a somber look.

"They're pushing us to find the motive before they kill someone else."

Chapter Forty-three

"Who do you think you are?" snarled Ratcliffe. "Backwater PI's acting like you're the FBI."

"We don't have to tell you anything," said Sophia.

I glared at them. I was tiring of their childish outbursts.

We had all gathered inside the dining hall.

This scenario was becoming disturbingly familiar. It seemed like we kept discovering a grisly killing or an attempted murder, after which we congregated in one spot to lie to each other.

From their reactions, I could tell they were more interested in saving their skins than giving one iota of thought to Jason.

After the initial panic, everyone had scrambled to put the fire out.

Javier, Mary, and Katy brought buckets of water from the kitchen while Elliot and I shoveled dirt on the fire. Oliver and Tetyana pulled the heavy-duty water hose from the side of the building and turned it on full blast.

The logs had been wet when we'd piled them on the lawn, but the gasoline had easily kick-started the fire. The wind had been strong enough that it had to turn just a few degrees to the left for the flames to travel toward the main building.

But, little by little, the fire died, leaving the black remains of half-scorched logs on the lawn.

Tetyana, Oliver, and Elliot had carried Jason's body into the house and deposited him in the walk-in fridge.

Katy and I had rooted around the pantry and found the box of oversized black garbage bags so we could cover the body.

I shuddered at seeing Jason laid out next to Camilla Carter. Both stiff and silent.

For good.

It wasn't smart to move the bodies from the crime scenes, but we had no choice. We didn't have anything to take photos, but our memories would have to do.

We couldn't leave Camilla in a hot room or Jason outside, near the cliff, until the authorities came, if they would ever come.

I hated to think of how much valuable resources we'd lost. Half of our precious provisions for the week had evaporated in less than an hour.

The driest logs on the island had gone up in diesel-soaked smoke and the flare gun had been emptied. Whoever had used it had emptied the chamber. They'd been keen to cut our ties and draw the net tighter around us.

I wondered how many more days we had on the island.

Now everybody was in a foul mood.

My plan to question them separately wasn't going to work. Acerbic, suspicious emotions swirled heavily around the dining room, like an ugly dark fog had crept inside.

Nobody wanted to talk. They hardly wanted to be in the room with us.

Everyone was sitting apart, in a bubble of their own, not making eye contact with anyone else, looking as wretched as the weather outside.

Even the normally placid Javier, who until now had looked more like an observer, was hunched over, a sullen expression on his face.

He was in his jeans and camouflage jacket, though I was sure he'd said he was going up to his bedroom. Sophia wore an old-fashioned nightgown and fluffy slippers, her hair down, looking more flustered than usual.

Ratcliffe was dressed in checkered pajamas but instead of slippers, he had muddied boots on. I wondered if he'd changed before running out of his room or if he'd been prowling around the lawn before.

Elliot was also in street clothes and sat at his usual spot at the table with the pair of kitchen scissors placed squarely in front of him, as if in warning to all of us.

Tetyana was standing at the door with her own knife in hand. She was prepared but wasn't going to create any more drama than needed.

Katy and I were standing at the head of the table, while Mary and Oliver had taken seats at the other end. They sat close together, holding hands, looking grayer than ever.

I should have felt terrified, but one thing kept my mind whirring.

I was banking on the killer choosing us to solve the crime. Why they had chosen us to do this, I still had no idea. There was no guarantee they would have mercy on any of us, but I held on to that hope, like it was the last thing on earth.

I turned to the table.

"We're all in the same boat," I said. "We can pull ourselves together and work as a team, or we can keep playing games and watch as we all die."

"How do we know you haven't planned this whole thing?" said Elliot, gripping his weapon. "What games are *you* playing at?"

I sighed.

"I already told you. I run a bakery in Harlem which caters to high-society clients. Given my team's previous backgrounds, they hire us when they have problems no one else can solve. As far as I know, this invitation was just another client requesting our help. They even sent us a hefty retainer."

I paused and looked around the table.

"What I'd like to know was which of you hired us?"

They stared at me with blank looks on their faces.

"Which one of you sent that ten-thousand-dollar retainer asking us to come here? Which one of you send that photo of the dead man on the beach?"

Silence.

"Where's your proof of this?" growled Ratcliffe. "You can't expect us to believe a stupid story just like that. I don't know you from Eve."

He got me there.

I had nothing to prove we were legitimate, not even business cards. My PI business had grown by word-of-mouth referral only.

"If there's anyone we need to be suspicious about, it's you people," said Sophia, a nasty smirk on her face. "You don't belong here. You girls are the odd ones out."

"Not to mention your friend," said Ratcliffe, shooting a disapproving look Tetyana's way. "Coming here with guns and all that."

He had a point. To anyone but the killer, our arrival must have looked strange.

I spread my arms.

"We didn't do it. The three of us were in the kitchen with Oliver and Mary. We sat down for supper and didn't get up until we heard the flare gun go off."

Mary nodded.

"That's true," said Oliver. "They were with us. Never left the kitchen."

I looked around the table.

"So, who murdered Jason? Who lit that fire? Who shot that flare gun?"

"That's what made me come out," said Sophia. "I was doing my night routine when I saw the red flames shoot up in the sky from my bathroom window. I thought someone was playing with fireworks."

"Me too," said Ratcliffe, in a low-key voice. "I was in bed, watching TV when I heard the pops. I looked out of the window and saw the flares. When I got closer to look, I saw the fire on the lawn."

We all turned to Elliot.

He gulped visibly and clutched his scissors tighter. His eyes were down on the table.

"Elliot?" said Ratcliffe in an impatient voice. "Where were you?"

"I was in the dining hall when I heard the pops."

"What were you doing prowling around the house?" asked Sophia, her eyes narrowed.

Elliot gulped again. Beads of sweat had formed on his forehead.

I leaned toward him.

"Time to be honest."

"I... I was in here and was about to come downstairs," said Elliot, his lips quivering, His hands nervously turning the pair of scissors around and around.

I suppressed the urge to lean in and grab that weapon off his jittery hands.

"Speak, man!" shouted Ratcliffe.

"I don't know what's going on here!" yelled Elliot, shooting an angry look at Ratcliffe.

"I'm scared shitless! First Helen disappears, then Camilla dies, and now Jason. I heard the fire. I saw it from my room. I even saw the person who started it."

Chapter Forty-four

The room exploded.

Elliot's last words had taken me by surprise, so much so, I'd missed the chance to catch everyone's reactions.

If anyone had been shocked at being discovered, they had cleverly composed themselves again.

"What the hell?" Ratcliffe shouted. "Who is it then, my man?"

"You were sitting here quietly without telling us?" cried Sophia.

"My heavens," said Mary, her hand going to her heart.

"Tell us!" said Katy.

Elliot's eyes were wide, like he was still in shock.

"I only saw their shadow. But I saw them throw away the jerry can and put a lit paper on the logs. Then, I saw the flares go up to the sky."

He paused.

"By the time I looked back down, all I saw was someone running to the back of the building. I didn't see their face."

"Man or woman?" I asked.

"Man, I think. Hard to say. They were wearing pants. Could have been a woman too."

Ratcliffe's eyes bulged.

"For heaven's sake, can you be more cryptic? Was he tall? Short? Did you notice anything about their clothes?"

"Medium build. No, small, I think."

His eyes flickered, like he was confused.

"I... er... I wasn't paying attention to them so much...."

"Why not?" asked Oliver. "You saw who killed Jason and you never—"

"I didn't see Jason getting killed!" shouted Elliot, his eyes red with stress. "All I saw was the fire on the lawn. I swear I thought the building was going to catch on fire. I was debating whether I should open the window and jump out or run down. That's all I was thinking."

His eyes darted back and forth.

"Why didn't you alert us?" asked Oliver. "Didn't it occur to you to let everyone know there was a fire?"

"How the hell did I know it wasn't you trying to burn this place down with us all in it?" said Elliot. "I don't know any of you!"

There was silence in the room for a moment, as everyone withdrew into their bubbles.

I looked at Javier, who'd been sitting hunched next to Elliot. He was the smallest man in the group. I wondered if I'd been too hasty in writing him off as just another frightened guest.

"I thought you said you were going to bed," I said, turning to him. "Where were you just before the fire?"

Javier opened his mouth to speak, but nothing came out. He swallowed, then shifted. He placed his hands on the table as if to steady himself and spoke without looking up.

"I was in my room. I was just about to change and go to bed when I heard the flare gunshots."

All eyes were on him now. Javier was shaking so badly, Elliot put a hand on his shoulder.

"I don't think it was you, man," said Elliot. "It has to be these mean girls from New York."

Ignoring the remark, I peered under the table. Like Ratcliffe, Javier was also in hiking boots caked in dirt.

All of our shoes had become muddied as we struggled to put out the fire. I couldn't make a proper deduction from them.

"Did you go straight to your room from the kitchen?" I asked.

"Y...yes," Javier stammered, shooting me a frightened look from underneath his lashes. "All I wanted was to lock myself in my room before anyone could get me."

"If it wasn't any of us, who was it?" cried Sophia, giving the room a wide-eyed look. "Who started the fire and killed Jason? The same person who killed Camilla? What's going on in this place?"

"I told you my theory," said Ratcliffe, turning to her. "It's this Jenkins woman."

"That was Javier's idea," said Elliot.

"I thought of it too," said Ratcliffe with a glare Elliot's way. "Don't you people see? I don't need to be a PI to figure this stuff out."

"What have you figured out?" asked Katy.

"This is Jenkins's way of getting notoriety. Imagine the book she could write after this. *Murder on Coffin Island*. The woman would make millions. Multi-millions. The best-selling book of the century. Heck, I'd fight to sign her up."

The entire room shot him a withering look, but that didn't seem to faze Ratcliffe. He was staring pensively at the wall, like he was already counting his chips.

"You think she's killing people so she can write a best-seller?" said Mary, staring at him. "That's the most outlandish thing I've ever heard."

Something stirred in the back of my brain.

"Didn't Jason say she's already signed up to an imprint of your company?" I asked. "That means you have first dibs if she writes a story, no?"

Ratcliffe turned my way, that pompous look coming over him again.

"Look, I'm a busy man. I don't have time to memorize all the names of my writers, unless they're celebrities. It's a bonus if she's already part of my stable."

"A lucrative bonus for you," said Katy.

"Be careful," I said, my eyes locked on Ratcliffe. "You could be next."

"She'd never do me in," he scoffed. "I'd give her a five... six, okay, a seven-figure advance, if she promised a book." Ratcliffe stared out the window again, almost salivating at the prospect. "This is gold."

For once, Sophia looked disgusted by her new frenemy. Elliot cursed under his breath and I thought I saw a sliver of anger cross Javier's face.

"You're a sick man," said Oliver, his fiery eyes on the publisher.

For a split second, his polite butler poise disappeared, revealing a dark interior I didn't know he had.

Chapter Forty-five

I scanned the group, wondering how they were going to take in the next bit of information.

"There's something you all need to know," I said. "We got something extra special with our invitation to the retreat."

They turned to me quizzically, but no one spoke.

"It was a photo. A photo of a dead man on a beach."

A collective gasp went through the group.

"A *dead man*?" said Elliott, his brow furrowed.

"An old photograph that had been digitized," said Katy, digging into her pocket and drawing out the printout. She handed it to Elliott, who peered at it.

"Helen Jenkins had the same photo inside the pages of her manuscript, which has now disappeared," I said.

Ratcliffe took the picture from Elliott and scrutinized it.

"This could be anyone," he said.

"Did any of you receive this photo with your invitation as well?"

The photograph went from one person to the next, each one examining it, and shaking their heads.

Javier waved the paper at me.

"What does this have to do with any of us?" he asked.

I'd love to know the answer to that question too.

"We believe there's a connection between this picture and the invitations you received." I paused to show the gravity of my next observation. "We also think this is the common thread that links you all."

Sophia took in a sharp breath.

Elliot went pale.

Javier stared.

Ratcliffe scoffed. "What are you talking about?"

"I've asked this before and I'm going to ask again," I said, hearing my voice rise, wishing I had the same calm demeanor Oliver seemed to have no trouble rustling up.

"Be honest. What's the connection between all of you?"

"You're mad," said Sophia. "I never met any of these people before in my life."

She looked away when she spoke. Sophia was hiding something. But did it have anything to do with Camilla and Jason's murders?

"This is a writers' retreat, for goodness' sake," said Ratcliffe. "That means we're all writers. There's your connection."

"That's not all, is it?" I said, narrowing my eyes. "Some of you have had other careers in other industries. Did you know each other from before?"

"I'm a prominent publisher and have been in this business for thirty years," said Ratcliffe. "When I say I've never met this bunch of idiots, I mean it. I regret coming here. I'm reconsidering my screenplay. If this is what happens when writers get together, I want nothing to do with them. I'm done."

He sounded sincere, but I knew I had to keep an eye on him.

I turned to Elliot.

"How do you know Camilla and Sophia?"

Elliot's eyes widened for a split second, but he caught himself.

"I met them the same time you did," he snapped. "I know them as much as you do."

All along, I'd been sure Elliot, Sophia, and Camilla were a clique. I'd suspected they were behind Helen Jenkins's disappearance and the boulder pushed down the cliff. But now one of them was dead, I was no longer certain of their role or their friendship.

I turned to Javier.

"You're a good observer, and I'm sure you have an excellent memory," I said. "Have you met any of these people here before?"

Javier turned to me, his face pale but stoic.

"No, ma'am. I've never met anyone here before in my life, and that's a promise I make on my dead sister's grave."

Why did that send a chill down my spine?

There was something odd about this young poet. He presented himself as sincere, but those boyishly innocent looks helped him on that front. Something told me he also wasn't sharing everything.

Given my past encounters with evil men in shady businesses, I had a hard time trusting people. Every squint of the eye, every twitch of the nose, or downturn of the lips made me wonder what they were hiding.

Ratcliffe pushed his chair back and got up.

"I've had enough. We're getting nowhere with your moronic questions."

He turned around to stomp out of the room but halted in front of Tetyana. She was standing guard at the threshold so no one could get in or out without passing her.

"You're not going anywhere," she snarled.

"Let me go, you fool!" said Ratcliffe, trying to push her away.

She didn't budge.

"You think you can push me around like this?" he shouted.

With a roar, Ratcliffe raised a clenched fist.

His fist didn't get far. Tetyana slammed her hands on him, pulled his arms behind his back, and had his face pressed against the wall in seconds.

Ratcliffe let out a howl.

"Try that again, and I'll get serious," said Tetyana.

Javier and Elliot stared, their jaws open.

"I saw that!" shrieked Sophia, pulling her nightgown around her. She turned to Oliver, pointing at Tetyana. "That was violence. Do something!"

I sighed.

"Look, I'm sorry it came to this, but we can't go around punching each other. We're trying to help. We all want the same thing. To get us home safely."

I paused and looked at everyone's pale faces.

"Our priority is to contact the mainland however we can. Build the raft, fix the radio, call a passing boat, whatever we can think of. Either you chip in and help, or please stay out of our way until we find a solution."

"This is too much," said Javier, putting his head in his hands.

"This is crazy," said Sophia.

Tetyana took her hands off Ratcliffe and faced the room.

Ratcliffe swayed in his spot, looking disoriented, like it was the first time he'd been manhandled like that.

"I'll be happy to escort you all to your rooms," said Tetyana. "But your job will be to stay there till dawn."

"That's how Camilla died!" shouted Ratcliffe. "While she was in her room."

"It's not foolproof, but it's your safest option."

"You can't make us do that," said Sophia angrily, half rising from her chair. "You can't make us do anything."

"You want to go strolling around the island with a killer on the loose?"

Sophia sat down heavily and turned away.

"It's up to you," said Tetyana. "Stay safe in your rooms tonight or become the next body we find. Your call."

It didn't take long for us to get the guests into their rooms after that. I guessed they were all too frightened to put up a fight.

"I'm ready to do my part," said Oliver, when Tetyana returned. "Tell me when you want me to go on vigil and I'll do it."

"I'm scared, Oliver," said Mary, her lips quivering. "We can lock ourselves in our room for only so long."

"We're going to do our best," I said, wishing I could promise more than mere words.

She rubbed her face. "This is a nightmare."

Tetyana turned to Mary.

"Not to worry. I'll escort you to your quarters."

Tetyana's words were polite, but I knew she was only making sure they were going to where they said they were.

Motioning us to stay in the dining hall, she followed Oliver and Mary out.

Katy was staring out the window now, her eyes on the burned logs on the lawn below us.

"This is the most psycho case ever," she said. "And we don't even have a way of letting the others know what's going on."

My stomach felt like it had been tied into an impossibly convoluted knot. I was stumped, but more than anything else, I was mad at myself.

The message on our bathroom glass wall kept spinning in my mind.

If you can figure out the motive, I might spare the remaining guests.

I'd been in many sticky situations, but I'd always found a clue, a nugget of information that pointed me in the right direction. Things had happened so fast, I'd hardly wrapped my head around the first incident, before the second happened, then the third.

Three people had died. And I was nowhere near knowing why or who the culprit was.

I tried to suppress the guilty feelings bubbling inside of me. They had died because I couldn't figure out the solution fast enough.

"Maybe they're right," said Katy, turning to me. "It's like a ghost has taken over the island and is doing these things. That, or everyone's in this together. It can't be just one person doing this."

My mind flitted to Oliver and Mary, who'd sat at the end of the table.

They looked like the perfect, unassuming couple, the quintessential professionals, who were just doing their job. But I wondered if someone could have paid enough money to convince them to either pull off these gruesome killings themselves or help the true killer out.

I remembered how Oliver had locked the kitchen door, citing fear of the killer. Instead of locking them out, maybe it had been a ploy to lock us in, while the murderer did their thing outside, undisturbed.

"Help!"

A thundering crash followed the spine-chilling scream.

Katy and I whipped around.

Chapter Forty-six

We dashed out of the room.

My heart was hammering so loudly, I hardly heard Tetyana bound up the stairs.

"Javier!" cried Katy. "What happened?"

The poet was lying at the bottom of the steps on the second-floor landing. He was trying to raise himself with one arm, but his foot had twisted behind him.

We rushed toward him.

"What the frigging heck?"

I turned in relief to see Tetyana. Without a word, she jumped up to the third floor, taking three steps at a time.

I turned my attention back to Javier, who was grimacing in pain. I squatted next to him and examined his foot.

"Did you trip?" I asked.

He looked at me and moved his mouth but nothing came out.

Is he in shock?

He winced when Katy put a hand on his ankle.

"Sorry," said Katy, pulling her hand back. "I was checking if you broke anything. You okay, hun?"

Still mute, Javier shook his head.

Upstairs, I could hear Tetyana banging on the doors. Soon the anxious voices of Ratcliffe, Sophia, and Elliot came down to us. Ratcliffe was denying he'd been outside in the corridor and Sophia was saying something about being in bed.

"He needs ice," said Katy, getting up. "I'll go check in the kitchen."

As Katy dashed down to the kitchen, I turned to Javier.

"Just nod or shake your head, okay?" I said, watching him closely. "Did someone push you from behind?"

Javier didn't reply with gestures or words.

He was hesitating.

I wondered why.

If someone had pushed him, wouldn't it have been obvious? Wouldn't he have felt a hand on his back?

"What are you hiding?" I asked, boring into his eyes.

Javier settled back against the railing, wincing as his foot moved.

"I don't know what happened," he said, looking at me unblinkingly for a few seconds.

I stared back, not wanting to be the first to look away.

I also knew that trick.

It was the hallmark of a skillful liar. All you had to do was speak the lie and maintain steady eye contact. It was a good way to convince someone you're telling the truth, but the telltale sign was that unblinking stare.

Why would he lie about an incident that had handicapped him? An idea was forming in the back of my mind.

"Javier," I said, taking a harder tone. "Who are you covering up for?"

He shook his head rapidly.

"No one."

"Then, tell me what happened."

"I walked up to my room and locked the door," he replied, speaking haltingly as if answering my questions hurt him as much as the twisted ankle itself. "But then I couldn't find my glasses. Thought I left them in the dining hall."

"So, you came out of your room?"

He nodded. "I opened the door and peeked out to make sure nobody was outside."

"Did you see anyone?"

He shook his head.

"I thought it was safe to come out. But when I got to the top of the stairs, I...."

He paused.

He was lying again.

I suppressed the urge to shake him.

"Did you feel something on your back?"

He gave me a strange look. "No, I didn't. Maybe it was Helen who came back to take revenge."

I leaned away in exasperation.

This idea of Helen's ghost running around and strangling people or pushing them down the stairs was annoying me. This was the work of a live human being with a serious motive to kill.

An earlier image of Javier floating underwater flashed into my mind, and that unsettling feeling came over me again. Something about Javier troubled me, but I couldn't say exactly what it was.

I leaned toward him again.

"Why are you here, Javier? Why did you come to this retreat?"

"To write," he answered.

"When we first met you at the pier near town—" I paused, wondering how to put this delicately. "Did you fall, or did you jump in?"

He gave me a startled look.

The thump of footsteps from above made me look up.

Tetyana was coming down with Sophia, Ratcliffe, and Elliot. The three writers looked down at their colleague with more curiosity than sympathy and gave Javier a wide berth.

"Where were you all when he fell just now?" I asked the group.

"I was in bed, for heaven's sake," said Sophia.

"I was in the toilet," said Ratcliffe, his face dark.

"In my room," spluttered Elliot. "Like you told us to."

The idea in the back of my mind was strengthening.

Javier was protecting someone. He'd agreed to help one of them with the killings, but he had become a victim himself. He couldn't speak out, lest he gave away his role in the game.

I turned to the poet.

"You could have broken your neck and died. This is serious. If you have something to say, say it now."

"Leave the man alone," said Elliot. "He nearly dies and you're interrogating him like a suspect?"

I glanced up at Elliot.

"Where's your weapon?" I asked.

He made a face and pointed at Tetyana. "She confiscated it."

Tetyana nodded and held up the scissors.

Elliot stared at me. "You're crazy if you think I pushed him. I'd never do anything like this."

Footsteps coming up the stairs made us all turn. It was Katy climbing up with Mary and Oliver in tow. Mary had a bag of ice in her hands, and Oliver and Katy were bringing the stretcher.

I got up as they took over.

"I'm okay," protested Javier as Mary stepped up to ice his ankle. "I just want to go to my room."

"How are you going to climb upstairs?" asked Mary, pushing his hand away and reaching for his ankle.

A flash of pain went through Javier's face as she deposited the ice bag on his foot. I could see he was gritting his teeth.

Was this an act? If it was, he was an excellent actor.

"You can't climb up or down," said Oliver, staring at the poet. "We have extra rooms on the first floor. We can move you down there."

"No," said Javier, "I just want to go to my room."

But it seemed like Oliver had made up his mind.

"There's an old wooden wheelchair, which the former lighthouse keeper used in his last years. It's in the shed at the back. I can get it for you so you can get to the bathroom at least until the pain subsides. You'll thank me when it starts swelling."

Sophia, Ratcliffe, and Elliot returned to their rooms under Tetyana's orders.

When she came down, she had all the room keys in her hand. I was surprised they hadn't protested. Javier's fall seemed to have shaken them, even Ratcliffe, who looked drained.

Mary and Katy stayed with Javier, while I went with Oliver to find the wheelchair.

In half an hour, we'd brought Javier down on the stretcher to an extra room below, next to Oliver and Mary's bedroom.

After settling him in bed with the ice on his ankle and the wheelchair by his bed, we left, locking the door behind us.

Mary left a bottle of painkillers on his bedside table so he could take one if it got any worse.

"I'll monitor him," she said. "He's right next to our bedroom and the kitchen. His door will always be in my sight. Don't you worry about him."

Oliver turned his eyes up to the ceiling.

"I think the people we need to be worried about are all on the third floor," he said in a somber voice.

"Who do you think pushed him?" I asked.

Oliver hung his head.

"Damned if I know. I feel like we're getting picked off one by one."

Mary turned to us, her face ashen.

"Who's next?" she whispered.

Chapter Forty-seven

"There's a message here," I said, pacing the carpet.

Tetyana and Katy were leaning against the bookshelf, watching me, arms crossed.

"It's hidden in plain sight," I said. "We're just not seeing it."

The library was the last place Tetyana wanted to be. While Katy loved this room for its interior decor, she cared little for the contents held in between the pages.

I'd dragged them up to the lighthouse library only moments ago, and they weren't too happy about it.

"We need to think harder, girls," I said. "*Think.*"

"I think you're reading too much into these books," said Katy.

"I think we need to be at the main building, keeping an eye on those crazies," said Tetyana.

After leaving Javier in his room with Oliver and Mary promising to watch him, I'd asked my friends to follow me to the lighthouse.

Other than the missing whale-bone knife on the first-floor wall, nothing else seemed out of place in the tower.

Knowing the killer had snuck onto the ground floor and stolen the knife sent shivers down my spine. They could have even come in while we were sleeping.

But the lighthouse door couldn't be secured.

The door to the tower never had a lock as far as Oliver and Mary could remember. Fast and easy access to the lantern room had been a necessity in the olden days, and that tradition had continued even though the light was out of commission.

Tetyana, Katy, and I were now standing around the library coffee table on which the guests' books sat neatly arranged.

"This is all part of the game."

I looked up at my friends who were staring at me, skepticism on their faces.

"The owner, whoever they are, placed these here for us to see them. There's one book by each of the writers. The question is, why these books? What's their significance?"

With a resigned sigh, Tetyana kneeled down and picked up the nearest book. It was written by Camilla and had been lying facedown on the table. I wondered if she knew what she'd just selected.

"So, you think these books will lead us to the killer?" asked Katy, settling down on the carpet and pulling Jason's graphic novel toward her.

"I think they will give us a clue to the connection between these writers and why they're being killed," I replied. "If they can also tell us who the killer is, that would be a bonus."

"But what does all this have to do with that photograph of Zimmerman on the beach?" asked Katy.

"That could have been a warning of what was about to happen here," I said. "Murder by the ocean?"

"Except Helen Jenkins had it on her too," said Katy. "It was with her unpublished manuscript."

"Didn't Ratcliffe say he was publishing unauthorized biographies of famous people?" I said. "Maybe that's what Helen was writing, an unauthorized bio on Zimmerman."

"What do you think?" asked Katy, turning to Tetyana.

Tetyana was leaning back against the nearest armchair, her nose buried deep in Camilla's book.

The eye-catching cover had a half-naked male model with a lingerie-clad woman straddling his hips. A dog collar and chain clasped the man's throat, and his hands were wrapped dangerously around the woman's skinny neck.

"Tetyana?" I said.

No answer.

Katy and I exchanged a glance.

"Yoo hoo," called out Katy, waving her hand in front of our friend's face.

Tetyana raised her head and blinked at us.

"Can't believe you like that crap," said Katy, making a face.

"I was looking for parallels to the murder," said Tetyana, a pink flush creeping up her neck. It wasn't often I saw my friend flustered.

Tetyana's romantic life was a secret even to us. She had many contacts in the martial arts and military communities and some who worked underground too, but we never knew if any were more than just friends.

"I'd never bring that book into my house," said Katy with a sniff.

"Don't be such a snob," said Tetyana, throwing Camilla's erotica on the table. "It's a quick read, and I was looking for clues."

"Different strokes and all that. Not up to us to judge," I said, picking up the novella, trying to stop the argument that was brewing. "Camilla made a chunk of change with these."

I flipped through the pages.

Tetyana was right. The chapters were short. The paragraphs were only a couple of sentences in length and the writing was at a second-grade level. I scanned the book.

It was when I turned to the last chapter that it dawned on me.

I looked up at Tetyana.

"Oh, my gosh," I said. "You're right."

"I always am," she said, her face stoic.

"What is it?" asked Katy.

"How did Camilla die?" I asked.

"Strangled," said Katy, "with Sophia's scarf."

"With that gas leak to confuse us," added Tetyana.

I pushed Camilla's book in front of them. "Read this para," I said, pointing at the last chapter.

With a sigh, Katy scanned the page.

"Death by asphyxiation," she whispered finally, her face clearing. "Oh, my gosh."

We stared at each other for a half a moment, as it sunk in.

Katy had Jason's book spread in front of her.

"Jason!" I said, a sense of urgency coming over me. "Check the last chapter."

Katy sat up and flipped to the back. His book was even easier to read, as it was in graphic cartoon format with few words.

"*Martian Knife Hunter* by Jason Taylor," said Tetyana as she read the title on the top of the open pages.

"Oh no," said Katy, turning the book toward us. "Look at this."

We stared.

If nothing else, Jason had had a weird imagination.

Images of humanoid-like beings lying half-naked in various poses filled the two pages of the book. They had all been stabbed to death with an elaborately decorated knife.

But it was the drawing at the bottom of the last page that drew our attention the most.

An androgynous body lay on their back next to a burning spaceship with an ivory knife stuck in their chest.

"This is so creepy," whispered Katy.

Tetyana grabbed Javier's poetry book from the table.

"Time to get reading, people," she said.

I reached for Ratcliffe's unpublished screenplay and read the title. Something about it made me turn to the table.

Camilla's paperback stared back at me, with the two adults in the front cover carrying on unabashedly.

Take My Breath Away.

What a title, I thought.

Wait.

We didn't have to spend hours reading these books. The information was staring us in the face all along.

"Hey," I said, waving Camilla's book in front of my friends. "Read the title."

"Yes, I know. That's what happened to her," mumbled Katy, going back to her reading.

"Okay, now check this one out."

Katy squinted at the manuscript in my hands.

"*Jaws of Death*?" she said, making a face. "How unoriginal."

"Remember what Ratcliffe said at dinner the first day?" I said. "All the people in his story get killed by a shark."

Tetyana gave a smirk.

"That solves my problem. That should stop him from fighting for a spot on the raft tomorrow."

"What about Sophia?" I said, reaching over to pick up her book. "She writes children's books, so she can't have murders and things, can she?"

I looked at the title on the cover.

A Spoonful of Syrup.

An adult elephant dressed in an Old Mother Hubbard costume was leaning over with a spoon in front of a baby elephant wearing a pink baseball cap. Cute.

I couldn't imagine how this book would fit into my hypothesis.

I flipped to the back.

"A fun and stress-free way to persuade your kids to take their medicine," I said, reading the blurb on the back cover.

"That doesn't make sense," said Katy, giving us a wide-eyed look. "Maybe *she's* the killer."

"We need to think deeper," I said. "Think in metaphors."

Tetyana raised an eyebrow.

"Medicine," I said. "Medicine that kills. She's going to be poisoned."

"Wait a minute," said Katy. "Does this mean Sophia's innocent?"

"It's a hunch for now," I said. "That goes for Ratcliffe too. Though I can't imagine how anyone can force him to die of a shark attack. Besides, there aren't any sharks in this part of the world."

"You said to think in metaphors, right?" said Tetyana, a thoughtful look in her eyes. "If it's not medicine, it's most likely poison. If it's not a shark, it's probably something with sharp, jagged teeth..."

We sat around the table for a few seconds, trying to wrack our brains.

"What about Helen Jenkins?" I said, sitting up. "Where's her novel?"

We scrambled to find it. Tetyana pulled it out from under the pile and turned the front cover toward us.

Katy and I gasped at the same time.

The Girl Who Lived.

Chapter Forty-eight

I stared at the book's dust jacket.

It was a literary novel. Beautiful multicolored squiggly lines wrapped around the book, an esoteric design I couldn't make head or tail of.

The golden award sticker shone under the dim banker's lamp.

The Girl Who Lived.

"As crazy as it sounds, maybe Ratcliffe is right," said Katy finally. "*She's the killer.*"

I rubbed my eyes, trying to think.

"What if I'm wrong? This is just a wild hunch. It's so out there. Maybe I'm making links where there are none."

Tetyana shook her head.

"I don't do woo-woo, and I like my evidence to line up." She paused. "But there's too much of a coincidence here. I feel like you hit on something."

"This means Helen's alive and kicking," said Katy.

"She's the killer, or she's in major trouble somewhere," I said. "Either way, we need to find her."

"What about Javier?" said Katy. "There's something funny about him that doesn't ring true. Something I can't pin down."

"I get those vibes too," I said. "He's too quiet. He's hiding something. It's like someone's coerced him into this and he's protecting them."

Tetyana turned to the book she'd picked up. It was a six-hundred-page tome, the one that had rocketed Javier to the highly enviable position of being Mexico's poet laureate.

"It's a depressing book and darn hard to read," said Tetyana, making a face. "Are all poets this morose?"

"What does the title say?" I asked.

Tetyana slammed the book shut and turned it to us.

I stared at the cover.

"*Sinless Suicides,*" whispered Katy.

"Strange choice of words," said Tetyana, frowning.

"Is he religious?" I wondered. "Suicide's a sin in some religions, but that's probably a play on words."

"I don't understand half of what he's written," said Tetyana with a sigh. "Can't even get through the first paragraph. Too high-brow for me."

I turned to Katy. "Remember when he fell into the water near the mainland jetty?"

Katy nodded.

"When I went to pull him out, he was floating just under the waterline like he was holding his breath. I can't shake that image off."

"You think he was trying to kill himself?" asked Tetyana.

"I can't say for sure, but now he's gone and fallen down the stairs. Was it a second try?"

"Come on," said Tetyana, shaking her head. "If those were suicide attempts, he sucks at it big time. He could have jumped off the boat when you were in deep water. He could have leaped off from the top of the lighthouse balcony, not down one floor of a set of carpeted stairs. He wasn't trying."

"Maybe I imagined it," I said, and sat up as a new idea formed in the back of my mind. "Or maybe he wanted to give us the appearance he was trying to kill himself."

"Why?" said Katy. "That smacks of self-harm. Maybe he's mentally unwell and needs help?"

"They all need help if you ask me," said Tetyana, rolling her eyes.

"Javier was super cagey when I asked him if he saw anyone in the corridor before he fell," I said. "It's impossible for anyone to sneak behind you in that open corridor. I found that strange."

Tetyana frowned.

"If we're going on this assumption that someone's trying to kill everyone using the themes in their books, one question remains."

"What's that?" asked Katy.

"How do you *get* someone to commit suicide? It's a decision someone makes for themselves," replied Tetyana.

"What if you know someone who's already considering it?" I said. "You could put them in the right place, at the right time and have all the ducks lined up to make them do it."

"That's psychological warfare," said Tetyana. "I thought only the KGB and the Mafia did things like that. Not everyday murderers."

"Whoever it is, they've spun a sophisticated game," I said.

"There's one missing," said Katy, shifting through the books on the table. She peeked under the table and then under the chairs. "Where's Elliott's book?"

"He writes screenplays for movies," I said, glancing around the room. "It's probably a spiral-bound book with printed papers, like Ratcliffe's script."

We scoured the shelves, looking for a printed manuscript.

I was on the ladder poking around the top shelf on one corner when I spotted it at the far end, next to the window.

"Up there," I called out. "Someone put it all the way up," I said, as I moved the ladder toward the end of the shelf and climbed to the top.

I pulled down the spiral-bound document and waved it at my friends down below.

"What's the title?" asked Katy.

"Retribution in the Big Sur."

"What the heck does that mean?" said Tetyana.

"A horrible title," said Katy. "That will never be a movie."

I climbed down, carrying the screenplay in my free hand. When I got to the bottom, I crouched on a lower rung of the ladder and flipped to the back of the document.

Katy and Tetyana huddled next to me as I tried to find a death scene.

"Wait," said Katy as I scanned through the last few chapters. "He already told us how he did it."

"How?" asked Tetyana.

"Someone pushes a man off a cliff, just like the one we're on. He falls screaming all the way down and smashes his head on the rocks below."

"Sophia hated it when he told that story," I said, feeling goose bumps on my arms.

"That's because it's the only realistic scenario," said Tetyana. "It's the easiest way to kill someone here. Lure them to the edge of the cliff and push them over."

"We need to tell him," I said, standing up. "I know this sounds crazy, but we need to warn them. Just in case we're right."

I got up and walked over to the coffee table to add the screenplay to the pile. I stared at the guests' books for a minute, realizing what this theory could mean.

"You know what our conclusion is now, right?" I said, turning to my friends.

"We have a good idea how everyone's going to die, but not why," replied Katy. "And we still don't know who the killer is."

"Maybe we do," I said. "Oliver and Mary aren't writers. There's no sign they're in danger."

Tetyana's eyes narrowed. "I was thinking the same thing. We gotta watch them like hawks."

"I can't believe it," said Katy, shaking her head. "I don't want to believe it. They're so nice. They're the only normal people here."

"Cold-blooded killers don't actually announce themselves as such," said Tetyana.

"We need to keep an open mind," I said. "They could be running the show here at the owners' bidding, or they're the owners themselves."

"What about us?" said Katy, a horrified expression coming over her face. "We haven't written any books with gory death scenes. Are we targets too?"

"Not if I have a say in it," said Tetyana, her face turning hard.

They had killed twice now. It was only a matter of time they'd want to eliminate all of us. We were witnesses to their deeds and that would be dangerous for them.

I let out a sigh of exasperation. "The thing is, some of these books could be a ruse."

"A ruse?" asked Tetyana.

"What if we're meant to believe they're all potential victims? One is the killer, but we won't know it because they've added their books to the pile, making us think they're also in trouble."

"Gosh," said Katy, shaking her head. "That means it could be *anyone*."

Tetyana stirred and turned a stern face at us.

"We can't stay cooped here all night, coming up with all sorts of scenarios," she said. "We need to get back in the main house and keep vigil. I have a funny feeling the night has just begun."

She pulled out two Swiss Army knives from her boot and handed one to Katy and another to me.

"Not great, but they're good enough. You remember the training David and I gave you, right?"

Katy and I nodded.

"All right, ladies. Time to move," she said, walking toward the door. "Let's hope no one else has died while we sat on our bums in this bookstore."

"Library."

"Whatever."

Chapter Forty-nine

Other than the security lights outside the resort building and the ornamental lights on the lawn, the house was dark.

I pulled open the main door with Tetyana and Katy behind me. I was sure we'd be the only ones up, so the strange grunt startled me.

Tetyana pushed me aside and stepped in.

"Come out," she growled.

I looked around, feeling the walls, trying to remember where the light switch was. Katy got to it faster than I did and turned it on.

The front foyer flooded with light.

Standing in front of us was Oliver.

"Thank goodness, it's you," he said, putting a hand to his chest.

Oliver looked drained.

He'd taken his jacket off and was in his gray waistcoat. He'd undone the top two buttons of his shirt and rolled up his sleeves.

His face was flushed and there was a row of sweat beads on his brow.

In his right hand was an iron firepit poker.

"What are you doing with that?" I asked.

He gave an embarrassed look.

"I didn't know it was you. I thought it was, er..."

"The killer?" said Tetyana.

Oliver shot her a frightened look and nodded.

"I thought you ladies had gone to sleep, so I took charge of the vigil." He raised his iron poker and gave a grim smile. "It was all I could find. Just in case the killer comes for me."

Katy and I exchanged a discreet glance.

"We're here now," said Tetyana, reaching over and prying the poker from his hands. "We'll take over."

"Where's Mary?" asked Katy, looking around. "Is she up too?"

"I told her to get some rest," said Oliver. "She was pretty shaken up. She's had heart problems before, so I told her to take her medication and go to bed. I didn't want her to...."

He wiped his brow and sighed.

"I've been worrying about this, but didn't want to alarm her. We can't have her get an attack in the middle of all this with no connection to the mainland."

"Seen anything?" asked Tetyana sharply, not even stopping to ask about Mary.

Oliver gave her another startled look. He'd noticed her change in tone.

"No... no. Everyone seems to be sleeping upstairs. At least the lights are turned off and I've not heard a peep since they all returned to their rooms. Javier's in his room next to ours and has been quiet all along. They're all locked in. I have seen nothing, except for you three now, of course."

He shuffled his feet like he wasn't sure what was expected of him.

On the surface, he looked like the least likely person in the world capable of using that iron poker. I could see Tetyana's glares had unnerved him. It was a tactic from her previous life.

She's playing the bad cop routine. Throw the suspect off to see if he'd give away his position.

But Oliver merely looked frightened.

My brain whirred.

What would Mary and Oliver gain by killing off their guests? If they had wanted to kill the writers, why invite us?

They would have known three inquisitive big city girls wouldn't sit quietly in the midst of a missing person and these murders. We'd ask questions and poke around, even if we hadn't been hired as private investigators.

I looked at the man standing in front of us.

Oliver had aged a decade since we arrived. He now looked like a deer caught in headlights. Confused. Frightened. Uncertain of which direction to turn.

"You look beat," I said, softening my voice. "Why don't you go to your room and get some rest. We can take it over from here."

He shook his head.

"I can't do that, Ms. Kade. This is my home. I feel responsible for everything that has happened. For the deaths of... of..."

His voice cracked. He swallowed and gave us a dismayed look.

"I just can't believe this has happened."

He rubbed the sides of his forehead like he had a headache coming on.

"I'm trying to stay strong for Mary, but I'm wondering if I'm going mad. In all my life I've never seen anything like this."

He choked on something and stopped.

Katy stepped toward him and put her hand on his arm.

"We can't explain it either, Oliver," she said in a soft voice. "But we have to stay strong."

"Maybe Mr. Ratcliffe is... is right," stammered Oliver. "Maybe it is Ms. Jenkins who is doing this."

Tetyana's eyes narrowed.

"Did you see her after she ran off that first night?" I asked.

"No, heavens, no. I wish I did. I would have tried to help her."

He looked up, tears welling in his eyes, a pleading look on his face, as if asking us to make this horror go away.

"Something bad has happened to her, but she's come back because she has unfinished business. Either that, or she's back to take revenge because we didn't help her."

"That's quite the story," said Tetyana, scorn in her voice.

Oliver stared at her, his blue eyes small and pointy. He swayed like he was about to faint. Katy put an arm around his shoulder and patted his arm.

"You don't believe in ghosts, do you?" said Katy.

Oliver turned to her in surprise.

"Ms. McCafferty, this is a lighthouse."

"So?"

"If you'd come at any other time, I'd have invited you all to sit around the kitchen fire, fed you doughnuts and coffee and told you all the stories about this place."

Oliver leaned against the wall and wiped his brow.

"Every lighthouse has a story. Not just ghosts either, but strange sightings out at sea, misty figures rising through the fog, haunting music coming from the shore in the middle of the night. It could be anything."

He crossed himself and looked up at the ceiling.

"If this is Ms. Jenkins, I beg you to stop doing this," he said. "If you're looking for some salvation, please don't take it out on us who are still here on earth."

Tetyana rolled her eyes.

I almost wanted to tell Oliver everything was going to be all right, that we'd watch over him and Mary.

But I knew better.

Everyone on this island had their deaths carved out. The only people exempt were Oliver, Mary, and us. Since I could strike the three of us out, that left only two possibilities for the murderer.

A lesson David shared with us from his days with the Mossad intelligence service came to mind.

Keep your friends close, and your enemies even closer.

Chapter Fifty

"Why don't you join us?" I said to Oliver. "You're probably not going to get much sleep tonight, are you?"

He gave a forlorn shake of his head.

"After you," I said, putting slight pressure on his back. Innocent or not, I wasn't about to have him behind us.

With a deep sigh, Oliver stumbled up the steps.

We walked into the dining room to see he had already rearranged the chairs, so we'd have the best view of the grounds.

Tetyana moved one chair to the side.

"I'd like you to sit here," she said to Oliver. "That way I can keep an eye on you."

He gave a wide-eyed look at her.

He opened his mouth, then stopped himself. With his shoulders hunched, he took the chair Tetyana had indicated. He sat down, chin against his chest, his eyes downcast, his hands clutching the armrests.

Either he was really good, and was having us on, or he was completely innocuous and was as terrified as he looked.

Katy and I were supposed to get some sleep while Tetyana kept watch for the first hour. But I was having a hard time keeping my eyes closed.

In the chair next to me, Katy was nodding, jerking her head up now and then.

Oliver had his eyes closed, but his heaving chest told me he wasn't getting any rest.

It was half an hour later that Tetyana called out.

"I saw something out there," she said, pointing.

I jumped up and ran to the window.

"What's going on?" said Katy, joining us.

"On the north side," said Tetyana, pointing in the lighthouse's direction.

I squinted through the darkness. We could only see part of the tower where the main door was.

"Could have been an animal or a bird," said Tetyana.

She turned to Oliver, who was sitting upright, watching us from his chair.

"Any feral dogs or cats on the island? Any animals?"

"No. Mary had a Golden Doodle, but we lost her six months ago. Buried her in the back. She was thirteen. She had a good life, and it was time for her to..." He looked away, his mouth turned down.

His eyes darted back and forth, like he was disoriented.

"Sorry, I mean to say there aren't any animals on the island unless you count the seagulls, the larks, the sparrows and the like. We also get the occasional Canada geese family that lands here on their way up north...."

Oliver was babbling, but I felt it was more out of the compelling human need to have a normal conversation amid this madness, than anything else.

He cut a pathetic figure, hunched in his seat, wringing his hands.

"I don't think it was a gaggle of geese I saw just now," said Tetyana, turning back to the window.

I peered out into the darkness, trying to spot whatever had caught her attention.

The skies had partly cleared, and a half-moon peered from behind a cloud, casting a shimmering yellow line on the water. The ocean seemed to have settled down.

I hoped this was a harbinger of what was to come. I hoped calm was settling on the island again. No more murders, no more fires, and no screams in the middle of the night.

"You don't have any night vision equipment, do you?" asked Tetyana, turning to Oliver.

He shook his head.

"No, ma'am. There's an expensive pair of binoculars in the lantern room in the lighthouse. The new owner put it there. But I have a small pair in my room for bird watching. Mary and I love to—"

"Would you get it, please?" said Tetyana. "Also, we'll need flashlights if you have any."

She turned to Katy.

"Keep an eye out and holler if you see anything."

"Sure thing," said Katy, walking over to the window and pressing her face against the pane.

I stepped up with Oliver while Tetyana came in from behind us.

"For the first time in my life, I wish I never set foot on this island," said Oliver as we stepped down the stairs.

"We'll figure it out," I said. "You just leave it all to us."

We walked along the first-floor corridor toward the kitchen at the end.

As we passed Javier's room, I leaned in to see if I could hear anything, but it was quiet inside. The painkillers put him right to sleep, I thought.

We stepped into the kitchen.

The lights were still on, and nothing seemed out of place. Oliver stepped into the walk-in closet next to the pantry while we watched.

He dug out four flashlights and a handful of loose batteries.

"I take the batteries out or they go crusty and bad," he said, placing the items on the kitchen table.

Tetyana inserted the batteries into the torches while Oliver slipped back into the small room to find his pair of binoculars.

I stood by the closet door, my ears and eyes on full alert. My right hand was in my pocket, gripping my Swiss Army knife, ready for anything.

Oliver popped out with an old pair of bird-watching glasses and a pink cloth. He sat down heavily at the table and started cleaning the lens.

"Haven't used this since last summer," he muttered. "Been collecting dust."

"Oliver," I said, sitting across from him, an idea forming in my mind. "I have a question for you."

He looked up and blinked a few times.

"What is it, Ms. Kade?"

"Do you know a Madame Bouchard?"

He gave me a puzzled look. "Madame who?"

"Madame Bouchard."

"Is she another writer?"

"No, but she was a celebrity of sorts. She passed away about eight months ago."

He frowned.

"Sounds foreign. Is she French?"

"Canadian. Her husband's American, from New Hampshire. She lived here for quite a while." I leaned across the table. "Are you sure you haven't had a guest here by that name?"

"If someone with that name came here, I would have remembered her," said Oliver, scratching his head. "But we haven't had visitors until now."

He squinted as if to think.

"It was mostly the construction crew who came to fix this place up. Two of their engineers were women. Very straitlaced and serious. I can tell you there was no one famous in that crowd or anyone who'd call themselves *Madame*."

There was no recognition of the name. No flicker of the eye or flinch. This meant Oliver and Mary didn't invite us here. This also meant they weren't the owners.

Oliver gave me a puzzled look.

"What's so important about her? Should I know her?"

There were some things I couldn't share with him, and one was our strange relationship with Madame Bouchard. Oliver probably thought of us as regular licensed private investigators working for our wealthy clients.

I couldn't muddy the waters by telling him there might be a connection between the new owner of this island and our former eccentric client who'd made me promise to help her friends out when they called.

I was about to dig some more, when a surprised yell came from upstairs.

Tetyana and I turned to each other in shock.

"Katy!" I said.

Chapter Fifty-one

We ran through the corridor and dashed up the stairs.

I could hear Katy hollering.

"The light!" she yelled as we burst through the door.

As soon as I stepped inside the dining hall, I realized what had spooked her.

For a moment, I wondered if the Coast Guard had sent their rescue helicopters and they were hovering above us.

But there was no sound.

Just an eerie, silent, football-stadium-strength strobe light that swept the ocean and part of the island.

I shielded my eyes and peered at the sky through the window.

The light.

The lantern in the lighthouse had come alive.

"Oh, my goodness gracious," said Oliver, his face white.

"What's going on here, Oliver?" I asked.

He gave me a frightened look, too frozen to speak.

"That..." he stopped and swallowed hard. "That's not worked in more than a decade—"

"Who turned it on now?" I demanded.

He gave me a mute stare, then shook his head.

A commotion behind us made me turn. It was Mary. She walked up to Oliver and grabbed on to his arm, like she was about to faint.

"It's Helen Jenkins," she said in a harsh whisper. "She's risen from the dead and has come to haunt us."

With an exasperated sigh, Tetyana pulled out her long Tanto knife from her boot.

"Let's go, girls!" she said, waving at us to follow her.

Pulling our smaller knives out, Katy and I broke into a run after her.

We scrambled down the stairs and out of the front door onto the front lawn. We didn't need the flashlights anymore. The lantern had lit up everything in the vicinity.

"Someone's up there," shouted Tetyana as we raced toward the lighthouse.

The killer!

Within minutes, the three of us had crashed through the main door of the tower. I scrambled up the stairs, trying to keep up with the long strides of my friends.

Tetyana was already on the third floor with Katy's footsteps thumping a floor behind her.

"Oh, my lord, oh, my lord," I heard Oliver panting from somewhere below me.

Did he come too?

I focused on my climb.

If someone was upstairs, they would hear us come up. My blood ran cold as I realized they might have Tetyana's Glock on them.

"Tetyana!" I hollered. "Be careful!"

As if I needed to tell her.

I doubled my efforts and jumped two stairs at a time.

If anything happens to her, they'll have hell to pay, I thought, gritting my teeth as I ran up.

When I got to the top floor, Katy was hovering at the doorway. She turned to me, a hand over her mouth, a horrified expression on her face.

My heart plummeted to my stomach.

Where's Tetyana?

I brushed past her and ran inside.

The room was so bright, I had to shield my eyes.

Tetyana was standing next to the light, her eyes on the floor.

That was when I saw him.

It was Ratcliffe.

But he was no longer alive.

Oliver came up from behind me. I felt him clutch my shoulder as he saw the sight. I stared at the scene, wanting to turn my eyes away, but unable to.

Ratcliffe lay sprawled on the floor, face up, next to the glass enclosure of the massive lantern.

Stuck on his neck was the swordfish. It was like the fish had dropped from the ceiling, its sharp beak pointing downward while he lay on the ground.

I recalled the first day at the lighthouse when I touched the end of that long bill. It had drawn blood on my finger. This was a more efficient murder weapon than any knife.

I looked at the rope dangling from the ceiling. Someone had removed the stuffed swordfish from the hooks and had rammed it on Ratcliffe like a spear.

Tetyana circled the body, shaking her head.

The swordfish was still upright, leaning against the glass enclosure, partly held up by what was left of Ratcliffe's muscles.

"I've seen many things in my life," I heard Tetyana say as I walked up to her. "This is the first time I see a fish bill used as a killing machine."

"My gosh," I said, trying not to throw up.

"I thought I locked the bastard up," said Tetyana, grimacing. "He should have stayed inside his room."

"What's that in his hands?" I said, as I spotted a small piece of paper Ratcliffe had been clutching in his right fist.

I bent down and wiggled it out from between his curled fingers.

I read the message, with Tetyana looking over my shoulder.

"Help me turn on the light. We can signal for help. Wait till lighthouse is empty. Can't trust anyone else."

"Signature?" Tetyana asked, bending down to scrutinize the paper.

"None."

The words were written crudely in black ink and in all caps, much like what we saw on our bathroom glass wall.

I stared at the dead body.

Someone had lured Ratcliffe here and killed him. The killer must have stayed hidden outside, waiting for us to leave, before sneaking into the lighthouse.

How did Ratcliffe get out of his locked room? How did we not see them?

"Watch out!"

I spun around to see Katy, who was still standing at the doorway. She was pointing at the body.

"Get away!" she screamed.

Tetyana pulled me back just in time.

We watched in horror as gravity took over, and the swordfish tipped.

We sprang away as it fell to the floor with a loud clatter. Red blood and globs of Ratcliffe's throat splattered on the glass case and Ratcliffe's head severed from his body.

I stood pressed against the wall, stunned. I vaguely heard Oliver run down the stairs, making retching noises. Katy stood by the threshold, clutching the door, her face the same color as the whitewashed wall.

For once, even Tetyana had gone silent in shock.

Blissfully unaware of what was going on, the enormous lantern kept shining toward the placid ocean.

I wished it would turn toward the mainland and act like an SOS beacon. I wished it would pulsate and flicker, and call for help. *Now.*

Instead, it shone calmly out to sea, as if mocking us, laughing at us.

I'd failed again.

Day Three

Chapter Fifty-two

"Should have seen it coming," said Tetyana, shaking her head.

"*Jaws of Death*," said Katy, with a shudder. "The connection was clear."

We stood under the electrical panel next to the light, our backs to Ratcliffe's body.

It was too gruesome to look at, even for Tetyana. I was sure this scene was going to give me nightmares for life.

"The killer had the key to this panel," I said.

The switch panel was locked.

Oliver had told us he didn't know how the light worked, and he didn't have the key to access the controls. But someone had known how to make that light work. Whoever turned on the light had also murdered Ratcliffe.

"It's the new owner," I said. "They had this renovated, and they held the key." I turned to my friends. "And they're here on the island right now."

"But who is it?" whispered Katy.

Tetyana gave us a grave look.

"We're left with Elliott, Sophia, Javier, and the Hudsons."

"Don't forget Helen Jenkins," said Katy.

We looked at her.

"We haven't found her body yet," she said.

That was true.

"There's a third option." I paused, feeling the hair on my arms rise as I contemplated the idea. "We may have not met the new owner yet."

"Are you saying they're on the island, hiding from us?" whispered Katy. "Gosh, how creepy can it get?"

"We've been here two days," said Tetyana. "If someone is here, they'd need a place to sleep, food and water. They had to have planned this well."

She frowned.

"Did Mary say any of the food or water bottles had gone missing?"

Katy and I shook our head.

"If they have, she didn't tell us," said Katy.

"What are the odds," I said, "that Oliver and Mary are in on it?"

"They look as scared as anyone else," said Katy. "They keep saying they don't know who the owner is."

"If they're the true killers, they won't talk," I said. "We can't trust their word."

"We need to find evidence and confront them. That way, they can't deny," said Tetyana, her eyes narrowing. "Let's start with the tower."

She turned to us.

"We have to stick close together. If things get hairy, follow my instructions, okay?"

"Roger that," said Katy and I at the same time.

Tetyana had saved our skins more than a dozen times in the past. When things got bad, I knew relying on her was the best way to stay alive.

I sent a silent thanks to David for sending her over. He'd have a heart attack if he knew what we were going through.

It took an hour for us to comb the lighthouse, as we looked for signs of the killer or anything that would give them away.

Was it Oliver? I wondered as we checked every nook and cranny. Or was it Mary? Was it both? Or someone we hadn't met yet?

But we came up empty.

"They're always a step ahead of us," said Tetyana, shaking her head in disgust.

"First the flare gun. Now the light," I said. "They're taunting us."

Tetyana grimaced.

"When I find the bastard, I'm going to wring their neck myself."

"If we get through this, we'll have a story to tell, that's for sure," said Katy. "Ratcliffe wasn't joking when he said a book about this would make millions."

"Let's make sure we survive first," I said. "Time to talk to the others."

We stepped out of the lighthouse to walk toward the main resort building.

"Gross," said Katy as the smell of fresh vomit wafted to us.

Someone had thrown up just outside the main lighthouse door.

"Oliver," I said, remembering how he ran out gagging.

"So, it wasn't an act?" said Katy, raising an eyebrow.

If someone really wanted to, they could have forced themselves to gag enough to throw up. It sounded excessive, but then again, this entire situation was extreme any way I looked at it.

We kept walking, shoulder to shoulder, staying close together. I was glad I had Tetyana and Katy with me. Whatever happens here, I thought, my goal was now to make sure I got them off the island unharmed.

Behind us, the massive lantern still shone brightly like an artificial miniature sun. I crossed my fingers, hoping it would alert a passing boat, or even the Coast Guard, who'd wonder why the old light had been lit in the middle of the night.

"What the hell?" said Tetyana, making me look up.

A small group had congregated near the front doorway of the main building.

"How did they get out?" asked Katy.

We were about fifty feet away from the building when Elliot came running toward us, his hair standing up like he'd been electrocuted.

"What the hell is going on?" he cried. "What's with the light?"

Then Sophia spurted toward us, her hair streaming behind her.

"What's happening?" she screeched, accosting us. "Tell me! What's going on?"

I stepped around her and kept walking. They were plainly on the verge of panic attacks and nothing we could say would calm them down.

It was only going to get worse.

Oliver and Mary were standing by the door, arms around each other, their faces pale. Next to them, sitting in his antique wooden wheelchair, was Javier, looking on with shock.

The three of us strode toward the main entrance, ignoring Elliot's and Sophia's angry yells and jabs.

"Tell us!" screeched Sophia in my ear.

Tetyana glared at the two writers. She was struggling not to push them away.

"Is it true?" said Mary as we walked up.

"Someone tell us what's going on!" yelled Elliot.

"Ratcliffe is dead," I said. "Murdered."

"Oh, my gosh," said Sophia. She wavered and slipped to the ground, holding her chest. "I'm next," she wailed. "We're all going to die."

"Hey, Sophia," said Katy, reaching over and taking her by her arm. "Panicking isn't going to help. We need to stay calm so we can all stay safe."

I turned to Elliot.

"How did you get out of your room?"

He didn't answer, still in shock at the news.

Mary turned to us.

"It was me," she said, showing us her key set. "Oliver told me one more person is dead in the lighthouse. I couldn't let everyone stay locked up in their rooms, in all good conscience. They needed to know."

My voice hardened.

"When did you open their doors?"

"Two minutes ago."

"Was it you who opened Ratcliffe's door earlier?"

"Of course not," she said. "His door was already unlocked when I went upstairs just now."

I looked over them carefully.

Whoever killed the publisher should have blood splatters on them. There were red splotches all over that glass enclosure, even before that swordfish fell over and decapitated the man.

But none of them had any red markings on their clothes or their skin. I wondered how long it would take to wash blood off your hands and change your clothes.

Not that long, I thought as I surveyed the crowd.

"Where were you all in the past hour?" It was a question I was tiring of asking.

"In bed," said Javier and pointed at his wheelchair. "I can't walk, plus you locked my door."

"Me too," said Sophia, shooting Tetyana a nasty look. "You locked me in."

"I was in... my bed," stammered Elliot. "Until Mary unlocked the door a few minutes ago and told me something bad had happened."

"I was trying to sleep in our room," Mary said. "Until Oliver came running to tell me Ratcliffe had died."

"What happened to him?" asked Elliot, his face ashen. "How did he die?"

Tetyana turned to him. "How would you like to take a guess?"

Chapter Fifty-three

"Was it your gun?" said Elliot. "Someone shot him, didn't they?"

"If you have any idea where my Glock is, I'd love to know," said Tetyana, a dangerous undercurrent in her voice.

"Of course not," spluttered Elliot, "but someone found it and used it on Ratcliffe, right?"

What had happened to the publisher was way too surreal to explain.

"Was he stabbed, like Jason?" asked Javier, eyes wide in shock. "Is that how they're killing us?"

"Ratcliffe died from a wound that punctured his throat," I replied.

Mary crossed herself.

"Was it one of my knives?" she asked, her voice high pitched. "I locked them up before I went to bed, even my shears. Did someone break in and take one?"

So Oliver hadn't shared the details. Was it to spare her the grief or to hide his heinous actions?

I shook my head.

"There are museum pieces inside the lighthouse. Old paintings, anchors, and stuffed fish hanging from the ceiling."

I observed the group, searching for any telltale signs of recognition or guilt.

"Near the light on the top floor was a big stuffed swordfish, about five feet long," I continued. "It had a long, sharp and pointy snout."

They stared, eyes affixed, faces in a daze, but nothing told me they knew what had happened inside the lighthouse.

"The killer took that fish down from the display and used the bill to spear Ratcliffe on the neck. He was, er, decapitated."

A shocked gasp came from Sophia. Elliot and Javier looked stupefied. Mary looked like she was about to buckle. Oliver pulled her in tight.

I looked at the bedraggled group of people in front of us.

It was time to share our theory with them, so the innocents could save themselves. If the killer was here, they'd know we knew, but we had no choice.

I cleared my throat.

"We believe the murderer is following a very specific pattern."

"What kind of pattern?" asked Javier, his forehead lined with worry and his cheeks sagging, making him look his age for once.

"What in heck are you talking about?" asked Elliot. "A pattern of what?"

"Remember the dinner conversation on our first day?" I said. "When you all discussed how people die in your books?"

No one answered.

"Camilla Carter wrote about asphyxiation," I said. "Jason Taylor had his characters stabbed in his books, and Ratcliffe's script is about a large fish attacking humans."

Javier, Sophia, and Elliot exchanged horrified glances.

"We found each of your books in the lighthouse," said Katy softly. "We think the killer is copying what's in them."

"Oh, my lord," said Sophia. "Oh, my lord. We die in the same way people die in our books."

"This is impossible. Unbelievably fantastical." Javier looked up. "Which book of mine did you find up there?"

I stared at him, unsure how to reply. I'd already seen him possibly attempting suicide. Twice. If we shared the truth, would it push him over the edge?

Or was this all an act?

"Thank goodness, I write kid's books," said Sophia, saving me from answering. "This means I'm spared."

She stared at us with pleading eyes.

"Am I right? Please say yes."

Elliot grabbed my arm and shook me.

"What about me? Which script of mine did you find? I want to know how I'm going to die," he shouted. "I need to know!"

"Wait," said Javier, pointing a finger our way. "If we're all going to die according to the scenes in our books, where does that leave you?"

He gave a wild-eyed look at Oliver and Mary in the corner.

"And *you*?" he said, pointing at them.

A look of terror crossed the faces of Javier, Sophia, and Elliot as this new realization set in.

Sophia and Elliot took three steps back toward the stairway, like they were preparing to make a run for it. Javier pushed his wheelchair a few feet into the corridor, closer toward his room.

"You sent the invites," said Elliot, pointing a shaky finger at Oliver. "You know the island. You know the house. It's you who's doing this!"

Oliver and Mary clutched each other even tighter.

"You deranged, psycho, sadistic murderers!" screamed Sophia.

Mary crossed herself again. Oliver looked like he was about to throw up. He swallowed and gave a weary look at Sophia.

"My wife and I have taken care of this lighthouse ever since the old keeper died," he said. "All we wanted was to enjoy the ocean and the outdoors, and finish our career here before we returned to Portland to be close to our grandkids."

He turned to Javier.

"Believe me when I say I've no idea why this is happening, or who's behind these killings. Mary and I can't wait to leave and never set our eyes on this island ever again. We're done. Please, I beg you to believe me. It's not us."

"Wait a minute," said Elliot, as if he'd just remembered something important. "What about Helen Jenkins? What was her book about?"

Katy and I exchanged a quick glance. If everyone wasn't creeped out already, we were going to make them now.

"The title of her book is *The Girl Who Lived*," said Katy in a flat voice.

"It's her then!" cried Elliott. "It has to be her doing all this. She's the killer!"

"Calm down, for goodness sake. We have no evid—" started Tetyana.

"Don't tell us to calm down!" shrieked Sophia.

"I want to see my script!" bellowed Elliott.

Elliot streaked past me and ran across the lawn, flailing like a madman. A screech from behind me told me Sophia was running toward the lighthouse as well.

"Get back here!" hollered Tetyana. "You can't go in there. It's a crime scene!"

"We just unleashed hell," said Katy, turning to me. "Maybe we shouldn't have told them."

"It was the right thing to do," I said. "If there was something in there with my name on it and how I will die, I would want to know too."

Tetyana was trying to corral the two writers, but they seemed to be too much to handle even for her. She let them go as they bolted, shrieking and screaming, toward the main lighthouse door.

"Let's go," I said as I raced over to the lighthouse.

By the time Katy and I got to the fourth floor, Sophia was collapsed next to the coffee table, poring over her book. Elliot was pulling tomes off the shelves and throwing them on the floor, muttering madly to himself.

Tetyana leaned against the doorway, a cross look on her face. There were fresh scratch marks on her cheek.

"They're worse than scrapping cats," growled Tetyana as we stepped inside. "Best not to get too close."

I turned around to see what the two writers were up to. At least they didn't go up to the top floor, I thought in relief.

"It's not worth it," I heard Tetyana say from behind me. "We just have to wait for them to calm down."

"What are you doing?" I said, walking up to Elliot, ducking as a book flew through the air, missing my head by two inches.

"Your screenplay is on the table," I said.

"It's not there. I looked," he grumbled as he lobbed another tome my way.

I scanned the shelves for the stack of printed papers I'd seen before.

"I see it," I called out, pointing at the topmost shelf at the end.

"Where?" shrieked Elliot, following my finger.

"Someone put it back where I found it," I said.

Who did that?

The killer?

"Wait," I said, a sick feeling coming over me. Something about this was wrong. So wrong.

"Elliot, stop!"

But he was already moving.

He grabbed the ladder, pushed it off the wall, and clambered up the steps while it moved.

We watched in horror as the ladder flew at lightning speed and slammed against the far wall near the open window.

Elliot didn't have a chance.

He stumbled as the ladder hit the wall. In a split-second, Elliot careened through the open window, screaming to the high heavens.

Chapter Fifty-four

Elliott's ear-splitting scream echoed across the grounds. It ended abruptly with a sickening splotch on the rocks.

Tetyana dashed to the window.

It took me an extra second to unfreeze myself. Katy and I joined our friend and looked out. All we could see was the inky black abyss below us.

Other than the waves crashing on the shore, there was no other sound. The seagulls were asleep. Even the wind had died down.

Elliott was gone. Just like he'd written in his story.

I don't know how long the three of us stood by the window, holding our breaths, staring into the darkness.

I strained my ears for any sound from Elliott, anything to tell us he was alive, as impossible as I knew that was.

It was Sophia's sobs that made me turn around.

She was still near the coffee table, clutching her book to her chest, crying uncontrollably.

"He's gone," said Tetyana, turning around, her face somber. "No one's going to survive a two-hundred-and-fifty-foot fall without a chute."

How much worse can things get?

I racked my brain, trying hard not to allow panic to set in.

We had two choices.

We could make our way down the slippery walkway and look for Elliott's body. But if he was already dead, there was no use putting more people's lives in danger.

I looked at the ladder leaning crookedly against the wall, one leg out of the tracks.

I stepped up to it and crouched down to examine the tracks. Tetyana came over to join me.

"What the frigging hell?" she said, pulling at the loose wheel at the bottom of the ladder. "Someone removed the brakes and took out the stopper at the end."

"Sabotage?" I said, the knot in my stomach tightening.

"Whoever killed Ratcliffe, came down and messed with this," said Tetyana. "They knew Elliot would look for his screenplay on the top shelf."

"But it could have been any of us," said Katy from behind, her face pale. She pointed at me. "Asha, you used the ladder earlier. You could have gone back up to retrieve his script for him."

I stood up, shaking at the close call. Katy reached over and clutched my hand. I squeezed hers back.

"The psycho is targeting us now," said Katy.

Tetyana shook her head.

"They're taking chances. Whoever planned this lined up as many ducks in a row to increase the probability it would be him. This is an intelligent, well-prepared killer who knows this place well. It wasn't some crazed psycho."

Katy gave Tetyana a horrified look. "But they're playing with our lives," she said.

"I knew something was wrong," I said. "I felt it in my gut."

"The question is," said Tetyana, "who is it? Is it a him or a her? Have we met them already?"

Camilla Carter, Jason Taylor, Elliott Ward, and Ratcliffe were all dead. Helen was still missing, and her book made her murder an inconclusive puzzle. If the killer had wanted to confuse us, they had done a good job.

I remembered the novelist's face. I recalled how she stared at us the first day she walked into the dining hall. That terrified glance, that recognition of someone that made her turn around and run off scared.

I was never one to believe in ghosts or ghouls. I had to admit, though, doing a disappearing act in such a small piece of land, cut off from everything, seemed almost supernatural.

I shook myself.

Tetyana marched over to the coffee table and towered over Sophia, her hands on her hips, a steely look in her eyes.

Still sobbing, Sophia didn't even notice her.

"Ready to talk?" snapped Tetyana.

Sophia looked up, wiped her nose with her sleeve and hugged her book even tighter to her heaving chest.

"Is he gone?" she sniveled. "Did he die too?"

"As good as dead," said Tetyana, not an ounce of emotion in her voice. I walked up, feeling a tinge of pity for the woman on the ground.

"It can't be her," said Katy, joining us. "She was sitting here all along."

"The ladder was tampered with a few hours ago," said Tetyana. "No one had to do anything now for that trick to work."

"What a horrible nightmare," Sophia warbled. "What a horrible, horrible place. I wish I never came. What's happening to us all? Why are they doing this? Who is it?"

"That's what I'd like to know," said Tetyana.

I kneeled in front of the crying woman.

"Sophia," I said, putting a hand on her arm. "I have some questions for you. Please be honest with us, okay?"

"Why are you asking me questions? I know nothing. I paid a lot to come to a luxury retreat, not to this hellish hole." She gave me a wild look. "Find the killer before he does me in too!"

"Take a deep breath," I said, trying to control my voice.

I wasn't fond of this woman. She had acted superior to everybody, gave off airs, and wasn't the nicest person to be around. But we had to glean as much background on everyone as we could.

"Can you please tell us how you know the other guests?"

With a large sniffle, she pulled her feet in and balled herself up.

I tried again.

"Have you worked with any of the others?"

She wiped her eyes and gave a few more sniffs. She shook her head, not making eye contact anymore.

I turned to Katy.

"The photo?"

Katy pulled out the crumpled image of the dead body on the beach from her pocket and smoothed it out. Squatting next to us, she thrust the photo in front of Sophia.

"See this picture?" I asked. "Do you recognize this man?"

Sophia shrank back in horror.

"Get that thing away from me," she said, turning around like she wanted to bolt from the room.

"Please answer this question honestly," I said, leaning in and holding on to her arm. "Did you meet Zimmerman in your past Hollywood career?"

Silence.

"Zimmerman was one of the most powerful producers in Hollywood. If you were an actress, you must have bumped into him, if not professionally, at a party or an event?"

Another sniffle came from Sophia, but she was keeping quiet, eyes on the floor.

"We think the body in this picture is Zimmerman. Whatever's happening here is linked to him, to this photo. This could be the clue to who the killer is. Please tell us, have you ever met him, talked to him, or worked with him?"

Sophia shrank farther into her bubble, but her lips were set in a thin grim line and her fists were balled tightly. I wasn't sure if she was in the depths of distress or simmering with anger.

That's interesting.

"Everybody knew Zimmerman," she said finally, in a low voice.

"Do you know what happened to him?"

Silence.

"Let me tell you then," I said. "Zimmerman had a circle of powerful men and women in his corner. They trafficked young actors and actresses who came to Hollywood to start their careers. They lured them in and abused them."

"The casting couch," said Katy. "His cabal perfected it. They even took videos and shared it online."

I nodded and turned back to Sophia.

"He was killed on this remote beach by one of those young actresses who'd had enough of the abuse. She took out an assault rifle and blew a slew of bullets through him."

I paused, wondering if I should also tell her we had been there when it had happened. But I doubted that would make her any more honest.

"Helen Jenkins had an unpublished manuscript on her bedside table," I continued.

"It disappeared with her. We found the same photo in between its pages. The working title of her book was *It's a Man's World*. We think it's an unauthorized bio of Zimmerman. Do you know anything about it?"

A calculated look had come over Sophia's face. It was like she was planning to take her secrets to the grave with her if she had to.

"If you help us," said Katy, "we can stop this killer. Please talk to us."

No answer.

From behind me, Tetyana let out an impatient sigh. I was sure she wanted to pick Sophia up by her shoulders and shake the truth out of her.

My voice hardened as I thought of an assumption that had been whirling in my mind.

"Sophia, were you in Zimmerman's cabal?"

Silence.

"Did you procure those young actors and actresses for him and his pals?"

Nothing.

That was when another tangent to this story came to mind. It was one I'd never considered before.

"Sophia," I said, softening my voice, "were you one of Zimmerman's victims?"

Chapter Fifty-five

With a shrill cry, Sophia sprang up.

Before we could do anything, she dropped her book and ran out the library door, sobbing.

Tetyana made a move to dash after her, but I pulled her back.

"She can't go far. We're on an island, after all," I said. "Besides, she's just going to scratch and scream. We need to find a way to make her talk."

"What if *she's* the killer?" said Tetyana, narrowing her eyes. "She could try to get the others too."

"I don't think she's the one. She's too hysterical to plan any of this. She's hiding something all right, but she's not the murderer."

"I don't think so either," said Katy.

"But from her reaction," I said, "I'm now sure this is connected to Zimmerman."

"He died years ago," said Katy. "I thought everyone had forgotten about him already. Why would anyone bring all that up now?"

"Someone here has a long memory," I said, staring at Sophia's book on the floor. "There's something else going on here, something more complex we can't see yet."

I remembered a valuable lesson I learned from my past life. *When things speed up and your head is spinning, that's the time to slow down. Way down.*

"We need to think through our steps or we could be next," I said.

I rubbed my forehead, trying to get my tired brain to work.

"The connecting link here is Zimmerman and something that happened in Hollywood ten years ago."

Katy held up her right hand.

"Okay, so here's what we have so far," she said.

"One, Elliott used to work as an agent to actors. Maybe he lured all those girls for Zimmerman. Two, Sophia used to be an actress and was in the thick of things in one form or the other. She was either part of the cabal or a victim. Three, Jason Taylor did video work for studio execs. Zimmerman could have been one of his clients. Four, Helen Jenkins had Zimmerman's photo inside that manuscript."

"And Ratcliffe?" asked Tetyana.

"Didn't Jason say he had an imprint for unauthorized biographies that were making him money?" I asked.

Katy nodded. "It was Ratcliffe who brought it up. Was smug about it too."

"I'll bet you everything Helen's unpublished book is a biography of Zimmerman," I said. "That's why she had that photo."

"Maybe she's behind this, after all?" asked Katy.

"Hard to say," I said, kicking myself for not having picked up her manuscript when we first saw it in her room.

"What about Camilla?" asked Tetyana, frowning. "She's from London. What's her connection to Hollywood?"

"She was very cagey about her past," I said, recalling my conversation with her that first day in the dining hall.

"You'd think someone who wrote erotica would be more hesitant to talk about their current work. But when I asked if she'd been an author all her career, she stopped talking and skedaddled. It was a little strange."

"That leaves Javier and the Hudsons," said Katy.

"Javier confounds me," I said, shaking my head. "He's the youngest. What's his connection to all this? Ten years ago, he was just in his twenties."

"Flimsy straws, ladies," said Tetyana, sighing impatiently. "We have a lot of assumptions, but nothing substantial."

"We need to talk to Javier," I said.

"What about Oliver and Mary?" asked Katy. "What do two lighthouse keepers who've lived almost all their adult lives on an island have to do with Hollywood?"

I looked at her.

"The best we can do is a process of elimination. If it isn't Javier, then it will have to be them."

"Unless the killer's not any of them," said Tetyana. "It could be someone else holed up somewhere on the island."

An icy shiver went through me.

"Let's get out of here," said Katy, walking toward the open door.

Leaving the library as it was, we climbed down the stairs and stepped out of the lighthouse.

Tetyana had her Tanto knife out and was clasping it in her hand, at the ready. We already had four deaths on the island, and there could be more if we couldn't figure this out fast.

The ominous message on our bathroom wall flashed into my mind again, and my brain swirled with questions.

Does that message mean none of the guests are guilty? Was there someone else hiding on the island, taking people out, one by one? Are Oliver and Mary as innocent as they say they are?

It was Mary who came running toward us when we walked in through the front doors of the main building.

"Come," she said urgently. "You have to see this."

"What is it?" asked Tetyana, suspicion in her voice. "What do you want us to see?"

"Oliver's trying to f—"

A loud clatter came from the second floor, making her stop in fright.

"What's happening now?" asked Katy.

It sounded like someone was crashing down the stairway. We all turned to look.

It was Sophia, hurtling down, looking like she'd seen a ghost.

"You have to do something," she screamed when she saw us. "He's coming to kill me!"

Sophia's hair was askew and her eyes darted back and forth. Her hand holding on to the banister was trembling. The self-assured, snobby actress-turned-writer we'd met on the first day at the dinner gala had vanished. She now looked like a trapped animal.

"Who?" I asked.

She lifted a shaking finger and pointed up the stairs.

"The killer," she whispered. "I saw him. Just now."

Stepping around her, Tetyana barreled up the stairs.

Katy and I dashed after her. From behind me, I could hear Sophia and Mary following us up.

When we got to the third floor, Tetyana was already checking Sophia's room.

"No one here," said Tetyana, turning to Sophia. "Where did you see them?"

"Him. It was a man." Sophia stumbled over to the window and pressed her nose against the pane. "I swear I saw him out there in the back."

"Outside?" said Tetyana with a glare. "Why didn't you say so?"

I stepped up next to Sophia and scanned the backyard.

"That's the woods," said Mary, coming over. "Just a clump of trees in the back."

"Are there any places for someone to hide out there?" I asked.

It was Ratcliffe, Jason, and Javier we'd sent out to the back to search for Helen. Did they find something? Is that why the first two were killed?

Mary shook her head.

"There's nothing back there, except for two graves next to the trees."

"Two graves?" said Katy. "We saw only one cross when we came by boat."

Mary nodded.

"That's for Jack Lieberman, the former keeper. He was a good man. Taught us everything we knew about lighthouse keeping."

"Who's in the second grave?" I asked.

Mary turned her eyes down.

"Little Sheila."

"Sheila?" Katy and I asked at the same time.

Sadness crossed Mary's face. She looked at the floor as if it was too hard for her to speak.

"It was tough when I lost her. I wasn't about to bury her anywhere but here. She grew up with me. She kept me company when the storms were bad. She never barked, and she always stayed—"

"Barked?" I said in relief. She was talking about her dog. Her Golden Doodle.

"Is there a structure or a building anyone can hide in back there?" asked Tetyana.

Stirring from her memories, Mary looked up and gave a slight shake of her head.

"The wind gets real rough on that end of the island. No one can bear to stay out there for very long. Nobody goes out there if they can help it."

Tetyana turned to Sophia, who was crouched in a corner, clutching her nightgown.

"You're three floors up. If anyone wanted to get you, they'll need a ladder."

Sophia's eyes widened.

"Oh, no," she said, taking in a sharp breath. "That's how he's going to kill me. He's going to come up here when I'm sleeping and do me in."

"Who's *he*?" I asked. "Did you recognize the person in the woods? Can you describe him to us?"

Sophia spun around.

"Why are you asking me all these questions! You're supposed to find him and stop him!"

Her face was flushed. She was losing her temper again.

"You people are useless!" she shrieked. "That man's going to come here and kill me and you just hang around asking dumb questions. You think I'm the one who did it, don't you?"

"I didn't say that," I said, putting my hands up in defense and taking a step back. "I was only trying to—"

"That's what you think! You think I was helping Zimmerman with his cabal!"

I stopped and looked at Sophia.

She stared at me unblinkingly, her face turning red.

I lowered my hands.

"I thought you might have been one of his victims, but you were the same age group as him, weren't you?" I said.

She spluttered, as if she was unable to compose an answer.

I leaned forward.

"Sophia, did you help Zimmerman carry out his evil work? Is someone now taking revenge for what you did?"

"Get out!" she screamed. "Get out!"

She advanced on me, fury on her face.

"You don't know me! You wouldn't care even if I told you. You'll blame me. That's what you're going to do. You're going to blame me for everything!"

"My goodness," said Katy, stumbling backward.

"Get out!" screamed Sophia. "Get out of my room!"

I heard Tetyana swear and stomp out.

"Asha, come out," she said.

I didn't turn around, keeping my eyes on the woman in front of me.

"Sophia—"

But I didn't get to finish.

She lurched toward me, put her hands on my shoulders and pushed me out.

"Hey!" I shouted.

The door slammed inches from my face.

Chapter Fifty-six

We heard her door bolt shut.

Then something heavy was dragged across the room, followed by a loud thud against the door.

Tetyana raised an eyebrow. "Securing her fort."

Mary shook her head. "Mrs. Knight's lost it. There was no one outside or I'd have seen them from the kitchen window."

She turned to me and tugged at my arm.

"Oliver made a breakthrough. You have to come downstairs."

"He knows who the killer is?" asked Katy in surprise.

But Mary had already turned around and was scurrying down the stairs.

"We don't have much time," she called out. "Hurry!"

Tetyana made a motion with her hands to say keep to the back. Katy and I kept our distance, our hands in our pockets, ready to take our knives out if needed.

"Where's Javier?" I asked when we got to the ground floor.

"Been in his room all the while," replied Mary. "He thinks we're out to get him, so we left him well alone. I can deal with only one basket case guest at a time."

When Mary got to the kitchen door, she turned around and gestured to us impatiently.

My eyes and ears were on full alert, as I wondered if we were walking into a trap.

"Come!" she said.

A strange static sound was coming from inside the kitchen.

What's that noise?

Katy and I stayed back, while Tetyana stepped up to the doorway.

"What the frigging...?"

Her face cleared, and she marched in before we could say anything.

Katy and I raced over to the door, our knives out, ready to come to Tetyana's aid. We looked in.

It was Oliver. He had got some of his color back.

He was at the kitchen table, a headset on his head and a black electronic contraption in front of him. It was a shortwave handheld radio that looked like it came from another decade.

Both devices looked like they were hanging together only by the copious lengths of duct tape wrapped around them.

He looked up as we walked in.

"Ah, there you are," he said. "I think I got it to work. Got a connection ten minutes ago, but it dropped."

I scanned the kitchen.

There was no one else here other than the Hudsons. Even through the crisis, Mary had kept a neat and clean kitchen. There was nothing untoward here at first glance.

But I kept vigilant, as I had no clue how or where the killer could strike next. Next to me, Katy had turned around and was watching the doorway, just in case someone would come in that way.

Tetyana reached over to the walkie-talkie.

"Don't touch that," said Oliver. "Please."

"Why?" said Tetyana, her voice hard.

"It took forever to piece the receiver together. Don't know if I can do it again."

She leaned over to examine his handiwork.

"Show me how it works," she demanded.

Oliver pivoted the black box toward Tetyana and turned a few dials.

A loud stream of static came through the half-broken speaker. He bent down and turned more dials, his full attention on the radio.

"Been at it for a while. I heard them speaking at one point," he muttered as he worked on the switches. "They didn't hear me but—"

"Who did you hear?" asked Tetyana.

"The Coast Guard team at the station back on the mainland. They were talking to a sailboat near the coast."

"Good work," said Tetyana.

"We just have to get a continuous channel up. It keeps dropping," said Oliver.

He increased the volume, and the static got louder. Mary covered her ears.

"If I can only open two-way communications," said Oliver as he tried to find the right channel, "I can send out an SOS."

"What about the lighthouse light?" I asked. "If that's not worked for decades, wouldn't it alert someone?"

Mary shook her head.

"They usually don't patrol the waters around here anymore. They'll come if someone complains or if they have time on their hands and get curious, but they won't make a special trip out here."

"Can we make it turn toward the mainland, and flicker to send an SOS message?" I asked.

Oliver looked up at me.

"It's a superb idea, but I wouldn't know how. The construction crew upgraded everything and put that fancy electrical panel. I think only the owner knows how it works. If you ladies can figure it out, please go ahead."

My mind buzzed.

Oliver had been with us when Ratcliffe died, so he couldn't have got to the lighthouse in time to commit the murder and sabotage the ladder. But we only had his word that Mary was asleep in bed.

Looking at the petite woman next to us, I couldn't imagine her killing Ratcliffe with such force.

Time to ask a few questions.

"This means whoever turned the light on, knew how that new installation works," I said. "If only the owner knows how it works, the owner should be here on the island."

I paused.

Mary and Oliver exchanged a glance.

"We were thinking the same thing," said Mary.

"What about your theory about the Mafia rival?" I asked.

"That was a silly guess," she replied, shaking her head. "Plus, Ratcliffe's now gone. This means, it has to be our new owner."

Oliver nodded. "They knew exactly how the place was rebuilt and how that light works. I don't know why they're doing this, but it's got to be them."

"Do either of you have any connection with Hollywood?" I asked.

Oliver and Mary looked up in surprise.

"Only what we see on TV," said Mary.

"When the construction crew came last summer," I said, "did you see anyone who looked like any of the guests?"

"We've never seen any of them before," said Oliver.

"Wait," said his wife, putting a hand on his shoulder. "Remember when the construction manager said we could take two weeks off because they were doing some jack-hammering?"

He nodded.

Mary turned to us.

"They gave us a ride to the mainland in their fancy helicopter too. We went to Portland and stayed with our daughter for two weeks. It was like a mini holiday."

"Two full weeks when you had no clue who was coming and going out of here?" I asked.

The couple nodded.

"To be honest, I never thought the owner would come until all the work was done."

The radio came to life, silencing us.

We could hear voices. The sound crackled, fading in and out. Oliver adjusted a few dials.

"Mayday. Mayday. This is Coffin Island Lighthouse. Over."

Nothing.

"I'll keep trying," said Oliver, fiddling with the buttons.

"Mayday. Mayday. This is Coffin Island Lighthouse. Police assistance required. Twelve adults...eight adults. In danger."

Silence.

Tetyana leaned over and lowered her voice.

"When you do connect, you can tell them we're down to seven now."

Oliver gave her a shocked look. Mary put a hand over her mouth.

"It's Elliot, isn't it?" she asked in a whisper.

"He fell through the library window to the rocks below," I said.

"How in heck can that even happen?" asked Oliver.

"Someone sabotaged the library ladder, and put his book on the top shelf, right next to the window," I explained. "They planned it so when he climbed up to get it, the ladder would slam against the far wall and he'd fall through the window. It was a risky idea, but they succeeded."

"You didn't hear him scream?" asked Katy.

"We heard Sophia shout about something when she ran inside," said Mary. "I tried to talk to her, but she was so upset. She ran up to her room and shut the door on me."

"I was here all the time," said Oliver, pointing at the radio, "trying to fix this. I didn't hear Mr. Ward... Mr. Ward... oh dear good lord."

We stood quietly for a while, contemplating Elliot's death.

"We're next, aren't we?" said Mary, looking at us. "We're doomed."

"If we don't find a way out of here, we're going to have more deaths in our hands," said Tetyana in a grim voice.

Mary got up.

"I don't know about y'all, but I'm going to make tea," she said.

She shot a determined look at us.

"If I'm going to die, I can at least have a good cuppa first."

As if waking up from a trance, Oliver turned back to the radio. His voice was now laced in panic.

"Mayday! Mayday! This is Coffin Island Lighthouse. Police assistance required immediately. Over."

Nothing.

My brain whirred.

Would the Hudsons try to get help from the authorities if they were the culprits? It had to be one of the only two writers left on the island.

Something crashed to the floor.

I spun around.

"Mary?" cried Oliver swiveling around. "You okay?"

She was staring out the back kitchen window. On the ground next to her was a broken ceramic cup.

"What is it?" I asked, running toward her.

"She was right," whispered Mary.

"Who? About what?" asked Katy.

"The shadow," stammered Mary, pointing at the tree line on the north side of the island. "I saw him. It's the killer."

That was when I saw it too.

A hazy shadow of a man next to the dark clump of trees.

Chapter Fifty-seven

I yanked the back door open and sprang out.

Katy and Tetyana dashed after me.

The second we ran out, the shadow melted into the trees. But I was sure what I had seen—the silhouette of a thin man on the small side. There was only one person who it could be.

"Javier," I said, as we ran toward the trees. "It has to be him."

I kicked myself for not thinking of him earlier. Katy had noticed it on our first day. There was something odd and familiar about the poet, she'd said.

Did he really get injured from that attempt to fall down the stairs?

The line of spruce trees stood in a semicircle at the north edge of the island.

The clouds had parted now and the half moon was out, but the moonlight was overshadowed by the light from the lighthouse lantern. That massive light was facing the ocean, but there was enough for us to see where we were going out here in the back.

The eerie light cast strange shadows on the ground and made the trees at the edge of the cliff look like giants hunkering down, hiding something from us.

"Where's that bastard?" said Tetyana, swiveling her head. "Where the hell did he disappear to?"

The cross in the far end reflected a ghostly white, the kind of white you'd see with black light in a dark room.

We had slowed down and Tetyana was now behind us, brandishing her knife in her hand, scanning the grounds. Katy and I walked stealthily in front, Katy keeping an eye to her left and me scanning the grounds to our right.

All we had on us were the Swiss Army knives Tetyana had given us.

If I survive this, I promised myself, I'm bringing my Glock with me everywhere I go. Even if it's to serve cupcakes at a birthday party.

We progressed forward, watching each other's backs, like a small SWAT team ready for combat.

I didn't know what to expect, but I couldn't shake that feeling something or someone was about to jump on us at any moment.

If it was just Javier, we could easily tackle him. The problem was our missing gun and the identity of this mysterious new owner.

Who had our gun? Was Javier in league with someone else? Were they armed?

We got to the cliff, and we still hadn't seen or heard a thing. Fifty feet below us, the ocean waves were crashing on the shore, much more subdued than before.

I felt goose bumps on my arm upon spotting the two graves. They lay silently, side by side, in front of the circle of trees.

They reminded me of Madame Bouchard lying in an exorbitantly priced cemetery reserved for celebrities and socialites in upstate New York.

She had carved out a fascinating life for herself. But even in her death, she hadn't stopped playing her games. What a woman, I thought, sending us on impossible missions like this. Putting our lives at risk.

We stepped up to the graves, one for a man and another for a dog. There was something eerie about seeing them with the pale moonlight from above and the lighthouse lantern shining from the side.

We scanned the area, but there was no one behind the trees or near the graves.

Unlike the sheer cliff near the lighthouse, the slope on this side of the island had a more gradual incline with a few scraggly trees jutting out of the ledges.

If Elliot had fallen down on this end, he would have survived.

"Check the shore," whispered Tetyana as Katy and I peered over the edge while she stood on guard behind us.

"Nothing," said Katy, shaking her head. "There's no one down here."

I got up and dusted myself off, my mind buzzing.

Did I imagine the shadow? Did Mary's reaction prompt me to see something I didn't see? Did she make it up to distract us from the real killer?

It had been dark near the trees, and I had an active imagination, but I wasn't stupid. I glanced around in frustration and turned to look back at the main building.

It rose behind us like a stately resort mansion. It was difficult to imagine so much horror was going on in that beautiful place.

Sophia still had her bedroom light on, but there was no sign of her near the window. I imagined her huddled under her covers, shaking with fright, waiting for the killer to climb up and get her.

The lights on the first floor were all on as well. Oliver and Mary were still in the kitchen, and, I hoped, making progress with the radio.

"This is fresh," said Tetyana.

I spun around to see her kneeling next to the grave without the cross.

"That one has to be Sheila's," said Katy.

"It's a pretty big grave for a Golden Doodle," said Tetyana. "When did Mary say that dog died?"

I racked my brain to think back to our conversation.

"Oliver said six months ago," I said, as I walked over to where Tetyana was.

I bent down and brushed my hand over the loose soil.

"This doesn't look like a six-month-old grave," I said.

"Someone dug this recently," said Tetyana.

"Why would anyone dig up a dog's grave?" I asked.

"I can think of one reason, and it's a pretty freaky one." said Katy.

"Tell us," said Tetyana. "You'd be surprised what I'd believe right now."

"They dug up the dog and buried something else in here," said Katy. "Or someone—"

"Frigging heck!" cried Tetyana, stepping back.

Katy and I looked at her in alarm. Tetyana's eyes were on the grave, staring at something in front of her.

"What is it?" I asked.

"Take a look at this," she said, gesturing to us to get closer.

"It's a black pipe," said Katy, kneeling down. "A PVC pipe."

She was right. There was something small and black sticking out of the loose soil on the dog's grave.

We scoured the area to see if any more pipes were sticking out.

"Just the one," I said, "whatever is it for?"

"Did you hear that?" said Katy, putting a hand on my arm.

I scanned the grounds to make sure no one was approaching us.

"Down here," said Katy in a hushed voice. "Closer to the ground."

I put my ear next to the pipe, wondering what she was talking about.

I pulled back, startled.

"Did you hear it too?" whispered Katy.

I bent over again.

The sound was unmistakable.

Knock, Knock, Knock.

"Oh my goodness," I said, pulling back, my heart hammering. "What fresh hell is this now?"

Tetyana pushed me aside and put her ear against the pipe.

She looked up, her face grim.

"I bet you every dollar I have, someone's buried right underneath here, and they're still alive."

"Buried alive?" I whispered in shock.

"We need to get them out," said Tetyana, jumping to her feet. "Shovels!" she yelled, running toward the house.

"In the back shed," I said, jumping up.

We ran across the grounds, helter-skelter, toward the house.

I was no longer thinking. I was no longer rationalizing.

Things had turned out so strange that if a bulbous-eyed, green alien dropped from the sky, I would not have blinked an eye.

All I knew was there might be a person buried alive, and we had to get them out.

When Katy and I reached the shed, Tetyana had already found two shovels and a large trowel. Picking up our tools, we raced back toward the graves.

I thought I saw something move behind the building. Maybe it was my imagination, maybe it was Oliver coming out to check on us, but I didn't have time to stop and look.

We dug as fast as we could.

The more we dug, the louder the knocking came.

My heart was thumping so hard, that at some point, I could no longer distinguish between the sinister knocking and my heart pumping in my chest.

Tetyana hit the wood first.

Throwing the shovel off, she jumped down, got on her knees, and scraped the soil away with her bare hands.

"There," she said.

"Heavy cardboard," I said, getting on my knees and peering down. "Looks like softwood."

"It's a coffin," whispered Katy.

That was when the knocking turned frantic. It was like they knew we were here, trying to get them out. They were struggling.

Then, an eerie moaning came from the box.

"Still there!" cried Tetyana. We picked our shovels again and dug frantically, using every ounce of energy we had in us.

"Aiee!"

Katy's screech made me jump, and I nearly fell into the hole.

"Jeez," said Tetyana, spinning around. "What the hell, Katy?"

Katy put a hand to her chest and pointed at something small and white she'd just uncovered. I leaned over and nuzzled it with the end of my shovel.

"A dog's skull," I said, with a shudder. "We found Sheila."

Chapter Fifty-eight

I set the skull to the side gingerly.

"Forgive us, Sheila," I whispered, feeling terrible for desecrating a grave, even if it only belonged to a dog.

The person inside the casket had gone silent.

My heart stopped for a second.

Did they die on us?

Please, no.

I thumped my fist once near the end of the box, where I assumed their feet were.

"Hey, you all right? Stay with us. We're getting you out, okay?"

A low moan came from inside.

"Keep breathing!" shouted Katy.

Another moan.

"The Girl Who Lived," I whispered.

I looked up at my friends.

"It has to be Helen Jenkins," I said.

"Helen?" Katy called out in a cracked voice. "Is it you?"

A frenzy of knocks came in reply.

A shiver went down my spine.

"Goodness me," said Katy, shaking her head.

"Get digging, girls!" called out Tetyana, getting back to work.

We moved fast, sweat streaming down our faces, talking to Helen, unsure what condition we'd find her in. Tetyana and I made another trip back to the shed to find straps, metal hooks, planks—anything to help us haul Helen out as smoothly as we could.

It was a relief to get the box finally to the surface, almost half an hour after we found her.

I ran my fingers along the sides of the coffin, looking for a latch, a lock. Nothing.

Did they seal her in?

Whoever did this had planned well.

It was an ingenious job, just as they had done with the gas leak in Camilla's room, the tampered ladder in the library, and the deadly swordfish in the lantern room. They'd prepared and executed with precision.

Evil. Horrible evil.

"Stay back!" shouted Tetyana as she grabbed a shovel and slammed it against the edge of the box. Once. Twice. Three times.

The cardboard splintered easier than I expected.

We scrambled to rip the lid open.

"Helen!" called out Katy. "Almost there!"

Pulling together, we pried the cracked lid open and threw it to the side.

Helen Jenkins was wearing the same suit she wore when we saw her at the threshold of the dining room.

Her eyes had been blindfolded, and her mouth had been gagged with a black rag. Her skin looked pale and sickly under the moonlight.

Katy leaned over and untied her gag while Tetyana worked on her blindfold. With the gag gone, Helen gasped for air, her chest heaving uncontrollably. She lifted a trembling arm up and clutched at the air.

I thrust my hand out and latched on to her hand.

"Helen," I said, "it's okay. You're going to be fine."

She squeezed my hand, but she was weak. She tried to say something in a croaking voice, but didn't get any words out.

I wondered how long she'd been inside of this hellish box, with no water and only a small pipe to breathe from. It was a miracle she had survived.

We helped her sit up, talking to her, reassuring her, while Helen looked around disoriented, blinking rapidly, still holding on to my hand.

"Where am I?" she whispered.

"You're safe now, hun," said Katy. "We got you."

I wondered if she knew what had happened to her. If she realized she was sitting in a casket in a graveyard on Coffin island.

She gave a confused look at us.

"Who are you?"

"We're friends," I said.

"We need to get you hydrated," said Tetyana. "Let's get you the hell out of here."

Tetyana and Katy helped her stand up and step out of the box. That was when I saw the stack of papers that had been lying under her shoulders all this time.

"The manuscript!" I cried, leaning in to pluck it out.

Next to the book was a white cloth the size of a handkerchief. I picked it up and sniffed it.

Chloroform.

Helen was having a coughing fit now. My friends led her to the nearest tree for her to sit and catch her breath.

I looked at the manuscript in my hands. This is the key to our mystery, I thought, as I flipped through the pages.

Helen was now sitting on the ground, leaning against Katy's shoulder, looking spent. She was staring at the opened box.

"I... I was in *there*?" she said, shooting us a frightened look.

We nodded.

"Somebody took you, blindfolded you, put you in this box and buried you alive," said Tetyana.

I hated we had to be so blunt after such a traumatizing event. But the killer was still out there, waiting to get us.

"Do you know who did this to you?" I asked, softening my voice.

Helen stared blankly at me for a moment, then nodded.

"Who?" said Katy. "Is it Javier?"

We'd been so engrossed with getting Helen out, we hadn't noticed the shadow that had crept up to the tree line.

I felt the sudden push on the small of my back, but it was too late. With a surprised yell, I stumbled over the box and fell face first into the open hole, clutching the manuscript to my chest.

I felt soil drop on me and covered my eyes.

"Asha!" screamed Katy.

"What the bloody hell?" I heard Tetyana shout.

I scrambled to sit up, shielding my eyes from the falling soil. I couldn't make out what was going on, other than a lot of yelling, screaming, and shouting.

I vaguely noticed a figure standing above me, at the edge of the hole. Putting a hand over my eyes, I glanced up to see Javier, a black handgun in his hands, pointed straight at my head.

Before I could do anything, a dark panther-like shadow jumped on Javier and threw him to the ground. The gun fell into the grave, inches from me.

It was Tetyana's Glock.

Katy ran over to give me a hand up, and I clambered out of the grave.

Tetyana had pinned Javier to the ground. Javier was struggling, but he could do little harm now. Tetyana's face looked so ferocious, I was sure she was going to beat him to a pulp.

Did he seriously think he could do me in with my friends watching?

"What the hell are you playing at?" I yelled.

He stopped wiggling and turned to me with a livid glare.

"This is all your handiwork, isn't it?" I said. "Why in god's name are you doing this?"

"This is all my fault," came a small voice from behind me.

I turned around.

It was Helen, leaning against the tree, speaking feebly.

"What do you mean?" I asked, my eyes narrowing, wondering if they were somehow both in this together.

"All of it."

"How?" I asked.

"I wrote the book," she said, pointing at the manuscript in my hand.

Javier's face had contorted into rage. If his eyes had been on fire, he'd have scorched Helen to ashes.

I looked down at the manuscript, trying to understand what made this so special to warrant four brutal deaths.

Someone didn't want this book to be published. I squinted to read the synopsis.

"This is a bio," I said, "of Zimmerman."

I looked at Helen.

She nodded weakly, as if too tired to speak.

I turned to Javier. A deathly fury had overtaken him, one I'd never have imagined the quiet poet to have in him.

What was the link between Zimmerman and Javier?

Javier saw me look.

"It's about the man who raped my sister," he said, anger boiling in his voice.

Chapter Fifty-nine

Helen was trembling.

I wasn't sure if it was from the trauma of being buried underground or because she was finally facing the man who had attempted to murder her.

"I did it because...because..." She looked down and went silent for a minute, her face drained of energy.

We waited.

Javier twisted around in Tetyana's clutches.

"You dragged my sister's name through mud," he said, his voice bitter. "You made Maria look like a prostitute!"

Maria?

I peered at Javier.

Maria Pablo?

"No," said Helen, looking up, shaking her head. "Believe me when I tell you. I never wanted to do that. I fought with my editor and my agent. I told them I wouldn't..."

"Then why did you take the job?" said Javier.

"I did it for my... because I had no choice...." stammered Helen.

Her voice was raspy. She needed water.

"You'll do anything for money," said Javier, spitting to the side. "That's all you care about. Just like the others."

"My mother had cancer!"

It was surprising to hear Helen shout, given her condition. Her face had gone dark, and she was no longer leaning against Katy. It was like she'd received a sudden burst of energy from within.

"My mother was dying. The only way I could fund her treatments was to sign that contract."

"What contract?" I asked.

"The publisher offered me a twenty-five-thousand-dollar advance to write this book. How could I say no when...."

Javier's face turned purple.

"Is that what my dead sister's life was worth? All that abuse and hell she went through?"

"That's what my mother's life is worth!" shouted Helen back. "I used every penny on her, so she'd get better."

She looked away, shaking. Katy touched her arm, but Helen pushed my friend away.

I remembered Maria Pablo.

She was an aspiring young Hollywood star, adored by the world, when she shot the director who abused her.

It had happened in public.

Katy and I had been at that awards gala. We had seen her pull out the revolver from her purse, and we had heard that fatal shot ring out.

The director had crumpled to the ground, his blood splattering on my lovely four-tiered cake he was just about to cut to open the ceremonies.

I turned to Helen.

"The first day when you came here, one or more of the guests shocked you. It was Javier, wasn't it?"

Helen didn't answer.

"How did you know him?"

She turned her eyes on the young poet, still pinned to the ground by Tetyana.

I knew Tetyana wanted to haul him away and lock him up somewhere inside the house till the authorities arrived. But this conversation was more revealing to us than any interrogation the police could do.

All we had to do was keep them talking.

"I didn't see him at first," said Helen, in a low voice. "But I saw the others. When I saw them all together in one room, I realized why I'd been invited. I knew what was going to happen on this retreat."

"None of them deserved to live," said Javier through gritted teeth.

"How did you get Helen from the shore up here?" I asked the question that had been bothering me all along.

Javier gave me a pained look.

"You never pushed her, did you?" I said, suddenly realizing how he had done it.

He shook his head.

"He got me when I was outside the building," said Helen. "He said he could show me a way out of the island, but brought me here instead. Next thing I knew, I was inside a dark box, a blind on my eyes and a gag in my mouth."

Helen shuddered and wrapped her arms around herself.

"Who did Camilla see down at the shore then?" asked Katy.

Javier shrugged.

"It was you, wasn't it?" I said. "You pretended to be Helen, and you had her coat on you, am I right?"

Another shrug.

"I bet you a hundred bucks, that coat is in his room," said Tetyana.

"Francesco Javier Quinteiro," I said, looking at him. "Is that your actual name?"

He glared.

"And your sister?" I asked.

Javier's eyes teared up, and he looked away. His head slumped against the ground.

"Maria Pablo," I said. "She had a different last name from you. That's why I didn't make the connection."

"It was her stage name," said Helen. "She changed it when she came to America."

"What about the others?" I asked. "Jason Taylor wrote graphic novels and did technical work in studios. Why was he killed?"

Helen grimaced and turned away.

"He edited those vile videos for Zimmerman and his crowd, am I right?" I asked.

No one replied. I turned to Javier.

"Maria was in those videos. You stabbed him because of his role in her abuse."

Javier didn't raise his head, but his silence told me everything.

"Elliot used to be a Hollywood agent and then went silent for ten years," I continued. "He represented Maria, didn't he?"

Silence.

"It's exactly ten years since Maria shot the director and hanged herself. Her agent knew what was going on. He was complicit in those crimes, so Elliot had to die too."

Helen nodded.

Javier stayed quiet.

"What about Sophia?" asked Katy. "She's still alive. Does that mean she's innocent?"

"You didn't invite everyone for kicks and fun, did you?" I said to Javier. "Everyone was here for a reason. Because of something they did to your sister."

"Sophia lured young actors and actresses into the circle," said Helen. "She pretended to be a mentor, someone who could teach them the ropes of Hollywood."

She paused and swallowed. She was getting tired.

"Isn't that what psychopaths like Bernardo did?" said Katy, her face scrunching in disgust.

"I swear to everything holy," said Tetyana, "I'm going to kill that sick woman myself."

Things were slowly falling into place.

Our initial hunches about Sophia, Elliot, and Jason had been right. There were still some missing pieces, but the picture we were building was a horrific one.

Javier was still silent. He was no longer struggling, but Tetyana had him in her vice-like grip just in case he tried to escape.

"Camilla," said Katy, turning around to Helen. "That British woman. What was her role?"

A flash of anger crossed Helen's face.

"Zimmerman's right hand," she replied. "She revamped herself as an erotica writer, but she was a personal assistant to powerful LA execs for a long time. She made the appointments, kept the books, and chose the girls."

That explained the chumminess between Camilla, Sophia, and Elliot. They had all played important parts in that perverse circle of predators.

A chill went through me as I realized we had sat next to some of the most evil people disguised as industry leaders and celebrated artists.

They were worse than the typical serial killer, like Paul Bernardo. Ten times worse. They created power structures and strong networks to commit horrific systemic crimes and get away with it.

I turned to Javier, and narrowed my eyes. I wasn't done with him yet.

"Why did you push me into the hole and point a gun at me?"

"I wanted you to tell everyone what happened to my sister. Instead you turned against me!"

Katy and I exchanged a confused glance.

"You wanted us to support your murders?" said Katy.

"I thought you'd be on my side," said Javier. "You fight for justice, don't you?"

"You've got to be kidding me," said Tetyana, shaking her head.

"And that message on our bathroom wall?" said Katy. "What was that about?"

"I knew you liked mysteries, so I gave you one."

I took a deep breath in to settle my nerves. I kicked myself for not seeing Javier for who he truly was.

"You planned all this last summer, didn't you?" I asked. "Bringing in that construction crew here to set it all up."

Javier gave a glum nod.

"The crew had no clue what you were planning, did they?" I said. "They probably thought you were just another eccentric millionaire who didn't know what to do with their money."

Javier let out a sigh.

"Only Mike knew."

"Mike?" said Tetyana and Katy at the same time.

"The boat captain?" I asked. "Did he help you? Why?"

"He had a lot of debt on that boat. He wanted to escape and make a new life in Mexico," said Javier in a low monotone, like he no longer cared. "He's probably there already."

"So the boat wreck," said Tetyana, "was deliberate?"

Javier looked at her. He didn't have to say anything.

He had planned everything well. Very well.

"What about Ratcliffe?" I said. "He was the publisher who was going to release the book, right? Your agent worked it out with him, I presume?"

Helen nodded glumly.

"My contract said I had to write Zimmerman like a hero," she said, her eyes dull, like the life had gone out of her. "A misunderstood man who had been unreasonably maligned by the public."

"Did Ratcliffe want you to write about the other guests too?"

Helen shook her head.

"All I had was unsubstantiated evidence, but Ratcliffe didn't care either way. It was all the same to him. Juicy gossip that would sell."

Helen paused to swallow.

"My agent was pushing me to finish the book this month."

"Why now?" I asked.

"Because Ratcliffe wanted to release it on the tenth anniversary of Maria's suicide."

"How cruel can you get?" said Katy, shaking her head.

"It was his inside joke," said Helen, her voice flat. "Ratcliffe thought it would be funny."

Chapter Sixty

But something didn't add up.

I turned to the poet.

"How did you know about the manuscript? Aren't these things usually kept in secret?"

Neither Helen nor Javier spoke.

Tetyana pulled Javier into an upright position and leaned back.

It looked like someone had pulled a pin on him and all the air had been depleted. I was sure he couldn't run now, even if he'd wanted to.

"It was me who told him," said Helen in such a low voice I wasn't sure I'd heard her correctly.

"You?" said Katy in surprise.

Helen nodded.

"I... I... didn't know what to do. I knew what I was writing was going to hurt many people, but they'd already paid me for the job."

She paused for a long moment.

"I was going crazy. I couldn't live with myself. One day, after I downed a half a bottle of vodka, I emailed a copy to Javier using an anonymous account."

We all turned to Javier, but he had his eyes cast down.

"I'm so sorry," blurted Helen, her voice cracking. Tears rolled down her face.

"I'm so sorry. I needed the advance. If my agent said Ratcliffe wanted me to write Hitler as an angel, I would have. I did it for my mother. I didn't have a choice."

She put her head on Katy's shoulder and sobbed.

"Javier," I said, lowering my voice. "Why did you jump in the water the first day, when we were on the mainland?"

He stayed quiet for a long time. All we heard was Helen crying.

"I wanted to end it right there and then," said Javier finally, his eyes focused on the grass. "I didn't want to go ahead with my plan."

An icy shiver went through me as I realized what I'd done. I'd saved one man, which had led to the deaths of four.

"And that fall down the stairs?" I asked.

He shook his head.

"I made it happen. I wanted you to think I couldn't walk." He looked down at his foot. "A swollen ankle is nothing compared to what my sister went through."

Tetyana glared at him.

"Here's what I want to know," she said, straightening him up. "Who is the owner of this godforsaken island? Is it you? How the hell can you afford to buy an island?"

"I'm the poet laureate of Mexico," he answered, tears streaming down his face. "I'd been planning for this for a long time. Helen's book only made me want to finish this job faster. I worked hard and by last year, I could afford to buy this place."

One with a decommissioned lighthouse a small town wanted to get rid of.

He got lucky.

"I wanted them all to suffer like my sister did," said Javier, crying now.

We waited, listening to Helen's sobs and Javier's lumbering breaths. The trees protected us from the winds, but they were picking up and the air was getting chillier.

I wasn't sure what to think.

Javier was our killer.

Would I have done the same, if the most powerful cabal in Hollywood had repeatedly raped my sister?

Maria Pablo had only been eighteen years old, still a teenager. How could she have saved herself when the entire industry had been against her?

A strange hum came from the distance. Tetyana let go of Javier and sprang to her feet.

The hum got louder until it sounded like a fleet of race cars were zooming toward the island.

"Coast Guard boats," said Tetyana. "Oliver's radio must have worked."

Another thundering sound came closer to the island. It was loud and getting louder until I felt like the entire island was shaking.

"Rescue chopper," said Tetyana. She walked across the graveyard toward the building, her face up, searching for the machine.

It appeared above us, whirring overhead like an enormous angry bird.

We all turned our faces up to watch the red helicopter hover over us. A blinding strobe light swept the island, splashed across the main resort building, the trees at the end, the open grave, and finally settled on us.

We stood silently in place.

Too shocked to react.

How are we ever going to explain what happened here?

Something from behind me made me spin around.

"Javier!" I shouted.

He was almost at the end of the cliff.

"Hey!" I yelled, running toward him.

"Stop!" hollered Katy from behind me.

We got to him just as he teetered on the edge. I grabbed him by the collar of his jacket. Katy glommed on to his sleeve.

He struggled.

We held on.

That was when I saw the brown rope ladder dangling against the cliff face. It was so dusty, it blended well with the cliff. No wonder I hadn't noticed it before.

The ladder registered in my mind only for a second, but I now knew how Javier had stolen Tetyana's gun and got out of sight without us noticing.

"What the hell are you doing?" I said, keeping my grip on him. "Trying to escape?"

He shot me an angry look.

Suddenly, he slipped out of his jacket, making us stumble back. I stared at the jacket in my hands, startled at what he'd done so swiftly.

"I'm escaping from *life,*" he said, taking a step back toward the edge of the cliff.

"No!" Katy and I cried at the same time.

He glared at us.

"Javier," said Katy, "please listen—"

"No, you listen to me!" he shouted. "I'm tired of everyone taking advantage of me. I'm sick of everyone treating me like some dinner party trophy. They all talk about me, but they never talk *to* me, do they?"

His face convulsed, like he was about to cry.

"Nobody asks me what happened to Maria or how I'm feeling. Nobody cares what happened to Maria. *Nobody!*"

"Javier," I said. "We'll work something out—"

He turned to me.

"That cake you brought was my sister's favorite dessert. I wanted to try it one last time before I...I..."

"You what?" I said, taking a small step forward.

He pointed at his jacket in my arms.

"Take that and save yourself. That's all you need."

What's he talking about?

Javier closed his eyes.

I took another stealthy step forward. Katy took one on her end.

"I will pay for my sins," I heard him whisper.

Before we could grab him, he spun around and jumped off the cliff to the shores below.

Katy and I screamed.

Chapter Sixty-one

"In the boat, now!"

"But—"

"No arguing!" bellowed the uniformed officer.

Her face told us she wasn't in the mood for a conversation.

I wasn't sure what Oliver had told them on the radio, but the Coast Guard and marine police teams that were scouring the island were all in a nasty mood.

Javier had made one mistake in his calculations.

If his jump from the cliff had been another attempt to take his life, he had failed again.

He'd stumbled down and landed on a ledge below, caught in the branches of a tree growing from the cliff face.

The helicopter swooped over him in a split second.

By the time Javier untangled himself and was ready to jump again, a first responder had descended from the helicopter. Within seconds, the rescuer had grabbed Javier by the waist and the poet went limp, like he'd given up.

Katy and I watched from the cliff edge as they hoisted him back up to the chopper. It had all happened so fast, I don't think I blinked through the entire operation.

But something about the way Javier reacted to his rescue gnawed at me.

He hadn't struggled. He hadn't even spoken to his rescuer, who had called out to him several times.

Javier was a man who had fooled everyone.

He had calmly and patiently planned the deadly revenge of all who'd hurt his sister a decade ago. Someone with that level of intellectual prowess had to have something up his sleeve when he went quiet like this.

The helicopter had scarcely lifted off, when half a dozen officers in uniform rushed toward us from the back kitchen door.

We stood rooted to our spots, petrified, as they ran up, handguns pointed our way.

It had been easy to identify the senior officer in the team.

With her hair pulled back into a smart ponytail, a scowl that rivaled any bulldog's, and a uniform with more stripes than the other men, I knew instantly who was in charge.

"Hands up!" she hollered.

We obeyed.

I wanted to explain everything to her, but she wasn't having any of it. She commandeered one of her men to pick up the manuscript and gun lying at my feet, another two to take photos of the backyard and the coffin, and ordered the rest of her team to march Tetyana, Katy, and me to their skiff on the shore.

"Why are they arresting us?" whispered Katy when the two junior officers escorted us to the largest boat tied to the island's pier.

"Stay calm and do what they say," said Tetyana in a low voice. "Don't make any sudden movements."

Katy and I nodded.

We took our seats on the hard bench on the deck while the two officers stationed themselves at the two ends of the police boat.

Where would we escape to, even if we had wanted to, I wondered, watching them, watching us?

I clutched Javier's camouflage jacket to my chest like a security blanket, still reeling from everything that had happened over the past hour.

At least they hadn't handcuffed us.

"Are they going to think it was us who did all this?" whispered Katy again.

Helen will get us out of this, I thought, crossing my fingers. *She will tell them what happened.*

But she wasn't here to help us. She'd instantly fainted at the sight of the Coast Guard rushing at us and had to be airlifted by the helicopter.

Only a few minutes after we watched the chopper take Javier, it picked Helen up on a stretcher. Then, it picked up a hysterical Sophia, who looked like she was having a hyper panic attack.

Within minutes, the helicopter turned around and took off in the direction of the mainland with Javier, Helen, and Sophia on board.

"Where are you taking them?" I asked, turning to the officer stationed nearest to us on the boat.

"Hospital," he said. "Medical emergencies. All of them."

I doubted Sophia had any medical issues, but I was glad Helen was going to be taken care of soon.

I hoped Sophia wouldn't get away with what she'd done.

A pang of guilt went through me to think I'd made Helen talk after being buried alive. She needed water, rest, and more psychological counseling than I could imagine.

"What about Javier?" whispered Katy. "Is he going to go scot-free?"

I reached over and squeezed Katy's shaking hand.

She was distraught, certain we were going to be thrown in jail for something we didn't do. I was anxious too, but I wasn't about to show it in front of the officers. That would only make them more suspicious.

"They have good forensics teams and investigators who know what they're doing," I said. "They'll connect the dots. Plus, Javier was alive when they took him. They'll make him talk."

"Unless he's got more games up his sleeve," said Tetyana, who'd been calmly watching the frantic police activity, with a grim look on her face.

"I can't believe what he did to poor Helen," said Katy, shaking her head. "Imagine getting buried alive. It's my worst nightmare. He'd better pay for that at least."

"Who's that?" said Tetyana.

Four figures had appeared at the top of the cliff, near the entrance to the walkway.

"Oliver and Mary," I said, perking up.

They were flanked by two officers and were making their way down the walkway. We watched as they came down slowly.

I crossed my fingers, hoping they'd join us in the boat so we could ask them what had happened.

What did they tell the police?

To my dismay, the officers ushered them into the smaller dinghy. Mary looked over her shoulder at us and gave a subdued wave.

I wondered if we'd been too trusting of them.

A police officer stood in between the two boats, discouraging any conversation.

The shoulder radios on the officers crackled to life and a female voice came through the air.

"Four deceased bodies," said the voice. It was their sergeant. "We need a coroner, a forensics unit, and a vehicle to take them back, once done. Get on it immediately."

The two officers in our boat exchanged a surprised glance.

"Did Sarge say *four* bodies?" whispered one to the other.

"What the hell happened here?" replied the other, turning to us.

"It was a nightmare," said Katy. "It was the poet from Mexico. He was going around killing everyone to avenge his sister's death."

"The *poet*?" said the second officer.

"We only learned about it now," said Katy. "You have to make him talk. He will tell you everything."

"A *poet*?" said the man again. "You've got to be kidding me. Did he go psycho or something?"

"If you didn't come," said Katy, "we would have been next."

"Jeez. What a horror show."

They were in a talkative mood. Time to strike.

"Do you know what happened to Mike, the ferry operator? He never came to pick us up."

The first officer nodded.

"Found his boat smashed on the rocks near the mainland," he said. "Got a call from a local kid who saw the wreck."

"Oh, no. Is Mike okay?" I asked.

"The boat was rammed and abandoned," he replied. "If you ask me, he's gone off to Mexico already."

If he only knew.

"Insurance scams are a dime a dozen," said the second officer, shaking his head, "nothing as spectacular as this usually, but they happen all the time."

So they don't think any of this is related?

I was about to reply, when we saw another figure come down the walkway.

It was their sergeant.

We fell silent. The officers got back to standing at attention.

Their sergeant ran down the walkway, surefooted and steady, a deep frown on her face. I felt a growing sense of dread, the closer she got to the boat.

Chapter Sixty-two

"Did you take their statements?"

The two officers jumped to attention as the sergeant approached the boat.

"No, Sarge," they replied in unison.

"Get to it, then. What are you waiting for?" she said in an impatient voice as she walked over to the dinghy where Oliver and Mary were sitting.

"Get the Hudsons back to the mainland ASAP," she said to the officer guarding the dinghy. "I will come in the other boat."

Mary turned and pointed at us.

"They helped us," she said in a shaky voice. "They were trying to—"

"I'll be the judge of that, Mary," said the sergeant as she marched to our boat.

That was when I realized the butler and cook no doubt knew almost everyone in town, including the local police and Coast Guard detachments. They had been on this island for over two decades.

It was us who were from out of town. We were going to be under suspicion.

The sergeant jumped up the plank and onto our boat. She came over and loomed over us, hands on her hips, while the two officers took their phones out to record our statements.

While Katy nodded and uttered encouraging uh-huhs, and Tetyana listened silently, I laid everything out. The more I told our story, the more unbelievable it sounded even to my ears.

And I'd seen the dead bodies, and I'd heard Javier's confession.

The officers' facial expressions vacillated from disbelief to intense shock and back again.

"The darnedest thing I've ever heard," said the sergeant when I was done. "Haven't heard anything like this in my entire career. This is too fantastical."

"Please talk to the Mexican poet," I said. "You should have handcuffed him and taken him to jail, not to the hospital."

The sergeant stared at me as if she was gauging my honesty.

"Please, believe us. We came here to help," pleaded Katy.

"Helen Jenkins, the novelist, will tell you what happened," I said. "She'll corroborate our story. Between those two, and Oliver and Mary, you'll find out what—"

A loud crackle from her radio stopped me. She turned away from us to listen in.

I sighed and sat back against the bench. I was drained and disappointed. I'd hoped to solve a puzzle and get recognition from the local police, not get arrested by them.

I pushed Javier's jacket behind me to serve as a cushion between me and the hardwood, when something jabbed my back. I pulled the jacket from behind me and felt its pockets.

Katy gasped as I pulled out a set of keys.

"Master keys," I said. "That's how Ratcliffe got out. Javier opened his door after opening his first."

"He had these all along," said Katy, taking the keys from me to examine them. "So, there were two sets of master keys, one with Mary and one with Javier."

There was something else inside the jacket. I put my hand in and pulled out Javier's phone.

Tetyana leaned in.

"Now, there's a find," she said in a low whisper. "Win can unlock that for us."

"If they don't confiscate it from us first," I said, holding my finger on the main button.

The screen flickered and came to life.

"It's unlocked," said Katy.

I looked up at the officers.

The crackled voice coming through their radios was speaking in code, but the tone was urgent. One of the officers raised an eyebrow. The other gave his colleague a surprised look.

The sergeant walked away from us and paced the pier, barking orders and shouting at the person on the other end. Something had agitated her.

I turned back to the phone.

Javier's email account was locked and so was the contacts list.

"Check the photograph app," said Tetyana. "Might be something there. Killers take souvenirs."

Javier wasn't a typical killer, I thought, but clicked on the camera icon, anyway.

"It's a video," I whispered, taking a sharp breath in.

The three of us bent over the phone on my lap and watched as a horror scene played out on the small screen.

Javier had left his phone in a strategic position in the lantern room.

We watched as Ratcliffe came up the stairs and walked over to Javier, who was standing by the balcony window. In the video, the publisher shows a piece of paper to Javier, the same piece of paper I'd found in his dead hands.

Javier takes it and turns around, as if he's reading it.

Ratcliffe walks over to the electronic panel on the wall, unsuspecting of what's about to happen next. Javier doesn't waste any time. He slips the swordfish out of its hanging hooks and rushes toward Ratcliffe.

Ratcliffe turns around in shock, but his fate has already been sealed. Javier rams the swordfish into his throat, slamming him against the glass wall. Ratcliffe doesn't struggle for long and falls to the ground with the fish bill still stuck to his throat.

Javier props the fish against the glass, wipes his hands on Ratcliffe's trouser pants, and walks up to the camera.

"Three down, three more to go," he says, wiping the blood splattered on his face. "This is for you, Maria."

Then the video is turned off.

We stared at the still of Javier's contorted face for a long time.

I sat back with a sickening feeling in my gut.

"Take that and save yourself," I whispered.

"What?" said Tetyana.

"That's what he said before he jumped," I said.

The police sergeant was yelling into her radio now, visibly upset at something that happened on the mainland. But I had a hard time paying attention. My stomach was churning and my mind reeling from seeing the video.

"There are more videos," said Tetyana, plucking the phone from my lap. She played the next one, but I'd had enough.

The scrunch of heavy boots on the pier made me look up.

It was the sergeant coming over, a perturbed expression on her face.

"You heard," she snapped at her team. "Hop to it."

One officer jumped from the boat and scampered to the railing where the boat had been tied. The second officer stepped into the cockpit and started the engine.

They were in a hurry, and it looked like they'd forgotten we were here.

Something is wrong.

"Hey, Sergeant," I called out.

She spun around.

I snatched Javier's phone from Tetyana and turned it around to show the screen to the officer.

"You need to see this."

With a deepened frown, she took the mobile from my hand and stared at the screen.

"It's Javier. He took videos of all the murders," I said, shouting over the engine noise. "He handed this to us just before he jumped off the cliff."

The sergeant looked up, squinting at me.

I held up the camouflage jacket. "This is his. The phone was in the right-hand pocket."

For a moment, I thought she looked even more suspicious of us than before. She leaned over and took the jacket and handed it over to one of the men.

"Well, that explains it," she said with a resigned sigh.

Something about her demeanor told me she already knew.

"What's going on?" I asked, hearing more force in my voice than I expected. I wanted information, but it wouldn't be smart to make this officer any more annoyed than she already was.

"This man in the video," she said, shaking her head. "This Javier. He just walked out of the hospital."

Katy gasped. "You let him get away?"

The officer gave her an angry look, but I could see her mind was miles away, wishing she was on the mainland right now.

"Javier escaped?" I said. "Why didn't you secure him?"

"I've called for a search," said the sergeant, turning away, her lips set in an angry line. "Come hell or high water, I'm going to find him."

"Sarge?"

We all turned to the junior officer, holding his radio.

"What is it, Constable?" snapped the sergeant.

"There's a David Basha waiting for these folks on the other side."

David?

David is here?

I let out a long breath I hadn't even realized I'd been holding. In that one moment, I felt all the heaviness of that weekend lift from my shoulders.

I couldn't wait to go home.

Four Weeks Later

Chapter Sixty-three

"More tea?"

Helen nodded.

I filled her teacup with the steeped Ceylon tea and put the pot down. Helen picked a sandwich and put it daintily on her plate.

"If I'd known about your bakery before, I'd have come here every day," she said. "Then, maybe I'd have avoided that hellish weekend in the first place."

"I can't believe we survived," said Katy, picking up a scone filled with jam that Luc, my chief baker, had brought to the table only moments ago.

"Fresh out of the oven, ladies," he'd said, as he'd placed the plate on the coffee table next to a tiered tray with mini cakes.

It was a sunny day, and Harlem was bustling as usual.

It was sizzling inside the bakery. The heavenly smells of fresh baking came to us and we could hear Luc and his team's high-spirited chatter as they worked inside the kitchen.

There had been no further prank calls or poison pen letters to the bakery. Life had gone back to normal. Though we were all still on guard, it was a relief to experience the ordinary things in life again.

I turned my attention back to the present.

Helen Jenkins, Katy, and I were sitting in the tearoom.

I'd designed this room as a reception area for guests to sit while they waited to pick up their cake orders. But very few clients came into our shop these days.

Our bakery's delivery superstar, Bibi, spent all her waking hours driving around New York, her favorite punk rock station cranked up to the hilt, as she delivered cakes to our online customers around town.

I was glad we were alone in the tearoom. It meant we could talk openly.

"I feel like I was responsible for all this," said Helen.

"Don't you think you're being a tad harsh on yourself?" asked Katy.

Helen stared at her cup for a moment.

"If I'd just said no to writing Zimmerman's bio the way they wanted—"

"They'd have found someone else to do it for even less," I said. "Zimmerman and his Hollywood cabal did what they did and most of them got away with it. If they hadn't set up a predatory network in the first place, none of this would have happened."

Katy leaned over and put a hand on Helen's arm.

"Hun, you just got thrown into the thick of things. Ratcliffe wanted to exploit what had happened and make some fast money. Javier murdered those people with his own hands for revenge. None of that was your doing."

Helen nodded absentmindedly, but I could see she still carried some guilt inside of her.

Our experience troubled me too, and I was happy to be back home.

Four weeks ago, David had made a fuss when I'd canceled our weekend plans and gone off on this trip. But the instant he'd heard what had happened to us on the island, he'd been more concerned for our safety than anything else.

Still, he wasn't happy. He wanted me to forget Madame Bouchard and her dangerous games. He wanted me to promise to never go on any more investigative calls again.

But I couldn't make such promises.

Being a PI was in my blood now.

These calls were a lifeline to me. Though I knew the risks, the work gave me a rush like no other. Besides, we'd never match the funding for our orphanages that came from these cases.

No, I couldn't give up my investigations in good faith.

But this meant I had to make it up to David. He was a good man, and good men like him were hard to find.

He and Tetyana were in the dojo next door at that moment. They were teaching a kickboxing class and had promised to join us in the tearoom when they were done.

Helen let out another sigh.

"I have something that will cheer you up," said Katy, getting up and disappearing into her office. She came out smiling and waving a small envelope.

I turned to the novelist. "I think this will settle your mind."

Katy sat down in her chair and pulled a letter out of the envelope.

Helen squinted at the paper, a wary look in her eyes.

"Something official from the police?"

Katy shook her head.

"Guess who wrote to us a few days ago? They still don't have an email account, can you believe it?"

Helen gave her a puzzled look.

"Oliver and Mary," said Katy.

"The Hudsons?" said Helen. "They didn't return to the island, did they?"

"The police cordoned off that whole place," I said. "Oliver and Mary didn't want to live there anymore. They were ready to retire, anyway."

"They're back in Portland," said Katy, opening the letter and reading pieces. "They're happy to see their grandkids. They had a decent pension from the Coast Guard for the time they took care of the lighthouse when it was still in the government books. They're with family now and are trying to forget all that happened."

Katy smiled brightly.

"See? All's well that ends well."

Helen's shoulders relaxed. A small smile came on her face.

"Thanks for sharing. I needed to hear that," she said, picking up her teacup. "Some good news at last. I was so sure they and y'all would end up in jail. And I was sure Sophia was already killed...." She trailed off, frowning. "Whatever happened to her?"

"Locked up," said Katy, placing the letter on the table. "They should have put her away a long time ago."

Helen looked at us in shock.

"Sophia Knight's in jail?"

We shook our heads.

"In a mental institution," I said. "Pumped up with antidepressants. Last we heard, she was barely talking or walking. Her lawyer said she's pleading insanity."

Helen let out another sigh.

"So she's going to get away with what she did?"

"Can you imagine her life now?" I replied. "She's essentially isolated herself in a prison for life, where everyone thinks she's insane. No more parties. No more jet-setting. All she has now are her memories of how she lured unsuspecting young people into torture."

"I'd never want to live with a heart as black as hers," said Katy. "If you think of it, she's got it the worst. The others have all died off. She has to live with herself."

"Karma gets you every time," I said, leaning back in my chair. "Thank goodness it's all over for us."

That wasn't entirely true.

You don't get over four murders just like that.

Katy and I were still recovering from what had happened in Oregon.

The police had brought us back to the mainland in their boat and let us go on condition we'd show up for questioning, when needed.

They'd had nothing on us.

We had been lucky Javier hadn't used Tetyana's Glock on any of the victims, or all signs would have pointed to her. Javier's fingerprints had been on the gun.

Tetyana had always kept in touch with her underground friends, people from her past, which usually made me nervous. But for that one moment, I was glad she'd brought an unlicensed weapon that couldn't be traced to anyone, not even her.

As far as the police were concerned, Javier's confession videos on his phone meant the case was closed shut.

Except they never found him in the end.

That's what I thought then.

Chapter Sixty-four

"Javier is probably somewhere deep in South America," I said.

"Given the stunts he pulled, I'm sure he had his escape figured out too," said Katy.

"Hey, ladies."

I looked up to see my fiancé, David, come through the door that connected the bakery to the rest of the building. Tetyana was right behind him. They were both still in their sweaty kickboxing gear.

With a kiss on my cheek, David sat down and reached for a sandwich.

"How are you holding up?" said Tetyana, taking a chair beside Helen.

"Hanging in there," replied Helen. "I still have nightmares, but I go to therapy every week. That helps."

She scanned our faces.

"Don't know what I would have done if you hadn't dug me out. I don't know how to thank you."

"Hey, this is what we live for," said Tetyana, turning to me with a wink. She knew about the continuous disagreement between David and me. "When someone's in trouble, you call us for help. That's what we do, right, Asha?"

"I really think we need to reconsider these calls," said David, shaking his head. "You might not get so lucky next time."

Tetyana picked the biggest cake on the tray, took a bite, and pointed the remaining piece at David.

"No offense, bud," she said, "but I'd get sick to death if all I did was teach kickboxing to a bunch of overpaid flabby executives every day."

"Me too," I said. "Catering to the upper crust day in and day out can get to you."

"I don't understand why you guys can't pick up Kung Fu or something where you don't bump into serial killers," muttered David.

"We're big girls," said Katy with a bright smile. "We got out safely. Besides, Javier wasn't after us. Plus, if we hadn't been there, who would have saved Helen?"

"Bummer about that Sophia woman getting away, though," said Tetyana. "I'd have loved to see her rot in jail. But the others. They deserved it."

No one had been more surprised than me to get a call from Madame Bouchard's lawyer a week later. As promised, he'd funneled a generous donation into our orphanage's account for us taking the case.

I wondered if it had been Javier who had contacted the lawyer. I'd been so sure he'd been unhappy with our actions. He had sought justice where the system had failed him. He had expected us to jump in and help him take his revenge, but instead, we had sought to expose him.

The attorney would never break client confidentiality and tell us who called, or how he even knew we had finished the case. The only thing I was sure of was Madame Bouchard's promise. She always kept her word, even when dead and buried six feet underground.

Helen Jenkins stared thoughtfully at her sandwich.

"From now on, I'm only writing what I love to write, no matter what. I'm going to write what moves me, what I feel good about sharing with the world."

"How's your mom doing?" I asked. "Much better?"

"Not perfect, but good. The doctors said she should have passed away months ago. They don't know how she's hanging on like this. I'm just happy she's still—"

She didn't get to finish. The bakery door banged open and Luc came bursting out, followed by an excited-looking Rosalie, one of his sous chefs.

We all turned.

"Need help in the kitchen, guys?" I asked.

"We think they spotted Javier," said Luc.

Gasps echoed around the room.

Rosalie and Luc rushed up to us, breathless.

"What have you got there?" asked David, pointing at the tablet in Luc's hands.

Rosalie moved the cake tray aside while Luc squatted next to the coffee table and placed the device in the middle so we could all see.

"Right here," said Luc, punching the screen with his index finger. I leaned across to see a tab opened to a popular online tabloid site.

"Rosalie told us this weird story she read this morning," said Luc. "I thought it sounded like the guy you met on the island."

"What does it say?" I said, suppressing the urge to grab it and read the article myself.

"Did they arrest him?" asked Katy.

"Nope," said Luc. "But someone went to the media with this crazy sto—"

"It's a woman from a shelter in Tijuana," said Rosalie, interrupting him, her words rushing. "She manages a place for survivors, women running away from the Mexican cartels. They give the women a safe place to stay till they recover and can leave town."

"What does that have to do with Javier?" asked David.

Luc jabbed a finger at the tablet again, more urgently this time.

"She says she got an anonymous donation from a priest a week ago."

"A priest?" asked Katy, frowning.

"Exactly," said Rosalie. "She got a letter saying to meet a priest at an abandoned church near the border who wants to give her a donation. When she turned up at the church, he was waiting for her with a briefcase full of loose cash."

"Sounds like something out of a movie," said Helen.

"It gets better," said Rosalie. "This priest gives her the briefcase and a note that says the donation is in the name of Maria."

"Maria?" gasped Katy.

"Maria's a common name in Mexico," I said. "Does she describe what the priest looked like?"

"It was too dark inside, supposedly. At first, she thought it was the cartel trying to get her, but she wanted to find out and went armed."

"Did he say anything to her?" asked David.

Rosalie sat up.

"That's the thing. He never spoke. She never saw his face. And the note said he was a traveling priest who'd taken a vow of silence and poverty for life and to never come looking for him."

"Could be a coincidence," said David.

"Why did she go to the media with the story?" asked Katy.

"Says here that she wanted to thank him," said Luc, scrolling through the screen.

My stomach fluttered. It was a strange feeling, but my gut was telling me something.

"It has to be him," I whispered. "I've no idea how he got across the border, but he did. It has to be him."

"Will they ever track him down?" asked Katy.

"I bet you he's in some remote cave in the middle of a jungle by now," said Tetyana.

The room fell silent as we all contemplated Javier's future.

I remembered his pale, angst-ridden face. By the time we found him by the graves at the back of the island, he looked like he had lived a thousand lives in those two days.

"He's going to be okay," I said, more to myself than the others.

Katy's face scrunched up. "I know he killed people, but I feel so sad for him. Imagine what he has to live with now?"

"I don't know what to think," said Helen, shaking her head. "He tried to murder me. But after all that has happened, I can't rustle up anger. I just feel sorry for him. Does that make sense?"

"Does life ever make any sense?" said Tetyana.

"We're only human," said David. "All we can do in the limited time we have on earth is to commit the least harm and hold on to the best of intentions."

My mind wandered over to Javier's sister, Maria Pablo.

The events of that fatal day were still crystal clear in my memory banks.

I remembered how Maria got up from her chair at the gala ceremony, her shaking hand holding that small black revolver. I remembered how she pulled the trigger. I heard the shot ring out and saw the bullet hit the man who'd hurt her so many times, videotaping it and using it to control her.

Most times, I knew good from bad and bad from outright evil. Most times, justice was cut and dry.

But Javier had unsettled me.

Could I blame him?

We had all taken part in vigilante action in our youth. We had no choice if we had wanted to survive.

Javier wasn't innocent, but did he have a choice?

Did his victims deserve to die so horrifically? Should he have been pardoned, given what they had done to his sister?

I shook my head to clear it.

This case had challenged my intellectual capacity and my moral compass. Most of the people involved in hurting his sister were gone, and her death had been avenged.

My only hope was Maria was finally resting in peace.

David was right. We did our best.

My phone buzzed, jerking me awake from my thoughts. I pulled it out of my pocket.

"I think we all need more cake," said Luc, picking up the tray. "Too much of this crazy stuff isn't good for you."

"And more sugar is?" said Tetyana, giving a playful jab on his shoulder.

I looked down at my phone.

It was a text message from an unknown number.

Your assistance is required immediately. A girl has gone missing. Discretion imperative. Please meet me at the Red Lake Academy.

I raised an eyebrow.

Red Lake Academy? Was this another call for help from one of Madame Bouchard's friends?

I looked up.

Rosalie was now serving the cake to everyone while Tetyana was telling a funny story about how David had tripped and fallen in front of his jujitsu students after giving them a stern lecture on focus. David gave a wonky grin and a shrug. Luc punched him playfully, and Helen laughed.

I glanced back at my phone.

Now was not the time to let them know of this call. This would have to wait for another day.

The least I could give my dear family and friends was a brief respite from my adventures, so they could enjoy the simpler things in life.

Like jokes, laughs, and cake.

Continue the adventure!

Read the next Merciless Murder Mystery Thriller and find out what Asha and Katy confront in an all-girls' private academy set in the woods near Boston.

The dark underbelly of an exclusive school is exposed. A missing schoolgirl is the victim. But is she innocent...?

Flip to the end of this book to read the first chapter.

OR get Merciless Crimes right now, here:
www.tikiriherath.com/mysteries

Author's Note

D ear reader,

Did you enjoy Merciless Games?

My promise is to give you an exciting escape with every novel I write, and I sure hope I have done so.

If you have a minute, I'd much appreciate it if you would leave an honest review of this book on Amazon, Goodreads, or Bookbub. Just one sentence would do.

Honest reader reviews help my books get selected for international book promotions and I get to reach more readers.

Thank you so much.

One more thing.

If you'd like to learn the backstory of Tetyana, Asha, and Katy, flip to the end of this book to learn about the spin-off series that tells their stories.

The Red Heeled Rebels is an international crime series and is the origin story that shows how they all met. It spans four continents and features the back stories of everyone in this found family.

The Tanya Stone FBI K9 Thriller series features Tetyana as Special Agent Tanya Stone and her German Shepherd partner, Max, hunting a devious serial killer in a small seaside town on the West Coast.

Enjoy the reads!
My very best wishes,
Tikiri
Vancouver, Canada

PS: Did you know there is a bonus chapter for this book? Join my VIP reader club and receive your exclusive bonus gift.
Click here for the bonus scenes:
Get them all here: Bonus scenes for Merciless Games.
www.books.tikiriherath.com/mmmb2-bonus

PPS/ If you didn't enjoy the story or spotted typos, would you drop a line and let me know? Or just write to say hello. I would love to hear from you and personally reply to every email I receive.
My address is: Tikiri@TikiriHerath.com

Merciless Crimes - Chapter One

Message on the Girl's Bathroom Cabinet

"Don't come looking 4 me. Pls don't tell Mom & Dad. B back soon."

Written in blood-red nail polish on the back of the bathroom cabinet door in a missing girl's dorm room.

Private. Keep out. Violators will be prosecuted.

Katy and I stared at the large, red-lettered sign nestled in between the two pine trees.

We had stopped in the middle of a lonely country road that curved its way through a secluded part of the forest.

I'd already double-checked the locks and made sure the windows were rolled up.

Three times now.

"Is it me, or is it creepy here?" I said, pulling my jacket closer around my shoulders.

"You're such a big city girl, Asha," said Katy. "Any place with more trees than towers scares you."

My best friend was in the passenger seat next to me, exhausted after her driving shift from New York to Boston. I'd taken over the last leg of our road trip as we headed north of the city to our destination.

We were twenty minutes from the Red Lake Academy, where I had an urgent appointment with my latest client—a client I hadn't yet met.

Katy clutched my arm, making me jump.

"Did you see that?" she hissed.

"What is it?" I asked, swiveling my head, my heart beating a tick faster.

"I thought I saw something move over there..." Katy trailed off, staring into the shadows among the trees.

I peered over her shoulder, but saw nothing.

"Was it an animal? A person?" I asked.

Katy rubbed her face.

"Just my tired eyes, I guess," she mumbled. "All that driving has me beat. I really hope they have a nice place for us to sleep tonight at the school."

I was exhausted too, and a migraine was coming on. It always did when I felt uncertain in my surroundings.

Uncertain.

And uneasy.

I glanced around me.

Massive oaks and maples lined the road. The trees were in their shedding season, preparing for another long and cold winter, typical for this region. Their twisty, gnarly branches pointed up at the gray sky, as if they were calling to the gods above.

Other than a frightened white-tailed deer that had crossed our path ten minutes ago, we hadn't encountered any life for miles since I took the last turn on the road.

What an isolated place for a girls' school, I thought as I peered through the windshield.

The calls for help that came to my private investigation firm were usually unconventional, and my upper-crust clients were always idiosyncratic.

But this call had been downright peculiar.

How does a girl vanish from the most upscale boarding school in the country?

I checked the windows again and instinctively reached up to feel the roof of my cabriolet. I was glad I'd put the top up and secured it before we left Boston. I'd have hated to drive through these dark woods exposed to the elements.

And who knew what else?

A strange rustle above made me look up.

"We have company," I whispered, pointing through the windshield.

Katy craned her neck to see what I'd spotted.

Half a dozen black crows perched on a naked tree branch just above the sign, their beady, intelligent eyes watching us.

Waiting.

Suddenly, the entire brood flew off, cawing loudly enough to awake the dead. It was like they were warning us.

"A murder of crows," I whispered to myself as I watched them take to the stormy gray skies, flapping their dark wings.

A murder of crows.

I wasn't the superstitious type, but I couldn't shake that feeling. Like a premonition of what was to come.

To be continued....

Continue the Adventure!

MERCILESS CRIMES, the next book in this series, will give you more spine-tingling intrigue, mystery, and lurking killers who Asha will ferret out in the end.

Get the book here: **www.TikiriHerath.com/Mysteries**

A missing schoolgirl. An exclusive academy. A devious murderer out for vengeance. IF YOU SAW HER DISAPPEAR, YOU COULD BE NEXT...

A high-tech tycoon's fifteen-year-old daughter vanishes from a private girls' boarding school.

In desperation, the principal turns to Asha Kade's detective agency.

Asha takes on the case, despite the fearful nightmares of her dark past as a trafficked survivor surging through her mind.

She must keep a steely resolve as death and danger await.

An unseen killer strikes just as Asha steps onto the secluded grounds of the academy. These hallowed halls of ivy hide disturbing secrets no one wants her to see.

Asha is no longer just searching for a girl.

She's hunting a tormented criminal mind who must be unmasked before they kill again.

And her instincts tell her the elusive killer is closer than everyone thinks...

Get the book and find out what Asha and Katy confront next. Available around the world, on Amazon stores everywhere. www.TikiriHerath.com/Mysteries

Available globally in e-book, paperback, and hardback editions on all Amazon stores. Also available for free in libraries everywhere. Just ask your friendly local librarian to order a copy via Ingram Spark.

The Girl Who Knew Their Names

Would you like to know what really happened to Zimmerman and Maria, and how Asha found herself on that remote Mexican beach the day the Hollywood Executive was killed?

Turn the page right here to find out how Asha got a coveted catering contract to a Hollywood awards gala, only to witness a cold-blooded murder streamed live around the world.

Get The Girl Who Knew Their Names to read the explosive story that started it all.

www.TikiriHerath.com/RedHeeledRebels

A haunted young actress. A glittering Hollywood gala. A cold-blooded murder among the stars. IF YOU KNEW THE TWISTED TRUTH, WOULD YOU TELL?

Asha Kade is thrilled to snag the most coveted catering job in Los Angeles. But she doesn't know she'll face a brutal predator on her first day....

Emma Foster holds a raging dark secret that can bring an entire industry down.

But the most powerful man in the city is on to her.

And he has one aim. To silence the terrible truth, no matter what it takes.

But Asha saw what he did that night, and she's not going to let him get away with an unspeakable crime.

Not now.

Not ever.

But when Emma vanishes without a trace, Asha realizes she's plunged deep into a scandal so horrifying, even the local authorities hate to touch it...

But it's too late to turn back now.

Will Asha face the same terrifying fate as Emma....?

What readers are saying:

"*This is truly a ten-star read!*" ~Goodreads Reviewer

"*A fast paced, action filled, page turner you won't want to miss! (I)t's a have-to-read if you like action filled thrillers!*" ~ Amazon Reader

"*There is an exciting finish to this novel that will make your heart pound in your chest!*" ~ Amazon Reader

"*Excellent writing AND amazing storyline means these books are un-put-down-able!*" ~ Amazon Reader

"*Drama, mystery, backstabbing, glamor, fashion and glorious cakes, bikinis, yachts and guns, this book has it all. It shows creativity at its best.*" ~Advance Reader.

Get **The Girl Who Knew Their Names** here:
www.TikiriHerath.com/RedHeeledRebels

Available globally in e-book, paperback, and hardback editions on all Amazon stores. Also available for free in libraries everywhere. Just ask your friendly local librarian to order a copy via Ingram Spark.

Debate this Dozen

Twelve Book Club Questions

1.   Who was your favorite character?
2.   Which characters did you dislike?
3.   Which scene has stuck with you the most? Why?
4.   What scenes surprised you?
5.   What was your favorite part of the book?
6.   What was your least favorite part?
7.   Did any part of this book strike a particular emotion in you? Which part and what emotion did the book make you feel?
8.   Did you know the author has written an underlying message in this story? What theme or life lesson do you think this story tells?
9.   What did you think of the author's writing?
10. How would you adapt this book into a movie? Who would you cast in the leading roles?
11. On a scale of one to ten, how would you rate this story?
12. Would you read another book by this author?

The Reading List

The Red Heeled Rebels universe of mystery thrillers, featuring your favorite kick-ass female characters:

Tanya Stone FBI K9 Mystery Thrillers
www.TikiriHerath.com/Thrillers
NEW FBI thriller series starring Tetyana from the Red Heeled Rebels as Special Agent Tanya Stone, and Max, as her loyal German Shepherd. These are serial killer thrillers set in Black Rock, a small upscale resort town on the coast of Washington state.
Her Deadly End
Her Cold Blood
Her Last Lie
Her Secret Crime
Her Dead Girl
Her Perfect Murder
Her Grisly Grave
Coming soon!

Asha Kade Private Detective Murder Mysteries

www.TikiriHerath.com/Mysteries

Each book is a standalone murder mystery thriller, featuring the Red Heeled Rebels, Asha Kade and Katy McCafferty. Asha and Katy receive one million dollars for their favorite children's charity from a secret benefactor's estate every time they solve a cold case.

Merciless Legacy

Merciless Games

Merciless Crimes

Merciless Lies

Merciless Past

Merciless Deaths

One more to come.

Red Heeled Rebels International Mystery & Crime - The Origin Story

www.TikiriHerath.com/RedHeeledRebels

The award-winning origin story of the Red Heeled Rebels characters. Learn how a rag-tag group of trafficked orphans from different places united to fight for their freedom and their lives, and became a found family.

The Girl Who Crossed the Line

The Girl Who Ran Away

The Girl Who Made Them Pay

The Girl Who Fought to Kill

The Girl Who Broke Free

The Girl Who Knew Their Names

The Girl Who Never Forgot
This series is now complete.

The Accidental Traveler

www.TikiriHerath.com

An anthology of personal short stories based on the author's sojourns around the world.

The Rebel Diva Nonfiction Series

www.TikiriHerath.com/Nonfiction

Your Rebel Dreams: 6 simple steps to take back control of your life in uncertain times.

Your Rebel Plans: 4 simple steps to getting unstuck and making progress today.

Your Rebel Life: Easy habit hacks to enhance happiness in the 10 key areas of your life.

Bust Your Fears: 3 simple tools to crush your anxieties and squash your stress.

Collaborations

The Boss Chick's Bodacious Destiny Nonfiction Bundle
Dark Shadows 2: Voodoo and Black Magic of New Orleans

Tikiri's novels are available around the world, on all Amazon stores everywhere. The nonfiction books are available on Apple, Kobo, Barnes & Noble, Indigo Chapters, and all good bookstores around the world.

All these books are also available in libraries everywhere. Just ask your friendly local librarian or your local bookstore to order a copy via Ingram Spark.

Happy reading.

Asha Kade Private Detective Murder Mysteries

How far would you go for a million-dollar payout?

<u>The Merciless Murder Mysteries</u>

Merciless Legacy

Merciless Games

Merciless Crimes

Merciless Lies

Merciless Past

Merciless Deaths

More to come!

Each book is a standalone murder mystery thriller featuring the Red Heeled Rebel, Asha Kade, and her best friend Katy

McCafferty, as private detectives on the hunt for serial killers in small towns USA.

There is no graphic violence, heavy cursing, or explicit sex in these books. What you will find are a series of suspicious deaths, a closed circle of suspects, twists and turns, fast-paced action, and nail-biting suspense.

www.TikiriHerath.com/mysteries

A newly minted private investigator, Asha Kade, gets a million dollars from an eccentric client's estate every time she solves a cold case. Asha Kade accepts this bizarre challenge, but what she doesn't bargain for is to be drawn into the dark underworld of her past again.

The only thing that propels her forward now is a burning desire for justice.

What readers are saying on Amazon and Goodreads:

"My new favorite series!"

"Thrilling twists, unputdownable!"

"I was hooked right from the start!"

"A twisted whodunnit! Edge of your seat thriller that kept me up late, to finish it, unputdownable!! More, please!"

"Buckle up for a roller coaster of a ride. This one will keep you on the edge of your seat."

"A must read! A macabre start to an excellent book. It had me totally gripped from the start and just got better!"

"A great whodunit with a lot of twists and turns along the way. The story was amazing!"

"I could not stop reading it. It was as if I was there witnessing the murders myself. The characters had depth and personality and backgrounds that were explained nicely. It was awesome!"

"Nothing is more terrifying than the fear of the unknown. Do you have any nails left? Another NAIL-BITING story from a very talented master storyteller!"

———⊷⊶———

A brand-new murder mystery series for a pulse-pounding, bone-chilling adventure from the comfort and warmth of your favorite reading chair at home.

Can you find the killer before Asha Kade does?

———⊷⊶———

To learn more about this exciting series and download the FREE novel—HER DEADLY END—as a gift, go to www.TikiriHerath.com/mysteries.

Sign up to Tikiri's VIP reader club to get the chance to win personalized paperback books, chat with the author and more.

———⊷⊶———

Available globally in e-book, paperback, and hardback editions on all Amazon stores. Print books are available for free in libraries everywhere. Just ask your friendly local librarian or your local bookstore to order a copy via Ingram Spark.

Tanya Stone FBI K9 Mystery Thrillers

*H*ow far would you go to avenge your family's brutal murder?

Tanya Stone FBI K9 Serial Killer Thrillers

Her Deadly End

Her Cold Blood

Her Last Lie

Her Secret Crime

Her Dead Girl

Her Perfect Murder

Her Grisly Grave

To come!

A brand-new FBI K9 serial killer thriller series for a pulse-pounding, bone-chilling adventure from the comfort and warmth of your favorite reading chair at home.

Can you find the killer before Agent Tanya Stone?

www.TikiriHerath.com/thrillers

———✦———

Some small-town secrets will haunt your nightmares. Escape if you can...

FBI Special Agent Tanya Stone has a new assignment. Hunt down the serial killers prowling the idyllic West Coast resort towns.

An unspeakable and bone-chilling darkness seethes underneath these picturesque seaside suburbs. A string of violent abductions and gruesome murders wreak hysteria among the perfect lives of the towns' families.

But nothing is what it seems. The monsters wear masks and mingle with the townsfolk, spreading vicious lies.

With her K9 German Shepherd, Agent Stone goes on the warpath. She will fight her own demons as a trafficked survivor to make the perverted psychopaths pay.

But now, they're after her.

Small towns have dark deceptions and sealed lips. If they know you know the truth, they'll never let you leave...

———✦———

Each book is a standalone murder mystery thriller, featuring Tetyana from the Red Heeled Rebels as Agent Tanya Stone, and Max, her loyal German Shepherd. Red Heeled Rebels Asha Kade and Katy McCafferty and their found family make guest appearances when Tanya needs help.

There is no graphic violence, heavy cursing, or explicit sex in these books.

The dogs featured in this series are never harmed, but the villains are.

To learn more about this exciting new series and download the FREE novel—HER DEADLY END—as a gift, go to www.TikiriHerath.com/thrillers

The Red Heeled Rebels International Mystery & Crime

The Origin Story

Would you like to know the origin story of your favorite characters in the Tanya Stone FBI K9 mystery thrillers and the Asha Kade Merciless murder mysteries?

In the award-winning Red Heeled Rebels international mystery & crime series—the origin story—you'll find out how Asha, Katy, and Tetyana (Tanya) banded together in their troubled youths to fight for freedom against all odds.

The complete Red Heeled Rebels international crime collection:
Prequel Novella: The Girl Who Crossed the Line
Book One: The Girl Who Ran Away

Book Two: The Girl Who Made Them Pay
Book Three: The Girl Who Fought to Kill
Book Four: The Girl Who Broke Free
Book Five: The Girl Who Knew Their Names
Book Six: The Girl Who Never Forgot
The series is now complete!

An epic, pulse-pounding, international crime thriller series that spans four continents featuring a group of spunky, sassy young misfits who have only each other for family.

A multiple-award-winning series which would be best read in order. There is no graphic violence, heavy cursing, or explicit sex in these books.
www.TikiriHerath.com/RedHeeledRebels

In a world where justice no longer prevails, six iron-willed young women rally to seek vengeance on those who stole their humanity.

If you like gripping thrillers with flawed but strong female leads, vigilante action in exotic locales and twists that leave you at the edge of your seat, you'll love these books by multiple award-winning Canadian novelist, Tikiri Herath.

Go on a heart-pounding international adventure without having to get a passport or even buy an airline ticket!

What readers are saying on Amazon and Goodreads:
"Fast-paced and exciting!"
"An exciting and thought-provoking book."
"A wonderful story! I didn't want to leave the characters."

"I couldn't put down this exciting road trip adventure with a powerful message."

"Another award-worthy adventure novel that keeps you on the edge of your seat."

"A heart-stopping adventure. I just couldn't put the book down till I finished reading it."

"Kept me mesmerized and captivated with the rich descriptions which made me feel like I was actually inside the story."

"This is a fantastic read that will have you traveling the globe. I absolutely loved this book. You won't be able to put it down!"

"A real page-turner and international thriller. Reminds me of why I've always loved to read. Because I can visit worlds and places, I wouldn't ordinarily get to see."

Literary Awards & Praise for The Red Heeled Rebels books:
- Grand Prize Award Finalist - 2019 Eric Hoffer Award, USA

- First Horizon Award Finalist - 2019 Eric Hoffer Award, USA

- Honorable Mention General Fiction - 2019 Eric Hoffer Award, USA

- Winner First-In-Category - 2019 Chanticleer Somerset Award, USA

- Semi-Finalist - 2020 Chanticleer Somerset Award, USA

- Winner in 2019 Readers' Favorite Book Awards, USA

- Winner of 2019 Silver Medal - Excellence E-Lit Award, USA

- Winner in Suspense Category - 2018 New York Big Book Award, USA

- Finalist in Suspense Category - 2018 & 2019 Silver Falchion Awards, USA

- Honorable Mention - 2018-19 Reader Views Literary Classics Award, USA

- Publisher's Weekly Booklife Prize - 2018, USA

To learn more about this addictive series, go to **www.TikiriHerath.com/RedHeeledRebels** and receive the prequel novella - **The Girl Who Crossed The Line** - as a gift.

Sign up to Tikiri's VIP reader club and get short stories, exotic recipes, the chance to win paperbacks, chat with the author and more.

Available globally in e-book, paperback, and hardback editions on all Amazon stores. Print books are available for free in libraries everywhere. Just ask your friendly local librarian or your local bookstore to order a copy via Ingram Spark.

Inspiration

To my childhood superhero author, Agatha Christie. Thank you for whisking me away on magical adventures during those long dark days.

For Lighthouse Buffs

Note: These external links are shared for interest and fun and their active status cannot be guaranteed.

Lighthouses off Oregon coast

www.traveloregon.com/things-to-do/culture-history/lighthouses

History of Lighthouses in Oregon

www.embracesomeplace.com/lighthouses-oregon-coast

Oregon's Tillamook Rock Lighthouse

www.oregonencyclopedia.org/articles/tillamook_rock_lighthouse

The Spooky Story Behind the Gibraltar Point Lighthouse

www.torontoist.com/2017/08/spooky-story-behind-gibraltar-point-lighthouse

Don't Turn Off the Lights: Haunted Lighthouses

www.beachcombingmagazine.com/blogs/news/haunted-lighthouses
These Haunted Lighthouses Will Give You the Creeps
www.southernliving.com/travel/haunted-lighthouses
Oregon Islands
www.fws.gov/refuge/Oregon_Islands

Acknowledgments

To my amazing, talented, superstar editor, Stephanie Parent, thank you, as always, for coming on this literary journey with me and for helping make these books the best they can be.

To my fantastic international team of beta readers who helped me through this adventure, who cheered me on as I toiled, and who gave me their frank feedback, thank you. In alphabetical order of first name:
Blessmore Chikwakwa, Zimbabwe
Carolyn Pennett-Staresinic, Canada
Laura Edwards, United States
Michele Kapugi, United States
Natasja Smith, South Africa
Serena Soape, United States
Stephanie Smith, United States

To all the kind and generous readers who take the time to review my novels and share their frank feedback, thank you so much. Your support is invaluable.

I'm immensely grateful to you all for your kind and generous support, and would love to invite you for a glass of British Columbian wine or a cup of Ceylon tea with chocolates when you come to Vancouver next!

About the Author

Tikiri Herath is the multiple-award-winning author of international thriller and mystery novels and the Rebel Diva books.

Tikiri worked in risk management in the intelligence and defense sectors, including in the Canadian Federal Government and at NATO. She has a bachelor's degree from the University of Victoria, British Columbia, and a master's degree from the Solvay Business School in Brussels.

Born in Sri Lanka, Tikiri grew up in East Africa and has studied, worked, and lived in Europe, Southeast Asia, and North America throughout her adult life. An international nomad and fifth-culture kid, she now calls Canada home.

She's an adrenaline junkie who has rock climbed, bungee jumped, rode on the back of a motorcycle across Quebec, flown in an acrobatic airplane upside down, and parachuted solo.

When she's not plotting another thriller scene or planning another adrenaline-filled trip, you'll find her baking in her kitchen with a glass of red Shiraz in hand and vintage jazz playing in the background.

To say hello and get travel stories from around the world, go to **www.TikiriHerath.com**